A Love and Games novel

One ring plus one wild night equals one crazy love

Sherry Robicheaux loves men. She loves love. And she loves an adventure. So when she meets a mysterious man while working backstage at a country music concert in Vegas, she's all about what happens in Vegas staying there.

Country music superstar Tyler Blue just wants a weekend of anonymity...though there's something about the spunky waitress with the streaks of purple hair that tempts him like no other. Until the next morning, when they both wake up with fuzzy memories...and rings on their fingers.

Convincing Sherry to maintain the ruse for his public image isn't the hardest part—it's reminding himself that their time spent playing husband and wife in her small town of Magnolia Springs can't last. Tyler's first love will always be music—and the road is no place for a sweet downhome girl.

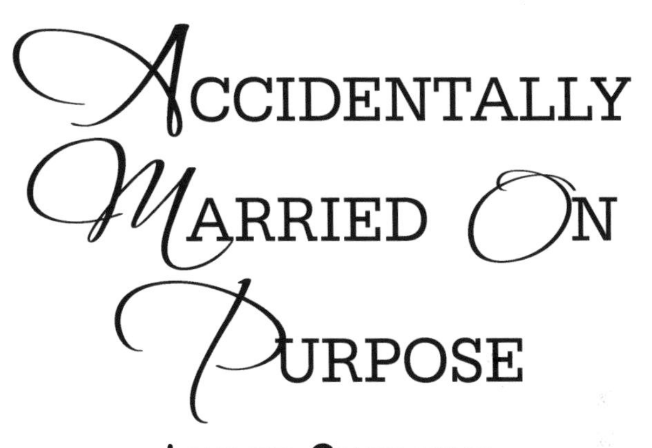

A LOVE AND GAMES NOVEL

RACHEL HARRIS

This book is a work of fiction. Names, characters, places, and incidents are the product of the author's imagination or are used fictitiously. Any resemblance to actual events, locales, or persons, living or dead, is coincidental.

Entangled Publishing, LLC
2614 South Timberline Road
Suite 109
Fort Collins, CO 80525
Visit our website at www.entangledpublishing.com.

Bliss is an imprint of Entangled Publishing, LLC. For more information on our titles, visit http://www.entangledpublishing.com/category/bliss

Edited by Stacy Abrams
Cover design by Jessica Cantor

Print ISBN 978-1-50097-982-9

Manufactured in the United States of America

First Edition July 2014

For Ashley Bodette, whose insight, humor, and eagle eye helped shape this book. Ashley, you've been my sanity this past year, and your friendship is such a blessing. Believing huge things for you, girl.

Also for my husband, Gregg, for the inspiration. You are my fairy tale.

Chapter One

Sad eyes tracked Sherry's movements as she said good-bye to the man in her life.

Their relationship was new, only a few months old, but their bond had been immediate and profound. It hurt leaving him now, knowing that he didn't understand. But Sherry needed a break. Not from him. From life. From her sister's luminous honeymoon glow and her brother's new sappy love. From the constant internal question of when it would be *her* turn to be just as luminously sappy.

When an out-of-town catering gig for their restaurant's biggest client yet suddenly presented itself, she'd practically tackled Colby for the opportunity. Sherry loved adventure—she craved it—and the star-studded getaway provided the perfect out from her sucky role as the Robicheaux family fifth wheel. Even if it did involve country music.

The hard part, of course, was explaining her desertion to Elvis.

"It's just for the weekend, buddy," she promised, smiling first at Elvis, then at the cute boy behind the counter of Tootsie's Pampered Poodle Day Spa and Boarding. A stinging mix of bleach and *eau de wet dog* permeated the air—certainly unlike any day spa Sherry had ever been in—but it was homey. Cheerful. The perfect place to leave her baby. Pressing her face against her Shih Tzu's cool, damp nose, she vowed, "You won't even know I'm gone. I've heard there's a hot Maltese here, too. Right up your alley." Scratching behind her puppy's fluffy ears, she leaned back with a sigh. "At least one of us should get our freak on."

She glanced up when the cutie waiting to take Elvis's leopard-print leash made a choking sound under his breath. Shrugging, she pushed to her feet and turned to the woman standing beside him. "My return flight arrives late," she told the doggie spa's namesake. "So Angelle's gonna pick him up once she gets back from Bon Terre."

Yet another reason Sherry was glad to leave town for the holiday. Cane and Angie were headed to Cajun country, and Colby and Jason were doing the family thing with Emma. If Sherry had stayed in town, she'd likely be ringing in the New Year with Ryan Seacrest on the TV and a pint of Ben and Jerry's in her belly.

That truth was more depressing than an eight-pound canine being the man in her life.

Tootsie fluffed her gray hair and pressed her ample bosom against the counter with a grin. "Vegas for New Year's Eve. Goodness, to be young again. Flirting my ass off, getting into mischief." She gave her a knowing wink. "I expect a full report when you come home."

Sherry snorted. "The only mischief I'll see is if I

accidentally put the wrong label on a heating tray." The spa owner raised an eyebrow, and Sherry explained. "We're catering the green room for a concert tomorrow night. A big new casino client we want to impress, so I'm going in to supervise."

"Concert, huh?" She bumped the file cabinet closed with her hip. "Anyone I might know?"

Sherry scrunched her nose. "Some country group called Blue?"

The name rang a slight bell, but she wasn't that up-to-date on the country music scene. Her style was more pop and dance, music she could shake her booty to at a club. Part of her felt guilty for not doing more research on her client, but really, she had a handle on the important things, like the number of people she was serving and if anyone had food allergies. As for the rest, she'd wing it. People and events like this were her specialty.

Too bad that doesn't transfer over to my love life.

Apparently, the name of the group more than rang a bell for Tootsie, as her big brown eyes grew even wider. "Blue? As in the ACM's Entertainer of the Year?" Sherry shrugged, her guess being yes, and the woman surged forward. "As in one of *People*'s Sexiest Men Alive? Seriously, how can you not know who he is?"

"His name sounds sorta familiar," she mumbled, a prick of unease tensing her stomach. Sexiest man alive? *Awesome.* Blue sounded just like the kind of guy she normally fell for. Hot, brooding, confident…and more than likely a man whore.

"You've *gotta* hit on him," Tootsie ordered, her enthusiasm raising her voice to wince-worthy decibels. The cutie on dog patrol shook his head and took Elvis's leash, smirking as he strolled toward the kennel door. Sherry blew her baby a good-bye kiss.

"If anyone has a shot with him, it's you," Tootsie continued. "You're gorgeous and confident. Fun and spontaneous. Shoot, you'll have him eating out of your hand! Just think…" Her eyes got a faraway look in them. "You'll smile. He'll come over. You'll kiss at midnight, and then fall blissfully in love. The two of you will live happily ever after." The woman giggled as a pinkish glow bloomed on her cheeks. "I read about that very thing in one of my romance novels."

Sherry sighed. She had too, and it was shortly after *the end* that she'd concluded happily ever afters belonged exactly there—in her beloved smut. They didn't exist in real life. At least not for her. Sure, her siblings were rocking it in the love department, but her luck flat-out sucked. That was where her New Year's resolution came into play.

"Not interested," she declared, shoving a thick section of purple hair behind her ear. "Celebrities are notorious players, and I've had enough of that nonsense for two lifetimes." She thought about it and then added, "But a little hot roadie action could be in the cards."

She wiggled her eyebrows with a grin, and Tootsie chortled. "Now there's the wild child of Magnolia Springs I know and love!"

Sherry fought to maintain her smile. Wild child, addicted to love, crazy chica—all names that fit her pretty damn perfectly…and traits that led to her current love*less* state. Always the fling, never the forever, but she had a new game plan to change that status going forward.

Of course, not before one last weekend to sow her *wild* oats.

Waving good-bye, Sherry donned her dark sunglasses and took a deep breath of fresh, crisp, pine-scented air. She had yet to share her New Year's resolution with her sister or best friend, and she doubted she ever would. Knowing them, they'd just try to talk her out of it. Or worse, give her pointers. She didn't need them to say her love life was a train wreck. She'd already diagnosed that particular problem and found herself a cure.

Fall for someone boring.

It was the solution to her heartache. Her desire to feel wooed and loved meant she always went for the exciting, mysterious types—only to find out later that those guys were mysterious for a reason. They were hiding another woman. Nope, it was high time she settled down with someone stable. A man who wouldn't cheat or charm her with a quick smile and swoony line only to turn around and charm someone else. She was through with being swept off her feet. Forevermore (or at least after this weekend was over), Sherry's feet would remain firmly on the ground.

Come Monday morning, her sights would be set on a guy like her brother-in-law. Jason Landry was the captain of the fire department and owned his own business. He was solid, dependable, hardworking, and loved her sister to distraction. Even Sherry's brother was an example. Sure, Cane liked to think he was big and bad with his tats and motorcycle, but inside he was just one big teddy bear. And that's what she needed. A *good* guy.

Someone like the nice, safe, dry-as-day-old-toast accountant who'd recently set up shop across from

Robicheaux's.

Sure, Will Trahan wasn't her usual type—both conversations they'd had thus far somehow led to them discussing Roth IRAs—but then that was the point. Any man more interested in the health of her investment portfolio than the size of her rack had to be good people.

Sherry threw her car into gear and turned the radio dial, blasting Rihanna as she reversed out of the parking lot. Gravel crunched under her wheels as she nodded with conviction at the reflection in her rearview mirror. Yep, next year she'd be a changed woman. No longer would she be the sister always getting in scrapes or making a mess of her life. The pathetic, relationship-disaster of the Robicheaux clan would be a thing of the past. A brand-spanking-new Sherry was emerging—one with her head on straight and her heart safe and secure.

But first, one last adventure.

One fun weekend in Sin City to live in the moment, embrace her unfortunate fling status, and store up exciting memories for the dull years to come.

Then, bring on Mr. Boring.

• • •

Tyler's calloused fingertips brushed against the thin piece of paper in his jeans pocket. He grinned as his publicist fought to stay in stride beside him, her click-clacking heels half drowning out her rant about the latest *development*, and began soundlessly mouthing the words he'd written only a half hour ago. He'd finally nailed it.

Catching sight of his bass player in the crowded hallway,

Tyler cut short Arianne's monologue. "Hey, man." Charlie raised his head, and Tyler withdrew the sticky note, wielding it as if it were a winning lottery ticket. "Got that last lyric."

His best friend immediately snatched the paper, and Arianne shot him an irritated smile. Oh, he'd pay for cutting her off. There'd be no escaping whatever had her bug-eyed and high strung—well, more high strung than normal. But for now, he'd gotten a reprieve. That damn line had been driving Tyler mad for a week, and Blue had an album to finish. Even the great Arianne Cruz, bulldog publicist to the stars, couldn't fault him that.

Charlie read the line and handed it back with a smile. "Hell yeah. That's it."

"Never doubt the power of a Post-it note, my friend." Tyler carefully placed the three-by-three square in the center of his wallet—that thing was pure gold—and blew out a relieved breath. "Back in the studio on Monday."

Charlie smacked his shoulder. "I'm there." His gaze shifted right, and the smile on his face altered. Tyler turned to find a smoking blonde in painted-on jeans standing along the wall, twirling her hair and eying his bassist. There went talk of their new album.

"Show starts in twenty," he called out as Charlie took off for the groupie. Really, he wasn't worried. A band didn't skyrocket up the charts, produce two back-to-back albums in as many years, and play to sold-out crowds in worldwide tours if the members weren't 100 percent committed. Especially as young as the two of them were.

But a reminder damn sure couldn't hurt.

Charlie shot him a wink in acknowledgment, and Tyler glanced back at Arianne. It was time to face the music. "All right. I'll listen to whatever it is that has you twitching, but can I at least stuff my face while I do it?" Usually he ate after the concert with the rest of the band, but today's rehearsals and interviews had run long, and he was starving.

Her thin lips pressed together, but with a curt nod, she led him down the hall.

As they made their way to yet another green room, the familiar buzz of adrenaline washed over him. The energy in the air was electric. Music, traveling the world, a new venue every night, this was Tyler Blue's life, and he loved every bit of it. It was a dream he'd held since his parents gave him his first guitar when he was thirteen, and he wouldn't trade it for anything. But as his stomach rumbled, he couldn't help thinking it came with a few drawbacks.

Living on the road—in particular, eating the crap food they tried to pass as gourmet at venues like this—was beginning to wear thin. What he wouldn't do for a bowl of his dad's homemade gumbo or a steaming hot plate of boiled Gulf seafood. But his career didn't leave much time for trips back home to Louisiana—a side effect of the industry that was both a blessing and a curse.

Brushing off the sudden sting of nostalgia and guilt, Tyler tried to psych himself up for another meal of pasta… only when he walked through the back room of the new Moonshine Casino, he discovered a Cajun feast laid out in the middle of the desert.

"What the hell?"

The question, obviously, was rhetorical. But after years of surviving on every variety of chicken known to man, he was certain the spread before him was a mirage. His mouth watered as he inhaled deeply, and the scent of cayenne hit his nose. It had been years since he'd sat down at his grandmother's table, and from the look of the heaping tub of jambalaya, this stuff was legit.

"Is there a problem?" Arianne surveyed the trays. "If you prefer something else, I can request it. But I'd think you'd be pleased. Isn't this the food of your homeland?" She widened her eyes as she said it and smiled.

"Cute." Tyler grabbed a Styrofoam tray, prepared to load that sucker down. "And hell yes, I'm happy. This is perfect. Just shocked to find it here of all places."

Moonshine was a country-themed casino owned by several of his music buddies. It was no secret they wanted Tyler involved, too, but tonight was his first visit to the Vegas resort. If food like this was a common occurrence, though, he might just be signing some papers after all.

"Well, they want you to invest, so of course they're pulling out all the stops." She shrugged, and the playfulness instantly fell from her eyes. "Now, fill your plate so we can talk strategy."

He almost laughed. Instead, he did as the lady requested and filled his plate to overflowing before the crew wolfed it all. Then, satisfied he'd added as much as it could possibly hold, he nodded at a passing sound technician, plopped his ass in a chair, and said, "Go for it."

"Tammy Paxton of *Country Music Weekly* has called your credibility into question." Tyler choked on his bite of Andouille, and Arianne handed him a napkin. "I can't say that I'm all that surprised. You flat-out refuse to be linked with anyone in the press, Ty, and I warned you it could bite you in the ass. As it turns out, Paxton's the snake for the job." She furnished a folded, torn-out piece of paper from her purse and handed it to him. "This article has already gone viral, and fans are starting to talk."

He set the paper down without reading it. He learned long ago not to read reviews or listen to critics. That was what he paid *her* to do. "Give me the highlights. What, exactly, does she claim I'm doing wrong?"

"Oh, the article starts off fine. She compares you to the greats. Johnny Cash, Tim McGraw, Keith Urban, Blake Shelton..."

That didn't sound bad. If Tyler had half the career they did, he'd be good to go.

But then Arianne continued. "Any guess what the rest of those men have in common?"

"CMA Male Vocalist of the Year Awards?" he replied helpfully.

"Wives." He shot her a look and shoveled in a forkful of jambalaya to keep from responding. It always came back to this. Arianne sighed. "More and more country artists are settling down and getting married, Tyler, and the fans are eating it up."

Spearing a plump Gulf shrimp, he asked, "Whatever happened to women loving the single celebrity thing? The mystery and 'no comment' about personal relationships spiel. The fantasy they love to spin that we're just sitting around, twiddling our thumbs, waiting for the right fan to rock our worlds?"

"Wrong genre." She grabbed a nearby empty chair and dragged it in front of him. "Country music is a totally different beast than pop or rock. With those clients, I actually advise them to do just what you do. Attend events solo. Remain an eternal bachelor in the press. Spin that dumb fantasy. But those artists sell a different *kind* of fantasy. You write and sing about forever love, and committed relationships lend credibility."

Relationships. Tyler set down his fork, the once flavorful rice now bitter.

Arianne rolled her eyes. "For the love of money, will you relax? I see you getting all riled up and twitchy. I'm not suggesting you get hitched to the next woman you see, but I am asking if it would *kill* you to go to an event with a date? Or let me at least leak a possible secret romance?"

He shook his head in irritation. It was the same song, different day. His management had been riding his ass about this for the last year—and they could keep riding it, because it wasn't happening. Music and long-term relationships didn't mix. You could ask his dad.

Other than music, Tyler liked things in his life to be easy. When he did have time for women, he preferred his interactions to be casual and without complication. He was an instant gratification kind of a guy. When he saw a woman who interested him, he went for it—but that was just it. He was rarely interested. There was no shortage of women trailing him, and they were all the same. Vapid, clingy, and superficial.

Across the crowded room, a side door pushed open, and a tiny brunette with crazy curves, purple-streaked hair, and sexy-as-hell lips strode through the entry, hauling a towering bucket of ice. Tyler froze.

"So, tell me, Ty, why should Suzy Housewife download your album instead of Luke Bryan's, huh? He's not hard on the eyes, either, and *he's* married."

Wisps of hair clung to the woman's forehead. She set the

ice down and swiped at her bangs with the back of her hand, causing the hem of her white fitted top to lift. Smooth, tan skin beckoned.

"Tyler, are you even listening to me?" Arianne huffed. "I'm saying that the competition is stiff, and this reporter is questioning if you even know what the hell it is you're selling. We need a rebuttal!"

Looking up from that strip of skin, Tyler discovered a set of gorgeous hazel eyes. They widened, catching his stare before a lighting tech crossed the path between them, breaking the moment.

"Love is my life," he said finally, transferring his gaze to his publicist. "Maybe not the act, but the feelings, the emotions. It consumes me when I'm writing. So, yeah, I'm a bachelor. So what? It doesn't mean I've never cared about anyone." He snuck another peek at the brunette, gratified to find her still watching him from across the chaotic room. "It doesn't mean I don't know what women want. And that's what I give them. I don't need to be in a relationship to do that."

His publicist squeezed her forehead with a manicured hand. "It takes more than going on an occasional date to understand love. Real relationships are complicated. They're messy. Something you would know if you'd ever actually been in one."

At the sarcasm in her voice, Tyler's jaw locked. Arianne winced. She was pushing it, and she knew it. Best in the business or not, this was his life she was talking about…and he controlled her paycheck.

The stirrings of a headache pulsed behind his eyes, which sucked, considering he had a show to do in less than twenty minutes. Rolling his shoulders back, he let out a breath and actually considered what she was saying. He wasn't an idiot. Public perception could make or break a career, and if Arianne was this fired up, then that meant the article posed a real threat.

Unfortunately, this was one area where he refused to budge.

Complicated, messy, *love*…those three words had no place in Tyler Blue's life. Especially since his life was his career. He'd done compromise and obstacles to overcome—that was his past. This right here was *his* time, and he planned to enjoy it.

"Look, I hear what you're saying," he told her. "But there weren't any complaints on the last two albums, and there won't be any on the next. This article will blow over, you'll see." Pushing to his feet, he stuck the damn thing in his pocket and handed Arianne his plate. "Here, finish this. There's something I need to do before the show."

Her lips pursed in annoyance, but she took the plate without a word. As he walked away, he felt her sharp gaze following him across the floor, but only one set of eyes interested him at the moment—hazel ones, currently lit in challenge.

From opposite the long table of food, the brunette gave him a blatant once-over as he came to a stop in front of her, twirling a strand of purple hair around her fingertip. When she reached his lucky belt buckle, her sinful lips twitched.

"If the words, 'Come here often,' leave your mouth, I swear I'll laugh you straight back to roadie-ville." Her words were harsh, but the smile that sprang free was playful, and Tyler found himself mesmerized by the familiar twang of her southern voice.

So much so that he'd almost missed what she said.

"Roadie-ville?"

"Sorry, do you prefer *techie*?" Her cute nose wrinkled as she stuck her hands in her back jeans pockets. "I heard someone else say that earlier, but I swear that sounds like a computer nerd." She looked him up and down again, this time her gaze lingering around his hips. Slightly south of the belt buckle. *Hot damn.* "I think roadie fits you better. Sounds sexier."

Tyler scratched the side of his jaw. Was she messing with him? He'd heard a hell of a lot of come-ons since making it to Nashville and had been propositioned in every way possible. But this was a first. The woman stared back, smiling that damn seductive smile, and he realized she honestly had no clue who he was. For some reason, he was in no hurry to correct that just yet.

He couldn't recall the last time he'd gone anywhere without being recognized, much less his own concert. But since the room was swarming with crew, Tyler could understand the confusion…*if* she weren't a hardcore fan, and clearly, this woman wasn't. Tyler swiped a hand over his mouth, hiding a smile.

"Sugar, you can call me anything you like," he drawled, laying it on thick even to his own ears. Her pretty lips parted, and he grinned. "And what can I call you?"

Her smile twisted into a smirk. "Who said you could call me at all?"

He laughed, shocked again, and for the first time in a long time, speechless.

She winked. "I'm Sherry." When she said her name, she

looked right into his eyes as if he should remember it, and he had no doubt that he would. The confidence pouring off her was sexy as hell. "And…you are?"

"Tyler," he replied, glad she'd gone with just her first name so he could do the same. The rest of the world simply referred to Tyler as Blue, the front man for the band bearing his last name. Even so, he stood back and waited for a sign of recognition.

It never came.

When it became obvious she really had no clue who he was, nor would she guess anytime soon, Tyler felt a knot of tension release between his shoulder blades.

"So, Sherry, you planning to watch tonight's show?"

She pulled a face. "I'm not much for country, other than the line dances. All those songs about trucks and trains and whiskey and dogs, though that last one I can forgive." Her smile softened and Tyler moved closer, wanting to be nearer the genuine warmth of it. "No offense to your boss or anything," she added with a slight grimace. "I heard he's pretty hot…even if he *is* the man-whore of country music."

A shocked laugh burst from his lips. "Excuse me?"

She waved her comment away, as if she hadn't just insulted him to his face—which, he guessed, she hadn't really. At least not on purpose. "Just a theory I have. I'm sure he's a perfectly adequate boss."

Now, Tyler laughed for real. "Yeah, he's…adequate." Shaking his head, he propped his hip on the table. This was the most fun he'd had with a woman in months—and they both still had their clothes on. "So tell me, if you don't like country, what *do* you like?"

"Mostly pop and dance music." She bit her lip and

studied him, lashes lowered as she scanned his body, before subtly nodding. Her smile took on a hint of seduction as she added, "And hot roadies."

Breath left his lungs at the look in her eyes. Their message was clear. Tyler stared back, knowing he could easily lose himself for a night in the mesmerizing kaleidoscope of amber and green. In that sweet, southern voice that reminded him of home. And in the refreshing reality that this woman had no clue who in the hell he was.

With Sherry, he wouldn't have to be *on* all night. Wouldn't have to fulfill a celebrity expectation or survive another conversation with talk of the industry and his musical inspirations. With this tempting waitress, he could just be Tyler, a Louisiana native, lover of Cajun food, and a man extremely attracted to the woman beside him.

Funny. Until that second, he wasn't aware he missed that sense of normalcy.

Reaching out, Tyler brushed away a strand of dampened hair from her neck. The muscles under the silky skin of her throat moved against his fingertips. Chill bumps pricked her skin as she tilted her head back, eyes locked on his in a silent question.

That article in *Country Music Weekly* was right—he wasn't a serial monogamous. But he sure as hell wasn't a monk, either. The fiery glow in her eyes said that if he was interested, she would be his tonight. And he was definitely interested.

"Tyler!"

Sherry jolted at the intrusion, and the moment was gone. Reluctantly, Tyler turned toward the doorway, gritting his teeth. "Yeah?"

His bass player glanced back and forth between them. "It's show time."

Of course it is. Any other night, Tyler was like an ADD kid hyped up on sugar before a performance. The wall of adoration that hit him smack in the face when he took the stage, the hot lights pouring from above—that was where he thrived. But tonight was proving to be far from ordinary. "I'll be right there."

As if they could start without him anyway.

Charlie smirked as he nodded and retreated a few steps, waiting until he was out of Sherry's sight to flash an opened palm. Whether that was code for five minutes or some sort of distant high-five was up for interpretation. Ignoring his idiot best friend, Tyler returned his focus to the woman in front of him.

The heat in Sherry's eyes had dimmed, but it was there, and the air between them still snapped. "Boss man calls?" Her voice was slightly breathless, and there was no stopping the smile crossing his face.

"Something like that."

He rocked back on the heels of his boots, delaying the inevitable. The feeling was apparently mutual because she asked, "Do roadies have to work the whole concert?"

A thrill of satisfaction warmed his blood as disappointment washed over her features. She didn't want him to leave. Glancing at the table, Tyler could tell only half the crew had eaten. There was plenty of food left over, which meant she'd still be here when the concert ended.

"Yeah, generally roadies are pretty busy during a show."

A slight prick of guilt hit him for continuing the ruse. But from what she'd revealed, the playful, simple way they were flirting would end the minute she learned his identity. It was selfish not to correct her. She'd probably be pissed as hell when she found out. But he wasn't ready to relinquish that easy feeling just yet.

Knowing Charlie and the guys were waiting, Tyler slowly backed away. "But don't you go skipping out on me. I'll be looking for you after the show." His gaze fell to her glossy mouth, and he almost groaned when Sherry bit the corner of one painted lip.

As excitement flared in her eyes, he turned on his heel. This was going to be the longest concert of his career.

Chapter Two

The moment Tyler's heavy footsteps faded down the hall, Sherry did a little booty shake. She couldn't believe her luck! This was *exactly* the kind of action she'd envisioned when she concocted her plan and begged to come here, and Tyler had just all but fallen into her lap.

Giftwrapped from above in one sinfully hot package.

Sherry threw her head back and smiled at the ceiling. Goodness, the things that man had done to her with one sizzling look of those bedroom eyes. Her knees were still weak, and her heart was doing the Cajun two-step in her chest. She'd always been the type of girl who jumped in feet first and fell in love at first sight—but this had squat to do with that emotion. This right here was chemistry, and precisely what the doctor had ordered. If a life with Mr. Boring and Dependable was to be her destiny, then a lust-filled weekend with Tyler-the-hunkalicious-roadie would surely fuel her fantasies for the next fifty years. Or longer.

Squealing into her palms, she turned around, eager to finish setting everything out so she could freshen up before Tyler returned…then jumped about a foot when she discovered she wasn't alone like she'd thought. "Son of a biscuit!"

A woman in a power suit appraised her from a good distance away. The same one who had been talking with Tyler before he strode his sexy self over to speak with *her*. One hand held a heaping plate of food—seriously, how on earth did she eat like *that* and still fit into that form-fitting suit of hers?—and the other hand gripped her hip. Her lips were pursed in an unreadable expression, and Sherry swallowed a sudden lump, hoping she wasn't Tyler's woman.

But he came on to me first.

Clutching her chest, she muttered, "Sorry about that." She smoothed back her hair and forced a confident smile. Warmth still spread across her cheeks, but she couldn't do much about that. "Apparently, I'm a sucker for a man with belt buckles the size of Texas."

Sherry waited, watching for a response, an indication the woman was angry, jealous, or simply staring because she'd shaken her butt and squealed like a moron. But the woman gave nothing. Motioning toward the full plate in her hands, she asked, "Can I get you anything?"

"No." The woman lifted her pointed chin, her look turning inquisitive. "As you can see, I have enough to feed an army."

Her lip curled slightly as she said it—not that surprising, since the chick probably never ate more than a crouton—and her whole vibe screamed polish and sophistication. Not at *all* whom she'd pair with the rugged roadie. That left the woman being a New York bigwig with a staring problem.

"I was curious about your catering company, though. The food seems authentic."

Sherry beamed—though she couldn't quite tell if the woman meant that as a compliment or not. "That's because it is. My sister, Colby Robicheaux—well, Colby Robicheaux *Landry*—has an Italian restaurant here in Vegas"—the woman's eyes flared with recognition—"which is how we got this gig, but our home base is in New Orleans. Our contact at the casino knew that and specifically asked for Cajun cuisine."

A horrible thought struck her, and she glanced at the heaping trays of food with a frown. While she'd been setting up, her contact said that the band wouldn't eat until after the performance. And to her knowledge, Blue hadn't even entered the green room before they went on. She'd been semi-stalking the door, curious to see what the hype was about. But maybe she'd missed him. Maybe her contact had gotten it all wrong. Maybe Blue *hated* Cajun food.

"Why?" she asked, trying to keep the panic out of her voice. Colby was a control freak and usually handled all the events, but Sherry had promised she had things under control. "Is Mr. Blue not happy with the selection?" She bit her lip again and took a quick survey of her ingredients. "My sister is the chef, but I can throw something else together if needed."

Cooking for Sherry normally involved cereal bowls and microwaves, but she was 68 percent sure she could whip up a meal in a pinch. Whether or not that meal turned out edible would be the question.

The kitchen had always been Colby-the-wonder-chef's domain. Even her brother had inherited their father's cooking gene to a lesser extent. Sherry, on the other hand, could burn water. When it came to food, her heart just wasn't in it to stay focused. *Her* specialty was customer interaction. Mingling, making people feel welcome. Working the front of the house at their restaurant was the closest she ever got to what she *really* wanted to do with her life.

"No, the food is fine," Ms. New York said, thawing slightly. Her gaze darted to the door Tyler had disappeared through and her brows lifted. "Interesting."

Okay. Obviously this woman was odd with a capital *O*. Something was churning in that über-polished brain of hers, but as long as it didn't involve the food or the job, Sherry didn't really care. She was just counting down the minutes until the woman left so *she* could get back to happy dancing over her future conquest.

"Well, if you're sure you don't need anything..." she said. The woman glanced back, blinking as if coming out of a daze, and Sherry jutted her thumb over her shoulder. "I have to make a run out to our van."

Ms. New York smiled, the intent stare softening to almost friendly. The transformation pricked her suspicion, but she had no clue why. "I'm good, thank you." She strolled forward, and now it was Sherry's turn to stare as she dumped the barely touched plate into the trash. *There goes twenty bucks.* "It was a true pleasure meeting you, Miss..." Her gaze flickered to Sherry's left hand.

"Robicheaux," she confirmed distractedly. It always bothered her to see people wasting food. When the show was over, she was donating the leftovers to a nearby shelter. That plate alone could've fed two kids.

"Enjoy your stay, Ms. Robicheaux. I expect it'll be filled

with amusements." Then the weird woman walked away, laughing softly under her breath.

One thing was for sure. Las Vegas was proving to be anything but boring.

When Sherry returned from the catering van with the last of the supplies, Blue's concert was well under way. Muffled cheers and a dull rhythmic thump shook the walls of the hallway. A pass swung around her neck, and she knew most people in her place would at least take a peek at the stage. But honestly, she had zero interest. Country wasn't her thing. And she was a woman on a mission.

Her eyes locked on the wall clock as she rolled the catering cart into the green room. Time was not her friend. Blue's concert tonight was a short set with an intimate crowd of a few thousand benefitting a local charity, an act she could definitely admire, but it meant she better haul butt. After her run-in with Ms. New York, she needed everything to be perfect when the band arrived.

Carefully checking the room for unexpected company and thankfully finding none, she yanked out her iPhone, selected a playlist, and set it on the table. The familiar beat of her favorite song filled the air, and Sherry set to work. With a smile on her face and a wiggle in her step.

Music was in her blood. Unlike Cane, she couldn't carry a tune in a bucket and instruments hated her with a fierceness, but Sherry could move her body with the best of them. Her mama was a dancer once upon a time, and she'd enrolled Sherry in every dance class in which she expressed an interest. That is to say, all of them. One song bled into another as Sherry twirled, pranced, and swiveled her to-do list into submission.

With a snazzy shuffle-ball-change, she restocked the silverware. A shimmy of her shoulders added flair as she topped off the jambalaya. And an elaborate mix of hip lifts, drops, and figure eights accompanied her adiosing a pile of crumbs and straightening out the tablecloth. She was so into the moves and the music playing on her phone that she actually failed to notice that the music elsewhere had stopped.

That is, until the hair on the back of her neck tingled to life.

Suddenly, the room surged with energy. Her pulse pounded in her ears. She didn't need to turn around to know he was standing behind her. Most likely with a smirk at catching her impromptu belly dance.

Smooth, girl. Real smooth.

Sherry closed her eyes tight, too mortified to face him just yet. "Good show?" she asked.

"The highlight of my night, that's for sure."

Chills skimmed down her spine at the sound of his voice. Deep, rich, and full of the very mischief Tootsie had hinted at back home. The salon owner had said it in reference to Blue…but Sherry doubted even the famous singer had a voice as tempting as Tyler's.

Slowly, Sherry turned around. The devil in denim was leaning against the doorjamb, gaze glued to her ass. Or where her ass had been. His lips were curved in a crooked, boyish grin, and when his green eyes moved to hers, the true meaning of his answer became clear.

Yep, he'd caught her performance all right. And he had

enjoyed every gyrating second.

Confidence rising, Sherry swirled her curvy hips in a slow, sultry circle, then ran her hands down her jean-clad thighs. "Shakira ain't got nothing on these hips."

Tyler's grin grew, and his eyes lit with amusement. Holy ovaries exploding. If Sherry had thought this man's smirk was sexy, the power of his full-wattage smile about knocked her on her swiveling butt. The electric air between them intensified. Seconds stretched in silence. When he finally opened his mouth to speak, she expected a flirty comeback or a naughty sexual innuendo.

Instead, he shocked the wit right out of her as he said, "Spend the weekend with me."

• • •

"Say what?"

The gorgeous brunette blinked up at him, clearly shocked. Frankly, so was Tyler. That request had come out of nowhere. But the more he thought about it, the more the idea of an incognito weekend thrilled him.

"I'd like you to spend the weekend with me," he said again, clearer this time, and with more conviction. Strolling forward, he realized he was actually nervous that she might say no. And wasn't that ironic. Countless women had offered him something similar, hoping for the fantasy, some not even caring if it was only for one night, and Tyler had been the one to gently decline. As much as he hated being in that position, this was worse. Gauging the look in her eyes and wishing like hell he could decipher their secrets, he said, "Unless you already have plans."

Tomorrow *was* New Year's Eve. Gorgeous women rarely spent that holiday alone. For all he knew, she'd come here with a boyfriend. The likelihood of that settled in his gut like a rock.

"Nope. No plans." Sherry's lips quirked as if she found something funny. "Nothing concrete at least."

Relief unclenched his fists, and a rush of anticipation warmed his blood. This was what he needed. An entire weekend with someone who wanted nothing from him, other than his company. And what he presumed would be one hell of a night between the sheets. No expectations, no pressure, just fun. The exact opposite of a relationship.

Arianne was upset about the article, but she'd just have to get over it. Blue's records were selling like mad, and they were about to drop their next album. Well, once they completed the last song and added a few finishing touches. His credibility was fine, and the band's future was bright. With or without a woman permanently planted at his side.

But temporarily was a whole different matter.

Reaching out, Tyler snagged Sherry's hand in his. "So that's a yes?"

She nibbled her lip, and a soft pink colored her cheeks. Her gaze darted to the room crowding behind them. She was stalling. Disappointment crashed over him, an emotion he hadn't experienced in quite some time.

He wasn't a fan.

Tyler gave a small nod, fixing to let her off the hook and back to work. But just as he opened his mouth to say forget it, Sherry's smile broke free, hitting him full force in the chest.

"No," she said. "That's a *hell* yes."

Chapter Three

Fluffing her hair in the hotel room mirror the next morning, Sherry tilted her glass to her lips and knocked back her mimosa. Room service seriously rocked. Another thing that rocked? Hot, mysterious roadies with a surprising romantic side. At least that's what Sherry decided to call Tyler's strange, secretive quirks. It was a heck of a lot better than believing that tiny voice in her brain, saying he was hiding something.

Honestly, so what if he *was* hiding something. They weren't building a relationship here. This was about fun, and they were both consenting adults. Even though it was weird that he'd disappeared right after he asked her to spend the weekend with him, only to return freshly showered after she'd packed up and practically written off their plans, she was all in. Maybe living on the road made him a bit dodgy. Maybe he had a James Bond complex. Maybe he picked up some weirdness from his equally secretive boss, who ended up being a no-show after the concert last night. All Sherry knew was that Tyler was exciting. He'd swept her off her feet with his flirtation and invitation, then shocked her right out of her shoes by not immediately whisking her back to his room. He also refused to tell her anything about what they were doing today, only that she should prepare for a day of adventure.

One she had no doubt would end with a *bang*.

Her tummy flipped, and she bounced on her toes. This would officially be the first time she aimed for a quick fling. Sure, she'd had them before, even claimed up, down, and sideways that was what she'd wanted—only to secretly hope for so much more. That was what happened with her ex, and he'd been the kick in the pants she'd needed. If she were going to change her fate, she'd need to change her type. Find a Mr. Boring. A cute/stuffy accountant type à la Will Trahan. And hot roadie or not, that was still her plan.

But with chemistry like theirs, this was the perfect setup for a fling…and Sherry wanted to go out on a high note.

Bring on the roadie!

Her phone buzzed with a text on the granite counter, interrupting her girl power playlist. She snatched up the phone, expecting it to be Tyler, and rolled her eyes at Angelle's message.

Get in any trouble yet?

Sherry tapped a fingernail on the screen, pondering how to reply. Anything she told her best friend would make it back to the woman's fiancé. And anything Angie told Sherry's brother, Cane, would most definitely circle back to Colby.

Not yet, she typed with a wicked grin. *But there's still plenty of time. Tell my siblings they best gather bail money now. Don't worry, you'll be my one phone call.*

Sherry checked for lipstick on her teeth as she waited for a reply. It didn't take long.

I'll be waiting eagerly for your call. Take lots of pics! Xoxo

It was a sad day when she lost the ability to shock her loved ones.

Smiling wide, Sherry sent her love back, and then locked her phone. The music was still paused, and the hotel room was quiet. *Too* quiet. But what if music drowned out Tyler's knock at her door? That would seriously suck. She glanced in the mirror a final time, deciding she looked presentable—no eyeliner smudges, hair falling softly around her shoulders, jeans and sweater the perfect blend between dressy and casual—and then plopped onto the bed. Hopefully the hotel's welcome binder would prove fascinating.

Ankle bouncing, jostling the bed, Sherry turned the pages. The menu already thoroughly studied, she flipped to the section about the casino. Glossy photos of themed slot machines, western décor, and women in cowboy boots set off a flood of memories. Despite the heady buzz that ran in her veins and snapped in the air between her and Tyler, Sherry had been a *good* girl last night. They hadn't even kissed, for cripes sake, but *that* was all on Tyler. For some reason, he was all about dragging out the anticipation. Reveling in the tension building between them. Making out hot and heavy on a lounge chair by the pool would've been fine with her, but her mysterious roadie had chuckled low in his throat and whispered, "There'll be time for that later."

But tonight, their time was up. No more waiting. No

more games. This was her last night in Sin City, and she intended to spend it doing sinfully yummy things.

A purposeful knock cut short her daydreams, and Sherry jumped to her feet. Shaking out her shoulders, she half skipped toward the door and threw it open.

"Mornin'."

And what a good morning it was. Tyler stood before her, six-plus feet of denim-clad hotness. A woodsy scent wafted toward her, and she inhaled deeply, loving the smell of his cologne. The man was gorgeous, and he was hers for the next twenty-four hours.

Closing the door behind her, she looked up into deep green eyes swirling with mutual desire and asked, "Do I at least get a hint *now* as to where we're going?"

Tyler shook his head and grinned.

• • •

"Okay, roadie-man, we're talking *serious* points here." Damp tendrils stuck to Sherry's flushed cheeks as she glanced back at the aerialist in flight. "I can't believe your boss hooked us up like this. Either Blue respects the crap out of you, or he's hella generous. Either way, this date freaking rocks!"

Tyler smiled, ignoring the stab of guilt that coincided with her praise. He'd tell her the truth eventually—he would. But was it a crime that he enjoyed this freedom so much? Yeah, so, he'd flubbed a few facts here and there. Claimed his big-shot boss had hooked them up. Got the Eiffel Tower to open for an early lunch and scored private lessons with Cirque du Soleil. But he hadn't lied about anything important. Other than his career and hinting at his pay grade, he'd been completely himself, straight up.

Only more so.

Sherry's energy was infectious. Her uncontained enthusiasm for life contagious. He felt like a kid again, laughing loud, chasing her around the auditorium. Music meant everything to Tyler, and nothing beat the rush of performing in front of a packed house—but spending the last eighteen hours with this woman, remembering how life used to be *before* the stress and pressure of expectation weighed him down was a rush of its own.

"I take it you enjoyed your aerial stunt?"

Sherry's face lit up in a smile, and he couldn't help feeling smug. He'd put that there. Sure, as far as first dates went, this was extreme. They could've easily laid low, gone somewhere simple, but he'd wanted to spoil her. Growing up, money equaled tension. Struggle. Deprivation. Finally, he had a bank account that allowed him to be a little frivolous, and he enjoyed taking advantage of that.

Plus, the private dining room and secluded auditorium kept Tyler from being outed by his fans.

A look of near awe crossed Sherry's face. "I've always loved dance and gymnastics, but that…Tyler, holy crap!" She laughed again, and the musical sound was like oxygen to starving lungs. "We *flew*!"

She reached out and fisted his long-sleeved shirt in her hands, beaming up at him with complete gratitude. Not with undeserved adoration or manufactured, starry-eyed lust, but with sincere pleasure and pure feminine appreciation.

That expression was addictive.

It made him feel like he could do anything. Like he was invincible. Worthy. And at the same time, it nearly brought him to his knees. All the groupies in the world couldn't replicate the satisfaction coursing through him, and suddenly, nothing mattered more, there was nothing he *wanted* more, than to kiss her.

To feel the lips that had held him captive since he caught her nibbling them in the green room.

To taste the mouth he'd denied himself last night.

Since becoming a man and accomplishing his dream, Tyler could count two times he'd deprived himself of something he truly wanted. The first was passing on the chance to open for Brad Paisley after his mom's diagnosis. The second was last night. The temptation to take Sherry back to his hotel room had been almost impossible to ignore—but he'd done it. Guilt over his lie of omission kept him from taking what they both obviously wanted. Later, as he'd tossed and turned in an impossibly large bed, he battled back and forth between admitting the truth, doing the right thing, and his selfish need to hold onto the freedom. The sensation of being wanted solely for who he was as a man and not what he could do for their career. Or for bragging rights. By the time the sun rose, Tyler had come to a decision.

This wasn't some sixth grade first kiss or crush. He and Sherry were adults, and they both knew the score. And right now, all he wanted was a taste.

He was almost positive he'd admit the truth before it went any further.

Before I take her to my bed.

Dropping his gaze to the object of his obsession, Tyler placed his knuckle beneath her chin. He gently tipped it toward him, and cinnamon-scented breath hit his parted lips. His mouth watered in anticipation. Snaking his other arm around her lower back, he tugged her still closer, lifting his eyes to hers.

"I've never seen anything so beautiful."

Sherry's eyes widened before letting her lashes fall heavily, covering the intoxicating swirl of amber and green. Licking her lips, she said, "Well, the aerialist did most of the work."

He chuckled. God, she made him smile. This was the happiest he remembered being in a long time. Hell, he was even flirting. When was the last time he'd bothered to do that? Lately, he barely said hello to a woman before she tried slipping him her room key.

Resting his forehead against hers, he breathed in her light floral scent and said, "You know damn well I ain't talking about your trapeze skills."

White teeth trapped her bottom lip. In slow motion, he watched her tilt her head and bring that lip nearer and nearer to his. He'd made it clear what he wanted, but she'd have to be the one to take it. He wouldn't force this, especially not since he wasn't being totally honest yet.

Sherry's dark lashes flickered, and Tyler was ensnared in the intensity of her stare. Focused questioning that softened into the sexy confidence of a woman who knew she was desired. A smile tipped her lips and she closed her eyes.

And his cell phone rang.

"Dammit to hell," he cursed, watching as Sherry skittered out of his arms. Wide-eyed, she unsuccessfully stifled a laugh as he shoved a hand into his pocket and snatched his phone in frustration. "What?"

"Dude, Nolan and Arianne are going ape-shit," Charlie replied, ignoring Tyler's bark. "Where the hell are you?"

Schooling his features, Tyler pressed the phone to his thigh and held up an index finger. "Give me a minute. Then we're picking up right where we left off."

His voice was a low warning, and Sherry's smile turned wicked as she winked and uncapped her water bottle. The sight of those lips wrapped around the opening was the cruelest type of torture. And she knew it. He clenched his teeth and hiked down the aisle so she wouldn't overhear.

"You've got impeccable timing, you know that?" He glanced over his shoulder and said, "I needed a personal day, all right? Sue me. What the hell do they care anyway? I checked the schedule. Nothing was on it. Blue has no commitments except studio time next week. So why have they been blowing up my phone all damn morning? Where's the fire?"

On top of annoying the crap out of him, the constant texts and calls from his agent and publicist had made Sherry suspicious. They'd also given Tyler ample opportunity to correct her misassumption, but he'd been too selfish to do that. He'd almost turned it off a million times, but his dad had this number. He'd told his old man to call any time, for any reason, if he or his mom needed him. The frustration and questions weren't enough to risk missing that call.

"The label got wind of the article," Charlie said. "They're using it to twist the system, man. Stone wants three new songs added to the album. One a duet with Kristen Wilson and two more that specifically hint at *committed* love." He made a disgusted sound, and Tyler imagined him flipping off the air. His friend hated this bullshit as much as he did. "And Ty, I hate to tell you this, but if you don't start playing along or find a woman of your own, it looks like they're gonna do it for you."

Tyler kicked the chair in front of him, watching the seat bounce with force. Suddenly, he couldn't breathe. He was in the middle of a date with an incredible woman, and Belle Meade Records was tightening the screws. That's what he was, too. *Screwed.* His career might just be in jeopardy after all. Now he had to come up with three new songs, sing one with a woman he'd barely met, and fake a relationship for the fans, or risk losing the one thing in this world he gave a shit about: his music.

Squeezing the bridge of his nose, Tyler closed his eyes. "Thanks for the heads-up."

They disconnected, and Tyler took a deep breath, then let it out slowly. The proverbial shit was about to hit the fan, and he had no clue what to do next. Other than finish his date.

"Everything okay?" Sherry's floral scent enveloped him a half second before her gentle hands closed around his shoulders. He craned his neck as she began kneading the knots. "Let me guess—that was the boss man?" she asked, giving him a sympathetic smile. "If we need to cut this date short, I totally—"

"No." Tyler shook his head. "We're not going anywhere." They may be about to mess with his life, but he refused to let the label ruin their date. Forcing a lighthearted grin he didn't quite feel, he said, "Wait till you see what I have planned next."

The concern on her beautiful face eased, replaced by excitement. The tension in his shoulders melted under her fingers. "Really? There's more?"

"Plenty," he assured her, taking her hand and bringing it

to his lips. "Ready to go?"

She flashed a smile and nodded, and threading their fingers together, Tyler led her to the exit.

He had no clue what tomorrow would bring or what his next step should be to protect his career. But those were decisions for later. Tonight was New Year's Eve. Tomorrow, Sherry Robicheaux was on a plane back to New Orleans, and he was, more than likely, off to Nashville to discuss his new fake relationship.

The thought twisted his insides.

One thing was certain. If this was going to be his last true night of freedom, he was going to enjoy the hell out of it.

Chapter Four

An incessant buzz drilled its way through Tyler's ears, rousing him from a deep sleep with the subtlety of a woodpecker. He blindly slapped a hand out to silence his cell phone but knocked it to the floor instead. *Great.* The room fell into silence for a nanosecond, and then the buzz began again. Groaning, he peeled open his eyelids to turn off the damn thing, only to have bright sunlight stab his corneas. He slammed them shut with a curse.

Hangovers sucked ass.

His mouth was drier than the desert outside his window. It tasted like tequila. Memories of *why* it tasted that way swam before the backs of his eyes like a tidal wave of booze.

Dancing. Liquor. *Lots* of liquor. Not nearly enough food to balance out said liquor. Fireworks. Sherry's laughter… blurred images of her head tipped back in passion.

Tyler's eyes popped open again.

Sherry. He jerked his head to the side, pain slicing

through his skull as he surveyed the rumpled sheets. No sexy brunette zonked out beside him. He glanced around the room, more carefully this time, and saw clothes strewn across every surface. A bra dangled from the television set. Definitely not his.

Slumping back against the pillows, Tyler swiped his hands across his eyes. He dug the heels of his palms into his eye sockets and tried to piece together exactly what happened last night. He distinctly remembered the call with Charlie—how could he forget?—then taking Sherry back to her room so she could freshen up. He'd picked her up an hour later, they hit the casino floor, and then…what?

A feminine moan, and not the pleasured kind he enjoyed, sounded from the bathroom. Tyler stopped rubbing his eyes. If Sherry felt anywhere near how he did, she was in a world of hurt. Yawning, he slid his hands down his face, preparing to head in and check on her…only to still as his gaze fell upon a silver band wrapped around his finger.

His ring finger. On his left hand.

No.

No, no, no, no, no.

His arm extended with a jolt. That wasn't there. He was imagining things. Delusional from dehydration. No matter how blitzed out of his mind Tyler had gotten, he'd never do something that stupid.

A second moan came from the bathroom, and Tyler shot to a sitting position. Pain exploded behind his eyes. Disbelief twisted with dread as he stared at the closed door, knowing what he had to do. Go in there. Check on Sherry.

See if her hand held a matching silver band.

"Shit." Cautiously, as if the damn ground was going to

latch onto his ankle and drag him into marital hell, Tyler set his feet to the carpet. Pushing to a stand, he took a tentative step—then stopped dead in his tracks when he spied two things on the nightstand.

A DVD boasting the title "Our Wedding."

And a photograph the happy couple had apparently taken in front of a chapel. Sherry in a white lacy veil over her sweater-and-jeans combo, him with a damn top hat, and both of them wearing matching, inebriated grins.

Wouldn't the tabloids love to get a hold of that?

Tyler swiped the evidence in his hand and did the first thing he could think of—dumped it into the nightstand drawer. Then he snatched his discarded jeans from the floor and hastily yanked them up his hips. Plans and scenarios ping-ponged in his mind as he zipped his fly. He was still dreaming. They were gag rings bought from a vending machine. Tyler stopped and tapped a finger against the metal. Jeweler he wasn't, but that shit looked and felt real.

His stomach rolled and cold pricked the back of his neck. His hand went limp and slapped against his thigh, crinkling paper in his pocket. He stopped breathing. Another memory flashed as he shoved his hand inside, not wanting to do it, but at the same time knowing that he *had* to, and he withdrew his death warrant. A Clark County certificate of marriage.

There it was, written in ink. Tyler Blue of Opelousas and Sherry Robicheaux of Magnolia Springs had gotten hitched at the Love Me Tender Wedding Chapel. Most likely by Elvis.

The words swam in his vision. It was like some sick joke. That or a cruel twist of fate. Never in his life would he want this. Marriage wasn't for him—at least not for another twenty years. Attachment, commitment, they got in the way of dreams.

His chest spasmed. God, had he even told Sherry who he really was? Had she seen the certificate? Tyler couldn't remember. It had been his intention to tell her everything after dinner—before sleeping with her. But since he was standing there married, he figured at some point along the way he'd decided to chuck his prior plans out the damn window.

Shit…he was *married.*

A cough came from the bathroom and he panicked. Quickly, he pocketed the paper declaring the owner of the voice Sherry *Blue*, wife of a world-famous musician, and looked around the room for a sign. An out. A silver lining of any kind. Other than the band around his finger.

The only thing that came to mind was that as bad as this disaster was—and it was a disaster—it could be a hell of a lot worse. This wasn't permanent. As shitty and unwanted as this was, people got out of drunken marriages all the time. And without anyone finding out.

But how many of them are celebrities?

The truth was that despite what his *wife* believed, he wasn't some Joe Schmo off the street. Was he dumb enough to think Tyler Blue could actually get married and divorced in a span of a couple weeks and have no one in the media ever find out?

And that didn't even factor in the bride.

Tyler didn't know much about Sherry Robicheaux. Barely anything, really. But he knew she was passionate and spontaneous. It was what drew him to her in the first place. Was it that much of a stretch to think she also believed in love at first sight? The very real possibility made his head pound harder.

Sherry could be in that bathroom right now, hungover and cursing the world, but blissed out about being married. He hoped to God she wasn't. Because for Tyler, marriage to any woman, gorgeous or not—*sweet* or not—was out of the damn question.

"Tyler?"

The rough question made him flinch. Sherry's voice sounded like she'd gargled rocks. Tyler blew out a breath and ran sweaty palms down the denim on his thighs. It was time to face the music. Squaring his shoulders, he took a breath and prepared to enter the bathroom. To greet—and console—his wife.

• • •

Waking up face-first on the bathroom floor may not be cause for alarm for everyone, but for Sherry, it ranked right up there. Especially since she knew the second her eyes cracked open that it wasn't *her* bathroom.

Fuzzy-edged memories pranced around her brain, just out of reach, as she hooked a hand on the toilet seat and pushed to a sitting position.

The world tilted.

As her stomach heaved, she dove for the porcelain throne, but nothing came up. Nothing other than slightly sharper memories. Ones that told of dancing, magical fountains, way too much alcohol, and some very, very sexy time between the sheets. The images pulsed like an old movie, blanking out too much for her liking, but a flush heated her skin at what she *could* recall.

Hot damn. She'd been right. A night with a roadie like Tyler would definitely keep her fantasies occupied for years to come. Shame she couldn't remember more.

Resting her head on the cool surface, she surveyed the fancy digs with half-lidded eyes. It was a hell of a room, particularly on a roadie's budget. Further proof that either Tyler was in tight with his boss, or Blue wasn't nearly the egotist she'd pegged him to be. Too bad she hadn't had a chance to meet him the other night.

"Tyler?" she called out again, wincing at the roughness of her voice. She sounded like an old lady who smoked a bazillion packs a day. Lovely. Grabbing hold of either side of the toilet, she wobbled first to her knees, and then her feet. The mirror was just a few feet away. Time to inspect the damage.

Eyes half closed, she fumbled forward and latched onto the counter to steady herself. Hangovers really didn't suit her. She turned on the faucet, and as she waited for the plastic cup to fill with water, Sherry raised her eyes to her reflection.

"What the freaking *hell*?!?"

She was wearing a wedding veil.

A wedding veil was on her head. It was white. It had lace. And it was on her freaking *head.*

She didn't have a single stitch of clothing on her body otherwise, but she did have that.

"Hubba, hubba, wubba…what?"

She blinked hard, repeatedly, thinking her reflection would change. It didn't. Cold water ran over her hand, and it didn't wake her from the bizarre dream. The door behind her started to creak open, and Sherry jumped, snatching a towel off the floor.

When she saw a huge honking diamond on her finger, she ditched the towel and screamed instead.

"Whoa!" Tyler walked in, shirtless with jeans riding low on his hips, holding up his hands. "Do you want people to call security?"

Ignoring his flippant response and her naked glory, Sherry thrust her left hand in his face. "Is this real?"

A muscle popped in his jaw, and his eyes glared at the ring on her finger like it was the bloody Ebola virus. "I don't think it's a cubic zirconia if that's what you're asking."

"Not the freaking diamond!" she screamed again. The sound echoed off the hard surfaces of the room and reverberated in her skull. Heeding his warning—seriously, the last thing she needed right now was witnesses—she lowered her voice and clarified through gritted teeth. "What it represents."

"Oh, yeah. That." Tyler's lips formed a tight smile that belied his casual approach to the horrible situation they'd found themselves in. "Apparently we're hitched."

Sherry turned and thumped her head on the wall.

Perfect. Just perfect. The one time in her life she actually attempted a fling—a *one*-night stand—and this was the result. Something permanent. She could never get it right.

"Ugh," she groaned, the sound half drowned by the wall. "How much did we drink?"

"Judging from my massive migraine and the fact you woke up in the bathroom, I'm going with a lot." Sherry shifted her head so she could peer at her groom with one eye. Tyler slid her a crooked grin. "Cheer up. We're not the first idiots who've done this. Getting wasted and waking up married in Vegas is pretty much a cliché, isn't it?"

Sherry blew out a breath. "My bookshelves are filled with that very thing," she agreed. Those stories also involved happily ever afters—an outcome that would *not* be happening here. "Okay, so what do we do? You have a life, a tour to get back to, and I, I have…" What? What did she have? A great family, a job that she enjoyed, even if it wasn't her dream, and a love life that was in the toilet. But… "I have a life plan!"

Picking up her head, she stared at him with what she was sure screamed desperation. "No offense, Tyler, but I was through with love screw-ups. This weekend was supposed to be my last hurrah. Starting today, I was going to be a new woman. A one-eighty from the relationship disaster of the past. I was going to find Mr. Boring!"

The squiggle on his forehead said he was either highly confused or extremely amused by her confession, but honestly, she was too distraught to care. Without breaking eye contact, Tyler bent at the knee, stooped down, and then popped back up. "Here."

She glanced down to see he had a towel in his hand, and she felt her cheeks go hot. *D'oh.* Conversations about screwing up your life and ways to dig yourself out of that mess were best handled clothed. He waited until she'd wrapped the terry cloth around her body and tucked it securely before speaking.

"Listen, I get it. This wasn't my plan, either. I like my life easy, and no offense to *you*," he said with a smile, "but marriage is far from that. Especially one to a stranger—no matter how gorgeous she is."

Sherry felt herself smiling, despite the extreme awkwardness of the situation. The man she married (married!) was a charmer, no doubt about that. In fact, that was the reason they were in this mess in the first place. He'd *literally* charmed the pants right off her.

A horrid thought struck the smile clear off her face. "Last night…did we…?" Chewing her lip, she stared at him and asked, "Did we use protection?"

Tyler frowned, and Sherry squeezed her eyes shut. How could she not remember? Could they have been that stupid?

Or, stupid-*er*?

"Yeah, we used protection." She opened her eyes to see him rake his fingers through his hair. "That much I do remember."

"Thank you, Jesus." Sherry made the sign of the cross, kissed her fingers, and pointed to the ceiling. "Okay, so no permanent damage done. Right? Not really. We can get out of this easily enough." She began pacing the length of the room. "I mean, not today. It takes time. And I have a plane to catch. And I still have to go back to my room and pack." She lifted her head. "What hotel am I in right now?"

"The Moonshine," he told her. "Same as yours." She nodded, and he placed his hands on her shoulders. "Listen, I need you to take a breath for me, okay? I know you're freaking out. I am, too. But honestly, this will be fine. I'll call the band's lawyers and get them on it, and we'll have this taken care of in no time. I promise."

"You think Blue will let you use his lawyers?"

An odd look washed over Tyler's face, but it was gone in an instant. "Yeah. But uh, like you said, you have a plane to catch. You let me worry about all of the other stuff, and you just lay low for the next few days. I'll call you as soon as I hear anything."

Sherry nodded again, the effects of the hangover and marital un-bliss making the edges of her vision fuzzy. *Lay low?* She wondered briefly why she'd have to do that, but then was distracted by the sight of his jeans slipping dangerously low as he trudged into the hotel room and grabbed his cell phone off the floor. Oh, right. She was married, and she didn't even have her husband's number.

She slumped against the door as he walked back.

"Here, put your information in." He handed her his phone, and she quickly called herself so that she would have his number, too. He took it back and shoved it in his pocket. The action made his jeans dip even more on his hips, and Sherry had to force her gaze back up. "Why don't you get dressed, and I'll order room service?" he asked.

The offer was sweet, but she could tell he was as twitchy about this predicament as she was. It seemed cruel and unusual punishment for the both of them to delay her leaving. Plus, even the idea of food right now made her want to hurl.

"Nah. I'll get out of your hair. I really do need to pack and get to the airport." Tyler nodded and turned to give her some privacy. "But, hey, Ty?" He glanced back with a raised eyebrow. "You'll call me the second you hear anything, right?"

He gave her a tight smile. "Absolutely."

And with that, he closed the door behind his glorious backside, and she was alone. In her *husband's* bathroom.

What in the hell have I done?

Chapter Five

"Sure, abandon me. I see how it is."

Angelle looked up from her opened bag, a worried line etched between her eyes. Sherry winked. "I'm just teasing, girl. If you want to shack up with my brother, go and live in a sappy, pre-marital squishy love fest. Who am I to complain? We're gonna be sisters soon. I figured you'd leave me eventually."

Sherry was well acquainted with being the odd duck out. Everyone around her was in love and settled, and dang it all, that's what she wanted, too. It was the entire motivation for her relationship makeover resolution. But for some reason, even though the bliss surrounding her was nothing new, it felt bigger post-Vegas. Knowing she was in a loveless mistake of a marriage—and that much further from her ultimate goal—made the depressing lonely truth sting all the more.

Being way too embarrassed to tell anyone the truth

didn't help any, either.

"Well, for now I'm only *semi*-abandoning you," Angie clarified with a grin. "Your brother and I have only been engaged for a month. I'm not ready to jump and move in full time. It's just that with Colby married and the house empty again, this felt like the right step." She grimaced. "Just don't tell my mama. She'd flip."

"My lips are sealed." Sherry made a locking motion over her mouth, and then pretended to throw a key behind her back. It was better that way, anyway, because all this talk of weddings and soon-to-be husbands had her seriously reconsidering unburdening her secret—and that would so not end well.

Knowing Angelle, once she got over the shock of Sherry getting married to a virtual stranger and the subsequent *non*-shock, since she was the family screw-up after all, she'd want to know all about the actual wedding. Only Sherry couldn't remember squat. What kind of bride can't even recall if she said, "I do," or "I will," or abandoned both options and sang an Elvis song instead?

Honey, you're my hunka hunka burning love. Kiss me.

Okay, so the hangover, weary flight, and the news that her best friend was moving out had her a little loopy. Even more of a reason to keep her mouth shut.

New New Year's resolution: no more alcohol. Or drunken marriages.

Zipping up her duffel, Angelle blew her bangs off her forehead and surveyed the room. "You sure you're okay with me leaving most of my stuff for now? I'm still paying half the rent, and don't even think you can stop me. Until I'm officially married, I'd still like a place to come back to if

I think your brother or I need some space, you know?"

Beneath her friend's anxiety, Sherry saw the unmistakable glow of bliss. "Of course it's okay."

The truth was, she was stoked that her big brother had finally found a good woman, and even more excited that Angelle would soon become her sister. Letting her own depression over being the Robicheaux family fifth wheel interfere was just selfish.

"So, what's left to pack?" Her voice was pitched exceptionally loud, and she smiled wide—probably *too* wide—to compensate. Evidently, she failed, because Angie looked at her as if she had two heads. "Have you checked the bathroom yet?"

She waved her hand in the direction of the hall and caught a flash of silver. *Damn*. The ring. Why hadn't she taken the stupid thing off yet? Oh, right, because she'd liked the look of it on her finger. How pathetic was that? Convulsively, she shoved her hand deep in her pocket and attempted to wiggle it off.

"Sher, you're positive you're okay? I don't want you to take this the wrong way, but you've been acting strangely since you got in last night." Angelle frowned. "Stranger than normal."

Sherry snorted. "Gee, thanks." With a sigh, she gave up on the wiggling—the ring was too damn tight to budge—and grabbed one of Angelle's bags with her right hand. "And yes, I'm fine. It was just...a very event-filled trip. I guess I'm still recovering."

That was probably the truest thing she'd said since she returned.

Nodding her head, indicating Angelle should lead the

way, Sherry began the trek to the front door. With every footfall, the word *stupid* rang out in her mind. As much as she hated to admit it, if this kind of thing actually did happen to anyone outside of romance novels or soap operas, it made sense that it had happened to her. Trouble followed where she tread. She'd gone in with a plan, a way to straighten out her life, and her drunken self had decided to say screw that and propose to a roadie instead.

But the roadie said yes.

That one puzzle piece didn't quite fit. Obviously, she must've been the one to suggest they do it. This had her written all over it. But had Tyler really been that drunk that he'd agree? Had he thought it was a game? They hadn't spoken since she'd left his hotel room almost twenty-four hours prior, and the silence was making her antsy. What if Blue didn't come through? Refused to lend Tyler his lawyers? What would be their next step?

No. She shook her head and adjusted the strap of Angelle's duffel on her shoulder. Everything would be fine. Her plan was still intact—just delayed a little—and in the end, she'd have a seriously crazy memory to cling to during her straight-laced future.

Feeling oddly better, Sherry wrapped her hand around the doorknob, stopping just short of opening it. "I know you're only going a few miles away," she said, a wave of emotion suddenly hitting her. "And that I'll still see you all the time. But chica, I'm gonna miss you."

Angelle's bright eyes filled with tears. Without permission, another pair of green eyes flashed in Sherry's mind, and she promptly whisked them away. "I'm gonna miss you, too."

They smiled at each other, relishing in the sappy sentimentality of it all, before Sherry exhaled a long breath. "Enough of that. We're supposed to be happy. This is awesome, girl, and you should be all smiles." She turned the knob and winked. "Let's do this thing."

She tugged open the door and barely got a foot past the threshold when a young woman appeared out of nowhere. "Are you Sherry?"

"Jesus, Mary, and Joseph!" Sherry clutched her chest, panting as she glanced around the front yard. "Were you, like, hiding in the bushes?"

"Are you Sherry?" the woman asked again, her blond head bobbing as she consulted her phone. She nodded. "Yep, it's her."

Before Sherry could respond, or ask whom she was speaking to, an older man materialized with a literal flash.

Blinking in surprise, she stared in confusion at the camera in his hand. Angelle clasped Sherry's shoulder and whispered, "Are you in some sort of trouble?"

"Uh, not that I'm aware of," she whispered back.

Angelle's eyes narrowed. "Excuse me, what exactly is this about?" Hand on jutted hip, her southern manners and newfound feisty personality made for an interesting combination.

The blonde held up her palm. "We're from *Country Insider* and just want the exclusive scoop about her recent trip." Behind her, the cameraman flashed some type of official-looking badge.

"Exclusive scoop?" Sherry asked with a laugh. "Do your readers really want to know the eating habits of roadies and crew members? Because I hate to tell you, sweetie, I never met Blue. If you're looking for dirt, you're barking up the wrong tree." *And flew a heck of a long way for nothing.*

Instead of looking disappointed, the woman rolled her eyes. "Sure you didn't. It was another purple-haired waitress from Louisiana who married him."

Wait…

"Married?" Sherry and Angelle asked at the same time. They looked at each other, and Sherry lifted her shoulders to say, *I don't know what she's talking about.* It wasn't a total lie, either. But Angie's gaze grew suspicious.

The weight of the ring on Sherry's finger grew heavy and she took a step back. This was seriously the oddest prank ever invented. With three pairs of eyes watching her with varying degrees of interest, she said, "Honey, for real, I don't know who your source is, but you got some facts confused."

Though not nearly as much as Sherry wished.

"So this isn't you and Tyler Blue outside the Love Me Tender Wedding Chapel two days ago?" She held up her cell phone displaying, in embarrassing full color, a picture of her and Tyler. Sherry was wearing that horrid veil, and he was in a ridiculous top hat.

Crap on a freaking, stupid, flaming stick!

Angelle's jaw dropped in Sherry's peripheral. The time for denial was over. Sighing, she admitted, "Okay, that *is* me, but that's not…" Her head snapped back and she snatched the woman's phone. "Hold on, what did you say his name was?"

"Tyler Blue," she replied with a huge smile, glancing back at her cameraman. She gave him some sort of signal and he stepped forward—just as the ground under Sherry's feet started to shift. "Lead singer of Blue, God's gift to country music. And your new husband. Am I right?"

Without thought, Sherry sunk to the ground, sticking out a hand for balance as she sat on her front stoop. This wasn't happening. He was Tyler, the roadie, not the lead singer.

The New York bigwig with a staring problem flashed in her mind. Along with the fact that Blue had never come in for food. And that Tyler had made himself scarce when others *were* there.

The nonstop phone calls.

The weird looks he'd given her.

The impossible, amazing, obviously *celebrity*/VIP-treatment-filled date.

"Holy crap." Slowly, she brought her hands up to her mouth and squeezed her lips, almost as if she could squish the words right back in. Saying anything aloud was like admitting the reporter's claims were true. But they were true…weren't they?

What in the heck did I step into this time?

A gasp broke above her head, and she glanced up in time to see shock wash over Angelle's face. She grabbed Sherry's left hand and thrust it out—at the exact moment that another flash went off.

Win!

• • •

"She's perfect. Seriously, I couldn't have handpicked you anyone better." The mile-wide smile on Arianne's face was almost as disturbing as the words coming out of her mouth. "Tammy Paxton's gonna eat her words."

Tyler grunted, and Charlie shot him a look. He'd joined

their come-to-Jesus meeting at Belle Meade Records for moral support—and to try to keep the fallout from his lead singer's drunken night to a minimum. Charlie was the one who'd convinced him to seek advice in the first place. It had been Tyler's intention to handle everything on his own. Contact his lawyers and not tell Arianne; his agent, Nolan; or the label a thing until the divorce papers were filed and the damage was done. But his friend was right. This was his career on the line. The one thing that mattered more than Tyler's freedom. It wasn't a situation to play fast and loose with the truth.

That's what got him in this shit in the first place.

The problem was that this marriage was a sham he wanted *out* of, and his team had all but thrown him a damn parade in the lobby. They'd completely glossed over the fact that it was a mistake. And now, huddled in a cushy meeting room with a full background check on one Sherry Elizabeth Robicheaux complete, their enthusiasm was off the charts.

Tyler rapped his knuckles against the tabletop. "Why's she so perfect?"

Charlie raised an eyebrow. Hell if he knew where that had come from. His mission today was to sway popular opinion *away* from the unholy union—but he also couldn't help a mild case of curiosity. In just forty-eight hours, the sassy woman had turned his entire world upside down. And Tyler hadn't stopped thinking about her since she'd left his hotel room.

"Other than a rumor of possible infidelity on her father's part," Arianne replied, opening the file in front of her, "her family is squeaky clean. They own a Cajun restaurant in a suburb of New Orleans, which appears to be the heart of the small town. She does charity work for every organization known to man. She pays her taxes, her credit rating is through the roof, and the people who live there love her. Her sister is even a bit of a celebrity in the culinary world." She closed the folder and smiled. "Tyler, you found yourself a somewhat edgy southern belle. Other than the hair and sass, which may even work in her favor with the fans, she's damn near perfect."

Well then. Would now be the time to mention he wanted out of the marriage ASAP?

And that the wife in this scenario wanted out as much as he did?

Charlie caught his gaze and shook his head. Apparently not.

Instead, his bassist spoke up. "So, how would this work?" Arianne smirked, and Charlie rolled his eyes. "What I mean is, is the hint of marriage enough for the media? Could they, I don't know, divorce quietly tomorrow? Hypothetically speaking," he added when Nolan's eyes narrowed. "They live in different states and we have a tour in the fall. What I'm asking is, is leaking the details enough, or do they have to be seen together, live together, what?"

All excellent questions. Tyler's gaze swung to the man at the head of the table.

David Stone, CEO of Belle Meade Records, held Tyler's career in the palm of his hand. Blue had come out of the bullpen swinging, and they'd knocked the last two albums out of the park. Their band scored the label a dozen number-one singles and more money than most of their other artists combined. But Stone was a shark with entitlement issues. Piss the man off, not deliver what he wanted? He wouldn't think twice about dropping you.

"Have you gentlemen glanced at Twitter lately?" David asked, leaning back and rolling a pen in his hand. "Stopped by your band's Facebook page? Your fans have started polls about whom you should be dating. Entire websites dedicated to the subject have sprung up."

It sounded to Tyler like people needed to get a damn life. "Oh yeah?" he asked, amused as much as he was irritated. "Who's in the lead?"

Stone looked at Arianne, who said, "Several celebrities and artists are in the running, but Kristen Wilson is definitely the favorite."

Ah. So that explained the duet the label was pushing. Tyler had met Kristen one time, for five minutes, at an award show. Some photographer had snapped a photo of them talking backstage, and gossip had swirled for weeks. He shouldn't be surprised.

Sensing blood in the water, or perhaps noticing something off in Tyler's eyes, David stood and grabbed his laptop. He walked the length of the table and set the computer down, hovering over him as he clicked the web browser. "Go ahead. Type in your name. See the fun you've been missing."

Tyler fisted his hands in his lap. Suit or not, the man needed to step the hell back. He shot David a pointed look and asked, "Think you could give me some room?"

Stone smirked and casually walked back to his seat.

On principle, Tyler never searched himself. When they first started out, he had Google alerts on his name and visited various sites, curious what the fans thought of his music. That didn't last long. He quickly learned that you can't please everyone, and some people lived to complain. But this was his dream. Not even just his dream—his dad's, too. Letting out a breath, Tyler typed in his name and clicked enter. Pages of sites appeared.

Charlie came around and read over his shoulder. Arianne was right about the article. It had definitely gone viral, and fans actually gave a shit about his personal life. It was ridiculous. But he couldn't argue with the facts staring him in the face.

After checking a few results, Charlie slid his gaze to Tyler. "Up to you, man."

But it wasn't. Any decision Tyler made affected his entire band. Charlie, their crew, Tyler's parents…this was so much bigger than just what he wanted.

Tyler had grown up believing relationships were a hindrance. That they got in the way of accomplishing your goals. But the team around him made the big bucks for a reason. They knew this business inside and out, and if they said marriage was what he needed to do to secure his future, well, he could do a hell of a lot worse than Sherry Robicheaux.

Unlike the countless women who threw themselves at him on a daily basis, she wasn't out for his money. Unlike most of the celebrities listed in the polls, she was honest and genuine and real. She'd been stoked over dating a roadie, for Christ's sake. Sherry had married him not even knowing who he was. True, she'd been blitzed out of her mind, but if she *had* known the truth, she wouldn't have touched Tyler with a ten-foot pole.

That was another thing about her—she was safe. For him to even consider this publicity stunt, he'd need a guaranteed out. With Sherry, Tyler had no fear of being roped into something permanent. She'd made it abundantly clear how she felt about his world; there was no way in hell she'd want this marriage to last forever.

The only trick would be convincing her to prolong it a little. Say, a year. Maybe two. Three, tops.

Tyler fiddled with the mouse, clicking on random sites as he questioned his sanity. Was he seriously thinking about doing this? Continuing this sham of a marriage for the sake of his career? And if he was, could he possibly convince Sherry to do the same?

He keyed in her name this time, unable to fight the smile when her face appeared on the screen. She'd organized an event a couple months back, a bachelor auction for charity. Her smile was wide and free. Her dress was killer. That same spirit was there, the one that drew him to her in the green room and demanded an entire weekend to explore. Staring at her picture now, Tyler realized a weekend hadn't been enough.

Tyler craved that easy feeling. The enthusiasm Sherry had for life. She was fun, and with her, this wouldn't have to be about messy emotions or getting lost in each other. It could be a business arrangement, pure and simple.

The more he thought about it, Arianne was right. Sherry *was* perfect. He just had to convince her of that. And find something she needed that he could offer in return.

"My wife's gone back to Louisiana," he said, still shocked as hell at hearing those words come out of his mouth. He closed Stone's laptop and glanced across the table. "Don't we have something coming up there soon?"

Arianne smiled and tapped the screen of her phone

with a smile. "Several somethings. In two weeks, you're being inducted into the Louisiana Music Hall of Fame, and following that, you're the captain of the Erato parade."

"You still have an album to finish," David broke in, as if Tyler had forgotten. "Kristen Wilson has agreed to the duet, and I want two additional songs as well. Maybe your new wife will inspire you. Luckily, New Orleans has many setups able to handle production. I'll call and schedule studio time."

Tyler caught Stone's triumphant smirk as he stepped outside, cell phone already in hand, but he ignored it. He had his own scheme in play.

Head to New Orleans, write some songs, get a few shots taken with the wife, and call it a day. Hell, he'd even squeeze in a visit home while he was in town. Then, image saved, he'd go back on the road with the band to promote the new album, and he and Sherry would get a quiet divorce in a year or so. By then, David couldn't say a thing. Marriages fell apart every day. Especially fake ones.

"Guess we're headed to New Orleans," Charlie said, standing up. "I can do some damage on Bourbon."

Tyler had no doubt about that. "Think the band will mind?"

His friend scoffed. "A two-week vacay in The Big Easy? I think they'll manage."

The buzz of his phone vibrating on the table stole his attention, and a genuine case of nerves hit his stomach. *Sherry.* Screw the band—she was the hitch in this plan. He had to convince her to play along.

And admit to her who he really was.

Charlie saw the name flashing on the screen and clamped a hand on his shoulder. "Arianne, what do you say I buy you a drink from the vending machine, huh?"

She nodded and stood from the table with an amused grin. "Tell Sherry I said hello." She sent Nolan a pointed look, and he got up from the table with an exasperated huff.

"Guess I'll be going, too."

Tyler gave him a tight-lipped smile and palmed his phone, waiting until the door closed behind them. Finally alone, he took a breath and hit accept. "Blue."

Shit. His greeting was automatic. Automatic and completely damning.

He heard a sharp intake of air on the other end. "So it's *true*?"

Tyler winced. That was one way to go about telling her. She mumbled an, "Excuse me," and he heard a scuffling sound in the background. A door closed and then, "I'm married to the freaking himbo of country music?"

"Not exactly," he replied, unable to stop his smile. She was sassy, all right, and he loved it. Another reason she was perfect for this. Sherry wouldn't take his crap. She wasn't some starry-eyed fan throwing herself at him. And she made him laugh. "Listen, sugar, I'm sorry we got off on the wrong foot. I should've told you—"

"Oh, you think?" she asked, and Tyler's smile grew.

"Listen, you have every right to be pissed," he said, leaning back and kicking his boots onto the spotless tabletop. "But I'm coming into town tomorrow, and I'd rather explain everything in person." He paused. "If you'd let me."

He held his breath and let the seconds tick. Everything depended on her agreeing.

"Town?" she asked, the feistiness in her voice replaced with uncertainty.

"New Orleans," he confirmed. "I have a couple events there this month. I don't know if I mentioned it, but I'm actually from Louisiana."

He fought to keep the amusement out of his voice. Okay, so now he was just pushing her buttons on purpose. For some reason, he couldn't help himself. She was passionate, and her fire turned on a dime. He knew she'd—

"Are you freaking kidding me right now?" she screeched, and his laugh broke free. "No, you *didn't* mention it. Just like you failed to mention that you're bloody famous, and that I'd have photographers staked out behind bushes and crawling around my front yard."

The smile instantly fell from Tyler's face. "Are they harassing you?" he asked. How in the hell did the media find out already? Had someone at the chapel recognized him? "How many are there?"

"Just one," she replied, voice lowered. "A reporter and a photographer."

Muffled voices were in the background, and a surge of protectiveness shot through him as he dropped his boots to the floor. "Are you outside right now?"

"Tyler, I'm not a complete idiot. I stepped inside after you blew your cover." He didn't miss the way her voice tightened, and he pictured her rolling those gorgeous eyes of hers. Yeah, he definitely had his work cut out for him. A noise like blinds moving crept over the line as she said, "My girl stayed out there to watch them, but the chick seems harmless enough. Overzealous perhaps, but harmless."

"I'm sure she is," he assured her. For the most part, the media was fine and even respectful. The kind that loitered on private property, not so much. "But for my sanity, can you please just tell the reporter no comment, grab your friend, and stay inside until I get there?"

She muttered something about paranoid celebrities, but then said, "Fine."

He listened as she stepped outside and waited until she told the reporter, "Sorry, no comment," before pulling the phone from his ear. It was already after four. Changing his flight wouldn't do any good. But he hated her dealing with this shit on her own. Especially without them being on the same page about the future.

He caught Arianne peering through the meeting room window and waved her in.

Covering the mouthpiece, he asked, "What time does my flight arrive tomorrow?" She held up eight fingers, and he nodded.

"Okay, music man, I did your bidding." A door closed on the other end, followed by a woman's voice in the background. "My pit-bull future sister-in-law has me securely locked inside my house and is standing as bodyguard. Happy?"

No. He'd be happy once she agreed to save his career. And once he got her a *real* bodyguard. "Thank you," he told her, squeezing the tight muscles in his neck. "You haven't dealt with these people like I have. I'll feel better once I'm there to protect you."

Sherry didn't say anything in reply, which Tyler took as a good thing. If she were annoyed, she'd have no problem letting him know. "So, my flight arrives at eight in the morning," he mentioned casually. "Any chance you can come and get me?"

"Gee, I don't know." Sarcasm dripped from her voice, but the anger had definitely lessened. With any luck, it'd be gone completely by tomorrow. A man could hope, right? "Pick you up from the airport? That seems hardcore, Ty. Normally, I'm married to a guy for at least a couple weeks before I take that big a step."

"Funny."

"I am, aren't I?" She released a sigh, and when she spoke again, she only sounded tired. "Fine. Text me your flight number, and I'll meet you at eight."

The call disconnected before Tyler could say anything else. He dropped his head into his hands. Their secret was out. The *truth* was out. And he suddenly had a migraine.

Chapter Six

Thank heaven for small miracles—the New Orleans airport was dead. Either the media didn't know the current heartthrob of country music was en route, or they were secretly hiding behind the luggage carousel. In view of the excitement yesterday, nothing would surprise her, but Sherry seriously hoped they weren't. Her poor nerves were frazzled enough.

After placating her overly protective bestie with tales of a whirlwind romance, flimsy excuses for her gobsmacked behavior on her porch, and promises to tell all soon, Sherry had feigned exhaustion and escaped to her room. If anyone would understand her predicament, it would be Angelle. She'd lied to her parents that Cane was her fiancé, way before they were even dating. Her friend deserved the truth. But Sherry had seen that look forming again, the sympathetic one that always trailed her "pulling another Sherry," and she just couldn't find the words. Because in this case, Angelle was absolutely right.

She'd pulled a doozy.

It took a special kind of person to land in this kind of mess. Sherry had learned a lot about Tyler Blue while hiding out in her bedroom. It was fascinating the things you could find on Google. She'd read about his modest upbringing in Opelousas and the amazing things he'd accomplished in the last three years. Critics said he had a unique sound, classic country mixed with a swamp pop flair that they credited as being his daddy's influence. Another article mentioned him being the captain of the Erato parade and that he was soon to be one of the youngest inductees into the Louisiana Music Hall of Fame. She'd also discovered that her initial assessment had been spot on.

Tyler *was* the himbo of country music.

Judging by the steady stream of women he was photographed with—never the same one twice—he was as big a player as any of her ex-boyfriends. What made it worse was that these women were mind-numbingly gorgeous, every single one. Blonde, ginger, brunette, the full spectrum had been represented—and with her in the mix, Tyler could even add purple-streaked. But the hair wasn't the only thing that made Sherry stand out like a sore thumb. It was the whole package. The women Tyler had been with in those pictures were glamorous and polished. They wore the right clothes, they stood the right way, and you could just tell they never accidentally dropped an F-bomb in public.

Sherry glanced down and tugged on her hem. The fabric was scratchy. She couldn't remember the last time she'd worn a dress. It wasn't that she was trying to impress Tyler. Hell no, that ship had sailed. He'd made her look like an idiot in front of strangers and was the reason a weird dude had been creeping in her bushes. But until they figured this disaster out, she'd wanted to look the part. It seemed stupid now. The little number she was rocking hit mid-thigh, was angelic-white, and was as far from her usual attire as she could get. An improvement from the photos snapped of her yesterday in ripped jeans and shrunken concert tee. Bra strap, no doubt, exposed.

A fresh batch of people made their way down the baggage claim escalator, and twinges Sherry hadn't felt since high school hit her stomach. She smoothed a hand down the back of her hair. She also hadn't been this nervous about a guy since the night of her ninth grade dance.

God…that night still nauseated her. It had been the beginning of a new year, and Sherry had just shed a ton of weight. She'd made the school dance team and had been primed and ready to take her place outside of Colby's shadow. Her date was two years older and a friend of a friend's from another school. Someone who'd never met the pudgy girl her small town knew, and would hopefully see the *new* her. As it turned out, she'd thankfully chosen right. Her dating debut had been magical. She received her first kiss and believed she was head over heels in love—that is until the guy came over a week later, got one look at Colby, and decided he wanted to be just friends. By the time the loser realized sisters stuck together, the damage had already been done. In more ways than one.

When the crowd broke and Tyler was still a no-show, Sherry's shoulders slumped. Was his plane delayed? Had he changed flights and forgot to tell her? That type of thing certainly fit the Blue she'd imagined originally…but not so much the man she'd gotten to know in Vegas. Deciding she'd give it another ten minutes, she walked over to the Starbucks stand. Times like these may not require caffeine—she was plenty edgy enough—but lemon pound cake was another story.

As she waited in line, she busied herself on her phone, twirling her hair as she checked for bad weather in Nashville. Nothing from what she could see. She sighed and dropped her phone back in her purse. The guy in front of her moved aside, and she'd finally made it to the front when an unexplained shiver rolled down her spine.

It was as if her body was attuned to the man. Damn, that was annoying.

Smiling stiffly at the woman behind the counter, Sherry shook her head and stepped away. She turned around, and there he was. Denim slung low on his hips, that damn belt buckle reflecting light, ball cap shading his eyes. But there was no missing that his gaze was locked on hers. He picked up speed, marching down the moving escalator as if he was that eager to be near her.

Don't be ridiculous, she scolded herself. *Thoughts like that are what get you in trouble.*

But that wasn't true. Heated looks like *that*, the ones her so-called husband was giving her right now, and the responding warmth that filled her belly, was what did her in.

Good grief. Celebrity or not—craptastic liar or not—the man was smoking hot. Memories of their weekend together slammed into her as he purposefully strolled toward her, now sliding past the crowd separating them, his long, lean muscles moving in fluid rhythm. Delicious, sexy memories of the many ways he could use those muscles…followed by breath-stealing memories of him deliberately withholding the truth.

Embarrassment burned as she recalled the times she'd alluded to his *boss* or asked about the hundreds of phone calls, and how he'd distracted her every time. *Deceived* her. Played her like a damn fool.

Tyler's small smile fell and his stride faltered as the desire kindling her blood doused, morphing into a hot streak of utterly pissed off.

This is better, she thought, rolling her shoulders back. Anger was easier for her to handle. And much, much safer.

• • •

Tyler detected the instant Sherry's passionate gaze ran cold. It smacked the smile right off his face and pumped the breaks on his momentum. The look was such an anomaly on her. As strange as the straight-laced dress she was wearing… and almost as unfamiliar as the sudden, fierce need he'd had to hold her.

Where had that come from anyway?

Sure, he'd been eager to discuss their situation. To get them on the same page about their marriage and find a way to make it mutually beneficial. Hell, it was all he'd thought about during the flight. But his career hadn't propelled him toward her like a dog in heat. Not even the memories of those exposed, curvy legs wrapped around him in his hotel room. It was *her*. Sherry. The tempting caterer with a sassy mouth and honest, unguarded eyes. And the brief instant that she'd turned and looked as though she'd missed him, too.

He stopped in front of her and placed a finger on her perfect lips, obviously ready to spit hate fire. "Shh. Not here."

Her mouth puckered beneath his finger and her eyes narrowed. The weight of her distrust hit him in his gut. He'd lost his *easy*. Forfeited the stress-free, infectious smiles he hadn't realized he'd been counting on. But he'd earn them back. It just became his mission, right along with regaining her trust.

"My assistant is bringing the rest of my things tomorrow," he told her, gripping the handle of his guitar case as he wheeled his carry-on between them. "I've got all I need right now, so might I suggest we move the fight you're clearly itching to have, and rightly so," he added when her gaze grew even steelier, "to your car?"

Sherry inhaled a breath, and for a moment, he was sure they were about to have it out right there in the baggage claim. That would make for an intriguing photo spread. But then she nodded curtly and spun on the heel of her shoes, her high, delectable ass swaying beneath the shape-hugging material of her dress. Oh, she was pissed, all right. And he damn well deserved it. But there was no stopping the grin on Tyler's face as he watched her go.

"Are you coming or what?"

She glanced back over her shoulder and frowned when she saw his smile.

Tyler ducked his head. "Right behind you, sugar."

Chuckling quietly to himself, he followed the lady through the doors of the Louis Armstrong New Orleans International Airport.

The air was cool, but not cold, as they walked across the access road. He kept his head down when a full shuttle drove past, on the off chance someone recognized him. To his knowledge, no one other than Sherry expected him for another two weeks. But after her recent brush with the media, he wasn't taking any chances.

They didn't speak a word on the trek across the lot, or even glance at each other during the tense ride up the elevator. It wasn't until she'd locked his luggage in the trunk of her magenta-colored Bug, and the doors slammed behind them, that she turned to him. With eyes that could kill.

"You lied to me," she accused. "Or at least omitted the truth, which *I* think is just as bad." Her voice broke on the last word and her mask of anger slipped. Revealing the raw hurt underneath.

That was Tyler's fault. His selfishness had done that. Closing his eyes, he dropped his head onto the seatback, never feeling less like a man than he did then. "You're right. It was wrong and selfish, and all I can say is that I'm sorry. But I swear I didn't do it to hurt you."

Silence met his confession, and he nodded. Had he really expected anything less? The plans and scenarios he'd cooked up on the plane didn't matter. His marriage was over before it even began. And, if his team was right, it could very well spell the end for his career, too.

"Why then?" she asked softly, and Tyler opened his eyes. She licked her lips. "If you didn't do it to hurt me or embarrass me, then why? Why not just tell me who you were from the beginning, or correct me at any point during the weekend?"

His mouth lifted in a halfhearted smile. "I couldn't chance it," he admitted. "I wanted to be the roadie or the super fan, or whatever-the-hell it was you thought I was, just for a night. I wanted to be with a beautiful woman who looked at me and saw *me,* not my reputation. Not my bank account. I wanted a night without the fame and any expectations."

Sherry's guard came down again, this time revealing sympathy, and his hand brushed against her cheek before he could stop it. "Don't go wasting your emotions on me, baby girl. I'm the jerk here. I don't remember everything that happened, or whose idea it was to get married. We were both wasted. But I should've told you the truth in my hotel room. I planned to tell you that night and I'm guessing that never happened. Afterwards…well, I panicked." He lifted a shoulder, knowing it was no excuse. "Even though I knew you were special, I had to get my team around me before I told you everything. Find out how to handle it. You know, on the off chance you were a crazed stalker or something."

He attempted a grin, and despite accusing her of possibly being psychotic, she returned it.

Blowing out a breath, Sherry glanced out the windshield. Her hands tapped along the steering column and Tyler listened to the beat, waiting, until she turned back. When she did, she said, "I guess I can kind of see your side."

That, he hadn't expected.

"It must suck being hot and famous all the time," she continued, with not a hint of sarcasm. "Not knowing whom you can trust. I get it. I don't *like* it, but I get it." The rest of her protective armor fell away, and a hint of the comfortable, laidback girl he knew in Vegas seeped through. She held up her ring finger with a smirk. "And clearly, this idea was mine. That night's a total blur for me, too, but this sucker has me written all over it."

She laughed at herself, and the tightness in Tyler's chest lightened a fraction more.

"So now what?" she asked, lifting a shoulder. "The

wedding may be a blank, but I do remember some choice moments of the wedding night. An annulment is out of the question." Their eyes met, and lingering heat snapped the air. Clearing her throat, she scooted away and rested her head against the window. "A divorce then?"

There it was. Tyler's opening. The question of how and when it would happen had kept him up all night, and she'd just presented him with the perfect opportunity. Shifting his weight, his boot crunched an old water bottle on the floorboard of her tiny car. He scratched the side of his jaw, prepared to lay it all on the line…and had nothing.

Shit. Why am I so nervous?

"I don't give a crap about alimony, if that's what you're thinking," she said, clearly misreading his silence. "I don't want a cent of your money. Just want the creepers out of my bushes."

The reminder of the cameraman firmed his resolve. He'd already gotten her in this mess. Marriage to him, out in the open, would offer Sherry some kind of protection. He could insist on a bodyguard and even defend her himself over the next month. Let that guy show up again on Tyler's watch. His jaw locked at the thought.

"I know you're not out for my money, sugar," he said, gazing at her from across the car. "You didn't even know I had any until yesterday. That wasn't why I hesitated."

"It's not?" When he remained silent, a curious smile touched her lips. "Okay, I'll bite. Why *did* you hesitate?"

Her smile widened, probably wondering what the big deal was. Perhaps even thinking he'd lost his mind. In some ways, it sure as hell felt as if he had. But that wide, gorgeous, *easy* smile finally prompted him to go for broke.

"What would you say if I suggested we *stay* married?"

Chapter Seven

"Stay…married?"

For one brief, hope-filled second, the romantic in Sherry fantasized that somehow in the forty-eight hours they'd spent together, and the forty-eight hours since, Tyler had honestly fallen for her. That insta-love was real, cute babies shot arrows at people's butts, and fairy tales existed in the real world. But then sanity returned, and she drop-kicked that part of herself to the curb. That had been the romance novels talking.

"Yeah." Tyler gave a disbelieving sort of laugh, confirming her thoughts. "I know it sounds insane. Hell, it *is* insane. But see, I have a business proposal for you."

Business proposal. The antithesis of the romantic kind. Sherry almost laughed aloud at her previous girlish hopes. *Silly, naïve heart, won't you ever learn?*

The pragmatic man in her passenger seat shifted and said, "Listen, I know it's asking a lot, but just hear me out, okay?"

Sheer, masochistic desire had her nodding, needing to kill any remaining hope. Tyler took a breath and let it out. "What I'd like is to deliver a press release and announce that we're happily married." Her eyes widened, and he rushed on. "See, the tabloids already got wind of the story. It's out there, and by tomorrow, it'll be everywhere. But what I'm saying, what I want, is for us to spin it *our* way. Control the story. Then after that"—he glanced away and then back—"well, I'd like to spend the month with you, here in New Orleans. Be photographed together. Really sell our version of the truth, you know?"

Sherry's mind raced to process the verbal vomit he'd just thrown at her. Unfortunately, at some point wires must've gotten crossed, because what she finally comprehended was complete lunacy.

She shook her head and closed one eye. "I'm sorry, what? I think my brain must be broken. I could've sworn you just confused me with an actress. Or a mindless, starry-eyed groupie."

Other than a slight wince, Tyler didn't appear that fazed by her reaction. He just continued watching her watch him, an expectant look in his eyes. Maybe her new husband had a few screws loose.

"I know what you're thinking—"

"No, I honestly don't think you do." She bit her lip and searched his face, trying to spot the crazy—and he laughed. That didn't help her opinion of his sanity at all.

"Let me back up and explain." He removed his ball cap and ran his fingers through his hair. It was long on top, and Sherry vividly recalled grabbing on to those strands. She shook the image away as Tyler twisted the cap around and replaced it on his head. Bright green eyes, unencumbered by hair or brim, worked their swoony magic as he stared into hers, and Sherry couldn't help but think, *At least he's a hot nutcase.*

"The day I met you in Vegas," he began, "my publicist gave me an article that called my credibility into question. Apparently, relationships are the new aphrodisiac. At least in country music." His upper lip lifted in a sneer that spoke volumes. "Sherry, I'm not sure how much you know about me, but I'm not what you'd call a relationship kind of guy. Music isn't just my career. It's my life. Emotional entanglements of any kind would just get in the way. But that's why our drunken mistake is sort of a blessing in disguise."

Sherry snorted. "Wow. Damn boy, you really know how to woo a girl. *Emotional entanglements.* Are you for real?" She shook her head, sure that she was either still asleep or someone had slipped something seriously funky in her morning coffee. The world no longer made any sense. For no other reason than utter curiosity, she tilted her head and said, "What *exactly* are you proposing? A press release and a month of staged photos, and then…what?"

Tyler regarded her for a moment, then exhaled heavily and scratched the side of his jaw. "First off, the photos wouldn't exactly be staged. We'd be out, living life, you going about your normal routine with me in tow, and the photographers would capture that. As for after next month…" He trailed off and cleared his throat. *Not a good sign.* "We'd stay married for a year or so, more than likely maintaining separate residences in different states," he added, lifting his hand in the air for emphasis, "with just a few targeted photo ops in select national magazines."

The boyish, innocent smile he slid her was at once highly confident and a touch uncomfortable. A mix he pulled off remarkably well. Sherry laughed aloud. "Oh, is that all?" With another shake of her head, she fired up the engine. "Why on earth would I agree to that?"

He was silent for a long beat before quietly answering, "Because you're the only one who can."

Reversing out of her space, she turned to look at him and saw that he meant it. "Seriously? A woman you barely know. Aren't women lined up in Nashville to fill this very position?"

"Maybe." He shrugged a shoulder and faced front to buckle his seat belt. "But I trust *you.*"

Dammit, that wasn't playing fair. Words like that called on every feminine instinct she had. Coming to a stop in front of the garage pay window, she searched for a way to reply without sounding like a bitch. Before she could, though, he added, "And I'd really like to help you, too."

"Me?" She slid the lady in the booth a ten dollar bill and accelerated past the gate after being waved on. "How can you help *me*?"

"With your event-planning business."

Sherry blinked. "I-I told you about that?" She wracked her brain, trying to recall when she'd revealed her biggest secret, let anyone in on that hidden wish, and came up with nothing. She hadn't even told her family about it, because there'd be no point. It was a stupid pipedream. Nothing would ever really happen.

And she'd told *him*?

"Yep. Mentioned it somewhere between the fourth

and fifth round of margaritas, I think." She looked over, surprised, and he shrugged. "Gets pretty fuzzy after that, but the job part I specifically remember. Your eyes lit up, a smile took over your face, and you said that if you could do anything in the world, that'd be it. You called it your dream." He paused. "That's what music is for me. And with my help, we can make your dream come true too."

A neighboring minivan honked, and she swerved back into her own lane. Embarrassment flushed her cheeks, and she fluffed her hair to cover her face. She suddenly felt exposed. And more than a little insulted.

"Tyler, this isn't freaking *Pretty Woman*. I don't need your white knight ass swooping in and rescuing me. I already told you I didn't want your money. If I wanted to do this, I could do it myself. I have a savings account."

An account she'd nicknamed "For My Dream" and had been building for years. Last time she checked, her nest egg had enough zeroes to make more than a decent-sized dent in her plan. She was just too chicken shit to do anything about it.

What if she told her brother and sister about it and they were disappointed? The restaurant had been in their family for *years.* A business they ran *together*. The thought of letting them down was too much. And that wasn't even the biggest stumbling block.

What if she did go for it, honestly try, and put everything into making the dream happen…only to completely crash and burn?

That would be too devastating to come back from.

No, it wasn't money keeping her from stepping out. Drive and heart weren't the problem either. The only thing holding Sherry back was herself. And a super-size portion of fear.

"I wasn't trying to insult you," Tyler said. "I honestly want to help, and if not with my money, then with my name. Plan events for me this next month, come up to Nashville at some point and throw a party. Build your resume, gain experience, and use me to get your own name out there." His voice sounded off somehow. Soft and sincere. Unguarded. "Hell, no one else has a problem using me. And unlike with the others, I actually *want* you to."

She snuck a glance, shocked to discover the look on his face was *hurt*. That didn't make any sense. Why did it matter to him if she did the business or not? They might be married in the eyes of the law, but in the space of her car, they were practically strangers. "Why do you even care about this?"

"Because I believe in you," he answered, surprising her with the conviction in his voice. "Because I saw your passion in action and read about that auction last fall. The article I read said you more than doubled ticket sales, and made a local charity a fat load of cash. That's impressive, sugar. More than that, it's good business. In my industry, you learn to trust your gut, and mine says you'd be incredible at anything you set your mind to. I want to be a part of it."

His words made the center of her chest ache. He believed in her, and he barely even knew her. She sat there, uncertain how to respond, and he shrugged.

"I just need your help too."

Sherry held his gaze for a second, then sighed and turned back to the road.

Tyler Blue, internationally famous country star, cared about her silly pipedream. Moreover, *his* dream was important to him. He'd called it his life. Colby felt that way about being a chef. Cane loved running the restaurant. Sherry had no clue what that kind of passion was like. Waitressing, managing the staff, it was a job. A paycheck at the end of the week, and a way to support her family. But if she ever *did* risk it all and go after what she wanted, how would she feel if it were suddenly threatened? And not even over anything she'd done, but because of her personal life?

She knew exactly how she'd feel—madder than hell. Talent and performance should be the only thing that mattered, and it sucked that wasn't the case for Tyler.

But what he's proposing...

Sherry frowned as she flicked her blinker and eyed the rearview mirror.

This was a classic no-win situation. Tyler needed to be *in* a relationship to achieve his goals—and Sherry needed out. Marriage put a major cramp in her plot to make Will Trahan, AKA Mr. Boring, hers. But what could she do? Her *oopsident* was already out there. A reporter had come to her door, and more would soon follow. If Sherry told them the truth, that her wedding hadn't been planned—that it was just some drunken fluke—she'd only confirm what her entire town already believed. She was a relationship disaster. Only this time, it wouldn't simply be Magnolia Springs pitying her. It would be the whole world.

Lord alive, she could hear the late-night monologues now.

Strangers in the supermarket would cast sad looks behind her back. And it wouldn't even matter if the truth came out or not. Divorcing quickly, as she'd originally planned, would be just as damaging as admitting it.

At least if they did what Tyler was suggesting, and stayed married for a year or two, she'd be slightly less pathetic. And after a respectable grieving time, she could get back to the main plan.

Sherry fiddled with the A/C vent and peeked at him from the corner of her eye. Clearing her throat, she said, "Okay, now I have a proposition." Tyler's head turned toward her. "If I did this, and that's a huge *if*, I'd need something out of it, too. And I'm not talking about your money or your name."

"Anything." He rested his back fully against the doorframe and held his palms up. "Anything you want is yours."

Sherry nibbled her bottom lip. She couldn't *believe* she was about to say this aloud. "I want the fairy tale." His eyebrows drew together, and she focused on the road. If she looked at him when she said this, she'd never get through it. "See, before you and that ginormous belt buckle waltzed into my life, I had a plan. I was gonna find myself a safe, dependable, *normal* guy. You were supposed to be my stolen weekend. But since we've found ourselves in this predicament, maybe we can make the best of it. Maybe before I accept the life of Mrs. McDull, or become some tabloid-like footnote on your Wikipedia page, I can experience the HEA."

Tyler hesitated. "The H-E-what-a?"

"Happily ever after." Heat spread across her chest, and she was positive she resembled a strawberry. But what did she have to lose? "You said we needed to make this look legit, right? I'm only suggesting we do a *really* good job of that. When we're out in the world, doing our thing, I want us to look like we're totally in love. For once, I want to feel what it's like to be wooed and swept off my feet. To be adored and appreciated. Just for show," she quickly added before he got any ideas. "Clearly we have different life goals, so this will be make-believe. A masquerade. A small taste of the fantasy."

The more the new plan took shape in her mind, the more Sherry loved it. Fairy tales may not exist for her, but for a short while, she could manufacture one. What made it even better was that she'd be in control of the situation from the beginning. There'd be no danger of falling. For the first time in her life, she could enter a relationship knowing her heart would be safe.

"So, you're saying you want me to court you." Tyler's handsome face grew thoughtful, as if he was honestly considering her suggestion. A streak of hope shot through her.

"Pretend court," she clarified. "And yes, that's exactly what I'm saying." The light turned red in front of her, and she glanced at him after coming to a stop. "Tyler, I heard what you said about your career, but you gotta understand. This isn't just damage control for *you*. My reputation is on the line, too. Either I can become the laughingstock of Magnolia Springs, or I can run with the hand I've been given and make lemon squares." His lips quirked at the mixed metaphor, and she grinned. "Let's sell this thing."

Tyler stared at her for what felt like forever, not saying a word. Her throat began to close. Maybe she'd been wrong. Maybe he *wasn't* considering her offer, but instead thinking she was a sad, lonely woman in need of intense therapy.

The car behind her honked, indicating the light had changed. She released the breath she'd been holding, her hopes plummeting to her shoes. It'd been worth a shot. She turned to face the road again and saw him nod slowly out of the corner of her eye. "That's the least I can do."

"Really?" she asked, ignoring the man now laying on his horn. Tyler nodded, and relief washed over her as fresh air refilled her lungs. "Awesome."

A smile broke across her face as she accelerated through the intersection. This was more like it. This she could enjoy. A weekend had been great, but she'd be lying if she said she was ready for it to end. That she didn't want a bit more adventure in her life before she gave it all up. She enjoyed spending time with him, and as long as she kept a good head on her shoulders, this could end up being even better than her original plan.

She smiled. "Of course, we do need to have a few ground rules."

• • •

"Ground rules?" Tyler repeated.

Damn, that sounded complicated. Arianne loved rules. So did his manager, his agent, and the label. Everyone wanted a piece of him, wanted to control him and tell him how he should act. But Sherry was different. Rigid rules were as out of place with her as the straitlaced dress she had on—not that he was complaining. During the drive, the thin scrap of fabric had ridden up her lap, exposing the tan skin of her upper thigh.

Definite benefits of their situation firmly in mind, he lifted his gaze to her profile. "What kind of rules are we talking about?"

A black-painted fingernail tapped against the wheel.

"Well, for starters, we need to decide how this is gonna end. What reason will we give for our eventual demise? Because I gotta tell ya, if it's anything embarrassing or tarnishing to either of us, then I'm out right now."

Hmm. That was a solid point. Honestly, he hadn't considered that far ahead. Getting her to agree at all had been his only priority.

"That makes sense." Tyler pushed back in his seat, trying his damnedest to get comfortable in the tin box she drove. "How about this. After the month is over, I have to leave anyway. There's a media circus for the new album and then Blue has a tour in the summer. That's how it always is. I'd imagine a few years of life like that would make any marriage difficult."

Actually, he didn't even have to imagine—Tyler knew it for a fact. His world made relationships impossible. It was the sole reason his dad had stopped playing.

He shoved aside the sudden weight on his chest. "So, when the time comes, we can file irreconcilable differences and cite my busy schedule as what kept us apart." He glanced at her. "It'd even be the truth, in a way."

What appeared to be sympathy washed over her face as her gaze slid over him. What she was searching for, he didn't know. Tyler loved his life and was happy with it just as it was. After a beat, she turned back to the road.

"I guess that works," she said. "It doesn't cast either of us in a bad light. It'll be mutual."

"Exactly." Shifting onto his thigh, trying one last time to stretch his legs in the cramped floor space, he asked, "So was that a rule?"

"No, *that* was our deal breaker."

She fell silent as an eighteen-wheeler sped up on her left, creeping too close to the driver side. The trucker made a hard cut in front of them to beat the light before the bridge, and Sherry's knuckles turned white from gripping the wheel. A string of curses went through Tyler's head as he glared at the fading license plate.

Lying about his identity to sweet southern women was one thing, but cussing in front of one was another. His mama had taught him right.

"Asshat."

Sherry lifted her middle finger at the windshield, and Tyler shook his head, chuckling under his breath. This *particular* southern woman kept him on his toes.

"Anyhoo, rules." She leaned back in her seat and sent him a look. "They're for how we're supposed to act around each other the next thirty days. Expectations for how this is supposed to go, what we have to do, our limits…"

"Limits?" The amused smile fell from his face. That didn't sound promising. "Like what?"

"Like, for starters, no one can know the truth about us. Other than that fancy team of yours," she amended with a twist of her mouth. The light turned green and she accelerated through the intersection, merging into line for the Lake Pontchartrain Causeway Bridge. "I assume *they* know, but no one else. Not even family."

She paused to let a car in front of her, anxiety tightening her normally animated features. "Look, I don't know how close you are to your family, but I'm really tight with mine. I don't want them worrying about me. It'll be tough enough keeping this straight between the two of us. Let's not involve anyone else in our madness, okay?"

That, right there, revealed so much about the woman he'd accidentally married. Stuff Tyler already knew, but it was nice to have confirmed. Sherry was genuine. She cared about other people, maybe even more than she cared about herself. In his world, that was rare.

"Fine with me." Unfortunately, Tyler didn't talk with his parents nearly as much as he should, but when he did, they discussed way more important things than his screwed-up love life. "And yeah, my staff knows. So does my bass player, Charlie. But they won't say anything. They want this staying quiet as much as we do."

A soft smile eased her anxiety as she exhaled aloud. "That's a relief."

She looked so relieved, in fact, that he hesitated to ask his next question. But he was too damn curious not to. "Is there a second rule?"

When the smile dropped, and she squirmed in response, Tyler cursed his curiosity.

"Actually, yes." Messing with the rearview mirror, she sat up tall and cleared her throat. "Well, first, we agreed on the fairy tale in public, right?" She glanced at him for approval and he nodded. "That should be a rule, too. Whenever we're outside, out in the world, we pretend to be in love."

"Okay," he said slowly, watching her fluff her hair. A low hum emanated from her throat. Sherry's energy was always a bit manic, but this was extreme even for her. Which meant whatever she had cooking up in that brain of hers was sure to spell S-U-C-K for him.

"But, I think if we do that, then it'd be only natural for that kind of, um, tension to seep into our private time…you know, when we're *alone.* And that would just be asking for trouble." Her gaze skittered to his and quickly away. "So I think the third rule should be no romance. When it's just us, no mixing of business and pleasure. It'd only complicate things."

Tyler shrugged. Despite the songs he wrote, he wasn't exactly the "hearts and flowers" type of guy. Sure, it sold records. That and the fairy-tale crap she mentioned earlier. But he was a man. This rule was no skin off his nose.

Then she cleared her throat again.

"Which leads to the fourth rule…no more sex."

Only when she said it, it came out more like, "*nomoresex.*"

His mouth fell open. A row of straight teeth clamped down on her full bottom lip as she looked at him, then away, and back again. "I know what you're thinking," she said with a grimace. "Been there, bought the T-shirt, so what's the big deal, right? But see, that's the thing. I don't *do* casual sex. Not normally at least. Our weekend was a first for me, and the only reason I escaped with my heart intact was because it was *just* for the holiday. But an entire month? *Years* together?" She shook her head and swallowed hard. "I can't do that, Ty. Not if I want to walk away from you unscathed."

Tyler was a man of no words. Their mutual attraction was a living, breathing, separate entity inside this shoebox car, and Sherry wanted to pretend it away. Ignore that it existed.

"You're serious?"

Those teeth worked her bottom lip so hard he expected to see blood. "I realize you probably have certain, uh, *urges*." Wincing, she flushed a light shade of pink and shook her head. "Good God, I feel twelve again. Why the hell am I sweating?" She raised an open palm to each cheek and left it on her forehead. "Look, I'm no nun, and I ain't saying this is gonna be easy, for *either* of us. Once you go out on the road, I-I guess as long as you're discreet, I can't say sh—" That opened palm came down to smack her mouth, and she squeezed her eyes shut for a second. Focusing back on the road, she said, "I'm sorry, I just…I can't…"

Tyler huffed a sigh. "Sugar, despite what you think, I'm not the himbo of country music. I don't do mindless, casual sex, either." He scrubbed a hand over his face, saying farewell to those benefits he'd imagined earlier. "Not anymore."

Back when he was young and stupid, and before Blue made it big, he'd indulged a few times. Okay, more than a few, but still less than most. Even then, though, it'd been empty. Those women barely knew his first name. The only thing that mattered was who he was, what he did, and where he was going. It hadn't taken long to grow old.

Unfortunately, that didn't leave him with many options. *Meaningless* didn't work and *casual* was all he could offer. Sherry had been his solution. Until her damn rules came into play.

Sherry reached over and squeezed his hand. "I'm sorry."

Tyler lifted his head, and she squeezed his hand again before placing it back on the wheel. "That was unfair. I made a snap judgment before I even met you, and I said a lot of unforgiveable things. I was speaking from my own pain, and the sad part is that I thought I was being funny. Folks from small towns know how harmful gossip can be. I should've remembered that."

A flash of emotion crossed her face. She'd been hurt before, and more than just some asshole breaking her heart. Protectiveness shot through him, stealing away his frustration, and leaving a subtle warmth in his chest. Sherry was a woman who straddled confidence and vulnerability, strength and sensitivity. It'd be easy to see the sass and sexy smirks and not delve any deeper. But he saw the cracks. Unraveling this woman's secrets would take a lot longer than a month, but Tyler was up for the challenge.

"No need to apologize…" He paused as if he were deliberating. "Unless it's for that last rule. Damn, girl, you sure know how to ruin a man's plans." He shot her a mock-glare and released a heavy sigh, feeling victorious when she laughed. "No lie, this is gonna be hard as hell. I want you bad, darlin', and I didn't get near my fill. But if *you* can hold out, I guess I can, too."

Amusement sparked in her hazel eyes, and he sucked in a breath. He hadn't realized how much he'd missed that playfulness.

"Oh, I think I can control myself," she teased. "I'll just imagine you dangling and then busting your ass at Cirque du Soleil, and my lust will be cured."

He chuckled. "Yeah, but I got it the second time, didn't I? Not all of us were born to fly."

She smiled, obviously pleased with the compliment, and they rode the next few minutes in comfortable silence. The north shore of the lake grew closer, and soon they exited the never-ending bridge. Tall green trees and New Orleans Saints billboards declaring "Bless You Boys" screamed that he was home. Tyler's head fell back against the seat rest. Opelousas was a good drive up the road, near Cajun country, but people were people, and these people were his.

Rolling down the window, he breathed deep and exhaled the tension from his shoulders. This was what he needed to finish his album. Get back to his roots, away from the madness. Find what he'd been missing.

"I have a rule," he said suddenly. Sherry looked over at him. "For the next month, we live in the moment. No talk of the future or expectations. No worries about what will happen next. Let's just live day by day and try to enjoy it, okay?"

She smiled softly and nodded. "I like that one."

They drove on for another minute, Tyler blatantly staring at the French-sounding names on buildings and the people in neighboring cars, snippets of potential lyrics already firing in his head. Digging in his back pocket, he grabbed his wallet and took out the pack of sticky notes he always kept inside. Inspiration flowing, he was a few lines in when Sherry suddenly pumped the break at a stop sign, causing his pen to scratch across the page.

"Crap! I was totally on autopilot." She smacked her forehead and huffed a breath before asking him, "Where's your hotel?"

Huh. He'd thought that would've been obvious. But then again, he'd also thought he'd be getting lucky tonight.

"Maybe I'm wrong, sugar, but I was under the impression married couples lived together." He watched realization dawn on her pretty face. "Don't they?"

Chapter Eight

Moss-draped oaks hugged either side of Main Street, a normally welcome and calming sight after a long day of work. Today it just sent Sherry's tummy into a free-fall. They were a block away from her street, her home where she'd be living with Tyler Blue, *alone*, just the two of them for the next month.

Shoot her now.

The fact that Angelle had moved out was a blessing and a curse. A blessing because at least she and Tyler wouldn't have to be *on*, performing all the time. They'd get a small reprieve behind her closed front door to stop the fantasy. Remember reality. It was a curse because the *front* door wouldn't be the only one she'd like to close behind them.

She already knew they had chemistry. Intense, set-your-sheets-on-fire chemistry, if her fuzzy-edged memories were any indication, which blew all previous sexual encounters out of the water. Her questionable ability to withstand a repeat performance was only one of the things locking her spine tight. The other was her house itself.

Sherry wasn't a pauper, and she was proud of what she'd accomplished on her own. Unlike so many of her generation, there was no failure to launch with her. At least not financially—love was a whole other boat. But after graduating college, she'd immediately gotten her own place, a rent-to-own home that she loved to pieces and was proud to call hers.

When fancy, millionaire celebrities weren't about to walk inside.

Had she loaded the dishwasher before she left? Remembered to pick up her dirty underwear from the bathroom floor? She'd been in such a hurry to leave, and a nervous wreck of a mess…and now, of course, she was worse.

Which was the only excuse she had for not realizing he'd be staying with her. It should've been a given. They'd established they were pretending this was real. A surefire clue their marriage was only for show would be him checking into a hotel. But for whatever reason, Sherry's mind hadn't gone there. And now here they were, turning onto her street, and Tyler Blue was about to walk into her house.

Her modest, old-style, southern house…that was probably the size of his kitchen.

Turning onto Maple Drive, Sherry glanced ahead to her driveway. It was clear, thank God. The last thing she needed right now was a well-meaning family member waiting in the wings, or another reporter chilling on her porch. She snuck a glance at Tyler's face, wondering how her simple, down-to-earth neighborhood looked through his eyes.

A small smile curved his lips. "This reminds me of home."

"Yeah?" He nodded as if he meant it, and Sherry swung her car into the driveway. As the engine idled, she fiddled with her seat belt, then said, "I mean, I know it's not much. It's only a rental, but..."

His hand closed around hers. "Sugar, it's perfect. My parents' place in Opelousas looks just like this. Just a lot older." She lifted her head, and he gave her a reassuring smile. Searching his face, the skin around his eyes seemed smoother. Lines of tension she hadn't realized had been there were now gone. Maybe he really did like it.

"When I got my first fat paycheck, I fixed up the place," he said. "Got my parents a new roof and better plumbing, a garden for Mom, more tools for Dad. But the old bones are still the same, and that house will always be home."

He glanced at the front porch and that beautiful, peaceful smile grew even wider.

Following his gaze, Sherry felt a surge of pride in her modest home. Hearing him talk, she got the impression he was close with his family. There seemed to be sadness there, but good memories, too.

Maybe helping Tyler reconnect with his past could be part of her mission this month.

"Well, all right then." Anxiety melting away, she turned off the engine and placed a borrowed high heel onto the concrete. She couldn't wait to kick the suckers off. She much preferred her boots or sneakers, but they hadn't gone with this dress at all. She'd tried. Tugging on her hem, Sherry stretched out the kinks in her back, and then met Tyler back at her trunk.

Popping it open, she laughed at his one carry-on and guitar case. "I can't imagine traveling so light. You should've seen what I lugged with me to Vegas. And that was only for a weekend."

Granted, most of that was makeup and hair supplies, but still. *One* bag?

"Don't get all impressed with me just yet," he said with a grin. "I've got more crap coming." He set his luggage on the ground and closed the lid of her trunk. A cool breeze blew her hair in front of her face, and Tyler tucked a strand behind her ear. The pads of his fingertips ghosted across her cheek as he said, "But I'm not here to inconvenience you. This is still your house. I'm simply a very grateful guest."

A tingle built beneath her skin, and as she leaned into his touch, it shot across her scalp. They stood there staring at each other, him looking down, his hand on her face, and her chin lifted toward him. It'd be so easy to push onto her toes and press her lips against his. It didn't even have to lead to anything. It could be a simple, friendly *nice to see you again* kiss, the kind she'd been too preoccupied—and annoyed—at the airport to give. Or an innocent brush of the lips to seal their new agreement.

But who was she trying to kid? She just wanted to kiss him. And it'd be wrong. A rule breaker. Technically, they were outside, and they *were* supposed to act hot for each other in public. But unfortunately, right now, they were very much alone.

Or are we…

A snap of a tree branch made Sherry jolt, and she twisted her head to look at the tall oak in her yard. Was the creeper back? A lump lodged in her throat, an icky feeling of being watched unaware stealing over her. Tyler cupped her elbow and growled under his breath.

"Cameras," he whispered.

His focus was trained on a distance beyond her, away from the tree. Meaning there was more than one camera aimed at them. A muscle jumped along his jaw. Fighting the urge to turn around, she stilled in his arms and asked, "What do we do?"

He lowered his gaze, and a new emotion joined the desire in his eyes. She couldn't name it, but the determined glint made her heart pound.

"Rule one." A smile lifted his lips as he slid his arm around her back. Sherry's breathing stuttered. This was what she wanted. For the world to believe they were in love. That he wanted her…though that part wasn't a lie. So why was her heart beating so fast? Cradling her cheek, he threaded his fingers into her hair as his gaze fell to her mouth. "Definitely my favorite one."

He brushed his nose across hers, and Tyler's scent hit her senses. An arousing mix of soap, cinnamon-flavored gum, and sandalwood. Sherry inhaled deep, letting it fill her head.

A dozen snapshot memories of their night together played in quick succession in her mind. No clear image remained, only unmistakable *want*. His grip tightened, and as his eyes burned into her, his eyelids grew hooded. He was remembering, too.

"Tyler…" Sherry swallowed, not knowing how to finish her thought. But this felt like a pivotal moment. There'd be no turning back tomorrow. Pictures would be everywhere, confirming their story. Tyler lowered his chin, tugged her up against him, and crashed his firm, unyielding lips onto her own.

Moaning, Sherry went on tiptoe. She threw her arms

around his neck and his hold shifted. His tongue traced the seam of her mouth. Gladly, she opened, wanting, *needing* more. She was intoxicated. Not on alcohol this time, but on him. His scent, his taste, the weight of him in her arms. Tyler Blue was hard muscle and velvet-soft touch, and his arms and chest engulfing her made her feel like a woman, feminine and wanted. His hands cradled her gently, and when he scooped her up, lifting her off her feet, the world dropped away.

Clicks and the murmur of voices brought her back to reality all too soon. Tyler must have heard the same because he slowed his kiss, fingertips now gliding in a circle over her skin. Instead of the frenzied hold of a minute before. When he opened his eyes and stared into her, nothing seemed more important than picking up where they'd left off, only inside and away from prying eyes. Which is exactly why they couldn't.

Breathlessly, she told him, "I think we got our point across."

His low, husky chuckle sent a fresh shiver down her spine. He set her back down and rested his forehead against hers. "I'd say so." He brushed his lips against hers again. "You sure about that other rule?"

"No," she admitted with a dazed shake of her head. "And that's why we need it."

Groaning, he closed his eyes and took a deep breath before straightening to his full, towering height. "I foresee many cold showers in my future."

Sherry put her fingers to her tingling mouth. "And I'll be right behind you." She lifted a shoulder. "But the way I see it, those are preferable to heartache."

His mouth pressed into a thin line as he nodded and gripped his guitar case. Pulling out the handle of his luggage, he nodded toward the house. "Let's see my new digs."

Grateful he wasn't pushing the situation, Sherry led the way, covertly glancing around her yard as they walked up the cracked concrete path. Was this what the next thirty days of her life would be like? People watching, capturing her boring-ass trek from the car on film? Videoing her slipper-clad hike to the mailbox?

What have I gotten myself into now?

On the porch, Tyler watched in amusement as she dug through her purse for her keys. She'd just dropped them inside, but the thing was a disaster as always. Eventually she found them underneath her hairbrush, and after fiddling with the lock until the stubborn thing turned, she threw open the door. "Home sweet home," she announced.

Tyler set his bags down on the porch and stalked toward her with a devious smirk. "What are you doing?" she asked, backing away in confusion at the mischievous look in his eyes.

That bad-boy smirk transformed into one of his crooked grins. The kind that sold millions of records and sweet-talked girls into trouble. "Carrying you over the threshold."

She widened her eyes and took another step back. "Uh, no, you aren't," she replied, a laugh bubbling up her throat as he advanced again, looking like a stealthy cheetah. For the most part, she was happy in her own skin. After years of battling her weight, she'd grown to love her curves. But a freaking feather she wasn't. "Really, Ty, that's not necessary."

"See, but I think it is. And you said you wanted to be swept off your feet."

He feigned left, she went right, and before she knew what was happening, Tyler had grabbed her up in his strong arms. She quickly yanked the hem of her stupid dress, trying very hard not to flash the cameras, as warmth infused her skin. He made holding her seem effortless. And damn if that wasn't hot.

Cradled against his chest, his shining eyes just a few inches from hers, Sherry's belly fluttered. And she felt giddy instead of annoyed. What was wrong with her?

"Traditions exist for a reason, baby girl," he said, voice like silk. "We don't wanna start this thing on the wrong foot, now do we?" At his teasing words, déjà vu hit. They'd definitely done this before. "In we go."

Laughing, they crossed the threshold and Tyler bumped the door closed with his foot. But he didn't set her down. Up close like this, staring into his eyes, she noticed a thin circle of gray around the green.

A silver lining, she thought like a dope, before almost groaning aloud. His kiss had evidently scrambled her brain.

After walking forward a couple steps, Tyler stopped and relaxed his hold, keeping their bodies connected as he slowly placed her back on her feet. She shook her head at his flirty smile, and he winked.

He popped back out for his luggage, and Sherry rolled her neck, giving herself a pep talk. There was nothing wrong with flirting, but she couldn't let herself get lost in the game. This was pretend, with a nice dash of potential friendship. As long as she stayed focused, kept her eyes on the prize, everything would be fine.

But keeping those giddy-making kisses to a minimum would be imperative.

"So where should I put my stuff?" he asked, returning with his things and looking around her living room. Sherry followed his gaze and winced at the dirty dishes and empty Coke cans cluttered around. Okay, so she was no Martha Stewart.

"Well, my roommate actually just moved out. Sort of anyway, so you can use her room."

She went to help with his belongings, and Tyler's hand shot out, stopping her from touching his guitar. "That's okay, I got it."

Lifting an eyebrow, she made a production of stepping away, palms in the air. "I don't have cooties or anything, I swear," she said, all serious-like. "And despite the tidiness of my humble abode, I'll even go so far as to say that I've yet to break things upon contact."

The left side of Tyler's mouth crooked in a grin. "Sorry. Guess I'm a little careful around my girl," he admitted, indicating the guitar. And wasn't that just the most adorable thing ever? "Dad got her for my birthday when I turned thirteen. She hasn't left my side much since."

A gooey part of Sherry's heart melted onto her toes. "She's your good luck charm," she said, noticing the slight aging around the case. Wikipedia had said Tyler was twenty-six—a year older than she was—which meant he'd had his guitar for thirteen years. A far cry from her longest relationship, that was for sure.

"Written all my best songs on her," he agreed, changing his grip on the handle. He hung his head, and the thick knot in his throat bobbed as he swallowed. Sherry got the impression he was working through a memory, something tied to his dad perhaps, so she stayed quiet until he lifted his eyes again. "You mentioned I can stay in your *sort of* roommate's room. Sure she won't mind me being in there?"

She shook her head. What she wanted to do was ask about his dad, offer to talk if he needed, but she didn't want to push. "She'll never know. Angelle is engaged to my brother, and yesterday she moved all the important stuff over to his house. Really, the only things left are a bed and some clothes. Now if you try those on, she might have a problem..."

The last trace of melancholy left his face, and she grinned.

"If they're engaged, why didn't she just take it all?"

"Angie's old-fashioned. She wants a place she can go if either of them needs space," she said, reiterating her friend's excuse. Then her smile grew, thinking of the *real* reason she suspected Angelle kept her things there. "And so she won't be technically lying when she tells her mama she still lives with me."

Tyler considered that. "What happens if she decides she needs that space and comes back while I'm here?"

The smile on Sherry's face fell away at the very real possibility of sharing a bed with Tyler. Again. Although she'd woken on the bathroom tile, the memories of the hour or two before that, fuzzy or not, were still pretty damn hot. "Then I guess you'd sleep with me. In my bed, I mean."

The look they exchanged made her want to douse herself with cold water, and she rocked back on her heels. With the feel of his lips still burned into hers, she was tempted to take him to her room *now*.

"But one day at a time, right?" she said, reminding him about their final rule. "If and when that happens, we'll deal with it then."

"Fair enough."

Silence fell between them, and Tyler looked around again, this time paying attention to the family photos on the wall, the framed concert posters and art. He grabbed a frame from the side table that held a picture of her and Cane at the bachelor auction. He shot her an amused look.

"That's my brother," she explained with a small laugh. "Which I realize may make it sound worse. He's shirtless for charity, just to be clear—that event you read about, actually. It was taken just after he won Best Abs." She smiled as the memories of that night washed over her. "As you can imagine, Cane loathes that picture."

Tyler chuckled. "Which is the reason you have it framed, right?"

She neither confirmed nor denied, simply smiled, and he set the picture down. "So let me see if I have this right. You have two siblings, Cane and Colby, and a best-friend-slash-future-sister-in-law, Angelle. Colby recently married a fire captain, who has a daughter named Emma. How'd I do?" Sherry nodded, impressed that he'd remembered her family tree, and he lifted his fist in victory. "Any other relatives I should be aware of?"

She started to say no. Tyler already knew both her parents were deceased, and she didn't have a lot of cousins or anything. But then his stance shifted, and her gaze fell to his guitar. His *girl*, as he called it.

"Only one," she said, widening her eyes. "Elvis."

• • •

Tyler was almost certain his new bride wasn't crazy, at least not in the literal sense, so he must be missing something. He stood there, waiting for the punch line, and she laughed with a mischievous smirk.

"Elvis is the man in my life," she said, backing slowly into the kitchen. "And I think it's high time the two of you met."

A cat-like grin crossed her face as she spun on her heel. The click of her shoes hit the kitchen tile like a drum beat. Soon an alarm beeped, letting him know she'd opened a back door, and he heard her speak in a low voice.

Despite what she'd said, it couldn't be another man. If someone were waiting at home, she wouldn't have needed to hook up with him in Vegas. She also wouldn't have made her grand plan for the future. So who was it? And why was he in the backyard?

A streak of white fur and energy shot around the corner seconds before two paws latched onto his jeans. Tyler laughed as he took a knee, scooping up the dog, and a rain of wet, slobbery licks fell over his face.

"Tyler, meet my baby, Elvis." At the sound of Sherry's voice, the chaotic ball of fluff in his arms went wild. She kicked off her heels and padded into the room, her voice turning into a singsong as she said, "And Elvis, this is Tyler. He's gonna be around for a while, yes he is."

When she leaned back, the smile on her face was radiant. God, she was pretty. She glanced at him and asked, "Please tell me you're okay with dogs? I would've mentioned it earlier, but I guess I got sidetracked."

"More than okay." He fell to the ground to play with the exuberant puppy, and Elvis immediately flopped on his back for a belly rub. His top lip curled like his namesake. "I've always wanted a dog."

Sherry scooted closer and smiled as the Shih-Tzu's tongue lolled out of his mouth. "You're obviously a natural, so what's kept you from getting one?" She sent him a teasing grin. "Something tells me you can afford it."

Tyler shrugged. "It didn't seem right. I'm always on the road, and a tour bus is no place to raise a dog."

"I can see that," she said softly, watching as he scratched under Elvis's chin. "Still, it seems so sad. So many dogs out there need a good home. What about when you were growing up? No dog then, either?"

Tyler kept his eyes on Elvis. He never spoke about his personal life, especially his parents, to anyone, and he wasn't sure this was the best time to start. Instead, he said, "Money was always tight," which was true. If not the entire reason.

"They're definitely not cheap," she agreed, falling to her stomach and taking over the belly rub. Leaning over the dog, she said, "Mama spoils you, doesn't she? Yes she does."

He chuckled under his breath. Cute girls who spoke baby talk normally drove him insane, yet somehow, with *this* cute girl, he found it adorable. Tyler doubted there was much Sherry could do that he wouldn't find adorable. Other than her housekeeping. He glanced again at the cluttered tabletops and the basket of unfolded laundry in the corner of the room. This would definitely be an adjustment.

"Knock, knock."

Sherry's widened gaze flew to the front door. A knuckle rap followed the muffled voice, and she bolted up, yanking the hem of her dress. Pity that. Assuming their visitor must be someone important, Tyler quickly adjusted the ball cap on his head. The show was apparently on.

Two seconds later, a cute redhead waltzed through the door, keys in the lock, trailed by a young girl and the same man from the picture frame. Only now, Sherry's brother was fully clothed.

"You must be Cane." Pushing to his feet, Tyler smiled and thrust out his hand. "Pleased to meet you. I'm Tyler Blue."

The man's eyes narrowed as he stood still, studying him. Leaving Tyler hanging.

Tyler didn't drop his hand an inch. He didn't date and wasn't the type who aimed to impress women's families, but he got the general gist. This was a simple case of big brother protecting his own. And when the person in question was Sherry, Tyler could appreciate it. But he also wasn't one to be scared off.

The redhead huffed and slapped Cane on the arm. "I swear you're the stubbornest man alive." She grasped Tyler's hand between hers and smiled wide. "Pay him no mind. I'm Angelle, and you're right, this is Cane, my ox of a fiancé. We hope we're not intruding; I know you just got in, but Ms. Emma here begged us to stop by." She glanced at Sherry and winked. "We'll only be a minute."

The young girl—Emma, he presumed—practically flew to stand in front of him, mouth agape. "When Dad told me Aunt Sherry got married, I was *totally* shocked. I mean, I assumed I'd be a junior bridesmaid. That's what I was in Dad's wedding, and Uncle Cane says that's what I'll be in his. But then I heard she eloped and married *you*, and I. Freaked. Out!" Her ponytail bounced as she did a little dance. "Ask my dad and Colby—I'm a *huge* fan."

Tyler smiled. "Well then, it sounds like you have excellent taste in music, young lady."

The smile that lit her face was pure sunshine—and had as much energy behind it as ten Red Bulls. "Aunt Sherry never liked your music much," she went on, earning a horrified, "Emma!" from Angelle. Tyler chuckled at her blunt honesty. "What, it's the truth. She said country music was nothing but complaining and sissy-baby whining, and that people needed to get over it already." She sent her aunt a wink, clearly enjoying herself. "But I'm guessing since y'all got married, she's changed her mind now. Can I have your autograph?"

It took a second to realize that last part was a question directed toward him. Once he did, Tyler shook his head to clear it. "Oh, of course. Anything for my biggest fan."

Sherry tugged the young girl's ponytail and said, "I'll get you some paper." A few seconds later, she emerged from the kitchen with a pad of paper and handed it over. She caught Tyler's gaze and mouthed the words, *Thank you.* He winked.

"You know, I'm actually not just a fan anymore," Emma corrected. "I'm your *niece*."

The joy in her voice, and the truth in that statement, hit him for some reason, and he paused in writing his name. He glanced at Sherry again. This was where their ruse got sticky. Smiling at the girl, he said, "I guess you are, sweetheart."

Tyler spent a few more minutes with Emma, giving her his full attention and talking about music and her favorite songs. At one point, he glanced up to find both Sherry and Cane watching him closely. Sherry with a soft, tenderhearted smile, and her brother minus a scowl. Tyler counted that as progress.

"Is that your guitar?" Emma asked, pointing to the case propped near the wall.

"It sure is," he replied with a nod.

"Uncle Cane just started giving me lessons. I don't totally suck, but I loathe having to clip my nails." She held up ten fingernails alternately painted purple and black.

Sherry mussed her niece's hair. "A girl after my own heart."

Cane shifted his weight closer to the case. "What kind you play?"

Based on the question and Emma's announcement, Tyler figured Cane must be a musician, too. Which meant Tyler's answer could be a make-it-or-break-it thing. "Takamine."

Three pairs of feminine eyes swung toward Cane, and when the man gave a small nod, they exhaled in unison.

Tyler's was a bit subtler.

"Nice." Cane's ramrod posture relaxed a fraction, and he propped his shoulder against the wall. "That's what I play."

Not much to go on. Grasping at straws, really. But hey, it was something. Sherry wrapped her arms around Tyler's waist, an action so natural it didn't feel like an act. In a way, it wasn't. Their relationship wasn't real, but the need to impress the people in the room was. Tyler slid his arm around his *wife's* shoulder and kissed the crown of her head.

"You two are so cute," Emma declared, taking a seat on the armrest of the sofa. "Angelle told us it was love at first sight and that you swept Aunt Sherry off her feet." She heaved a dramatic sigh. "That's so romantic."

"Also pretty reckless," Cane muttered, earning another slap from his fiancée. "Hey, I'm one to talk, I know. I asked you to marry me after a week." He tugged her into the circle of his arms and turned back to his baby sister, anxiety clear on his face. "But we at least knew each other for months, and neither of us is famous. I just have to wonder if either of you know what the hell it is you're doing."

Not a damn clue.

One thing he *did* know: the Robicheauxs didn't hold back. They told it like it was, and Tyler liked it. But he could also see why Sherry didn't want to admit the truth.

"I'm not saying life with me is easy," he admitted, squeezing Sherry close to his side. "When your sister married me, she inherited a lot of hassle. Paparazzi, journalists, gossip, long hours, and a husband who travels more often than not. But she also married a man who doesn't give up. Who respects and appreciates her, and who would do anything within his power to keep her from getting hurt."

Sherry lifted her head from his chest, and Tyler brushed aside a strand of purple hair. "Our relationship isn't conventional, and it sure as hell didn't start off like most. But we both know what we want and aren't afraid to go for it."

At that, Sherry winced slightly, her arched eyebrows drawing together. It hadn't been a knock on her business plan; he'd meant her confident nature in general. She was a go-getter, even if she didn't realize it yet. Somehow, he'd find a way for her to see it too, and help make her dream come true. All she needed was a little push.

"Well then, I think it's time we left the newlyweds alone."

Tyler looked away from her mesmerizing eyes and returned Angelle's smile. They said their good-byes, earning a smile from Sherry when Cane shook his hand, and Emma waltzed outside humming one of his tunes. Cane followed behind her, shaking his head. Just outside the door, Angelle paused with her hand on the jamb.

"Colby and Jason are sorry they couldn't come and say hello. They're both on shift tonight, and we're watching Emma. But I have a great idea. What do you say we have a big ole Welcome-to-the-family dinner tomorrow, yeah?"

Chapter Nine

The world makes all kinds of rules for love…

Sherry bolted awake, heart in her throat. "What the what?"

Hand to chest, she glared at her clock, happily singing away about crazy people in love. Perfect. Not only had she been yanked away from a hot dream (and just when it got to the good part), but country music was now blaring in her room. Like a dope, she'd set her alarm to the local channel before falling asleep in an effort to get to know Tyler better…and this was what she got. Love songs. *Perky* love songs about people who shouldn't follow a list of rules. Sticking out her tongue, she clicked off the rude thing and collapsed against her pillows.

That was better.

Staring at the popcorn pattern on her ceiling, she admitted the alarm clock wasn't the *only* thing that had her teed off. Her subconscious was on her hit list, too. She'd purposefully escaped to her bedroom last night, needing a breather from, well, everything. From the hunk of a man now living with her, and from convincing her family they were in love. From the awkward, charged silence that had fallen after Cane and crew left, and remembering Tyler's kiss out by her car. Along with those fuzzy images from their night in Vegas.

Only problem was, the instant she closed her eyes, those memories overtook her.

Normally Sherry had the good sense to dream about mystery men. Famous celebrities she could crush on from afar without bumping into them in the bathroom. But her brilliant self just had to go and marry one of those celebrities, which promised to make brushing her teeth a much more interesting experience.

With a sigh, she threw off her blankets. Time to get ready for work. After slipping on a bra and padding to the bedroom door, she quietly turned the knob, pausing to listen for any telltale noises. The house was utterly silent. Sticking her head out, she dared a glance both ways, but not a shadow moved. There wasn't a single peep.

Could Tyler still be sleeping?

Generally, Sherry was the last one up in any group. Morning person she was *not.* But it was possible her rock star husband was an even bigger slouch than she was. Slipping down the hall on tiptoe, she stopped before the bathroom and then leapt inside, wanting to get a handle on the bedhead. And the hideous dragon breath.

Yeah, Tyler had already seen her at her worst—did it sink much lower than waking up nude, hungover, and bedraggled?—but she'd rather erase that glorious impression from his memory bank, not add to it. Safely tucked inside, she released a grateful sigh and shuffled to the sink. As water sputtered and filled the basin, Sherry lifted her bleary eyes to the mirror.

Where a yellow sticky note was stuck at eye-level.

Hey gorgeous,

The label rented studio space downtown, so that's where I'll be all day.

Call my cell if you need anything.

Tyler

P.S. Elvis is sweet, but I prefer sleeping with you.

She left the water running. Heading down the hall again, this time in the opposite direction, she didn't stop until she reached Angelle's bedroom. With a palm placed against the partially cracked door, she peered inside…and there was Elvis. Sleeping curled in a fluffy white ball on a dented pillow. *Tyler's* pillow. That no doubt smelled of sandalwood. A groan slipped out of her throat.

The bad boy of country had cuddled her baby all night. The sweetness of that made Sherry's chest constrict. Damn it, this wasn't playing fair. She set her head against the doorjamb and stood there, watching Elvis sleep. His tail twitching mid–puppy dream and his tiny legs kicking the air. Tyler's cologne lingered in the air and Sherry closed her eyes, fresh images from their night in Vegas sweeping over her. Sense memories tingled to life.

The weight of his arms holding *her.*

The slip and tug of his fingers knotting in her hair.

The warm pant of breath on her already heated skin.

Releasing a jagged breath, Sherry opened her eyes and focused on Elvis.

Lucky bastard.

• • •

Walking inside Sherry's house was like entering a war zone. The same basket of clothes was shoved in the corner, fresh Coke cans were on the coffee table, and now, piles of paper littered the floor. Tyler waved at the bodyguard he'd had posted outside (and the cause of their first martial spat via text that morning. She'd said it wasn't necessary; he'd vehemently disagreed, and in the end, well, Tony was still there), then closed the door behind him. Maneuvering as best he could, his inner neat freak twitching to organize the chaos, he called out, "I'm home."

Home. Now there was an interesting concept. Several dwellings contained Tyler's stuff. A big one in Nashville that collected dust. A tour bus he'd spent half his life on the last few years. The house he grew up in a few hours up the road that held his childhood books. That one probably came closest to an actual *home*, but it wasn't his. It didn't tell the story of who he was today, or what he wanted as a man. It told where he came from. And illness permeated the air.

But this place was different. Bigger than a tour bus, smaller than the one he owned in Nashville, Sherry's house had a warmth and energy that wrapped around you the moment you opened the door. Even with the cluttered mess. The belongings weren't his—his stuff didn't arrive for another hour—yet somehow Tyler felt more at home here than he had in years. Giving it up in a month was going to suck.

"I'm in here," Sherry called back, and Tyler followed the sound to the kitchen. She lifted tired-looking eyes from her laptop, surrounded by even more papers crowding the counter. "Hey. What time is it?"

"Just after five." He'd spent almost the entire day at the studio, meeting the crew, getting the lay of the land, prepping things so that when Charlie and the band arrived they'd be good to go. Melodies and lyrics were already churning for the new songs, and Tyler was eager to get to work. Grabbing a barstool, he sat down with his guitar on his lap and waved a hand over the paperwork. "What's all this?"

She rolled her head in a slow circle. "Robicheaux's is having an event next week." Yawning, she rubbed the back of her neck and then said, "I'm finalizing a few of the details."

Distracted by the strain of soft cotton as she raised her arms, stretching her chest, Tyler was slow to comprehend her response. But forcing his gaze away, he looked over the paperwork and said, "A few details? It looks like a small tree gave its life here."

She mumbled something incoherent, continuing to work sore muscles, and he snatched the nearest papers off the counter. To keep his mind busy and his hands off her soft skin. As he gathered the sheets into piles, he realized that despite outward appearances, she clearly had a semblance of organization—each one had a giant letter written in marker on top. A, E, F…

"It just bugs the crap out of you, doesn't it?"

"Hmm?" Looking up, he found Sherry's eyes bright with laughter.

"I swear, music man, you make me feel like a slob. You woke up at an ungodly hour. You made your freaking bed around Elvis. And your things are all unpacked. Heck, even your toothbrush was tucked away in the cabinet." She set her elbow on the counter and leaned her chin into her hand with a *tsk*. "Dude, didn't you get the memo? Musicians are supposed to be rowdy and break stuff. I think you might have to turn in your rock star card."

"Funny." Tyler tapped a pile against the counter with a smirk. "What can I say? My mama raised me this way. No one came behind me to clean my messes. That was my job. Even if she tried, I wouldn't let her. She had enough to deal with."

The truth came out without thinking, and from the corner of his eye, he saw Sherry's eyes sharpen. Tyler bit back a curse. Tonight was her family's dinner; now wasn't the time to share their sob stories—*if* they ever would. Adjusting his guitar on his lap, he fixed his attention on the papers.

The pile in his hand was marked with the letter A. The top sheet was a bulleted list, highlighting the needs of the St. Tammany Humane Society. Under that was a detailed spreadsheet of different breeds, along with math equations scribbled in the margin. Curious, he picked up another pile, this one with the letter E, and found names of local DJs, bands, and media contacts.

"Sherry, this seems pretty major." After reading a press release listing her as the point of contact, he asked, "Wait, it's *Wednesday*? As in, a week from today?"

She nodded, and he reared back in his seat. "Tell me about it. Good thing I work well under pressure, huh? It came together rather quick, but Tyler, it's so worth it.

You've gotta see this center. What it does for the animals in our parish. I volunteer as often as I can, and during my last visit, I overheard they were several big donations shy of their goal. I had to do *something*. I'm telling you, this place is phenomenal."

Not a trace of exhaustion remained in her eyes by the end of her short speech, and her entire face lit with a smile. "And don't even get me started on the animals. I'd adopt them all if I could afford it. There's this sweet little Catahoula Leopard mix I've had my eye on…" She sat back with folded arms. "If that girl doesn't find a home soon, she's mine."

As usual, her enthusiasm was completely adorable. This right here was Sherry's passion, her *dream*, in action. And Tyler wanted in. "Tell me what I can do."

"Really?" Her voice pitched high, and if it were possible for her smile to grow even wider, it did. He grinned in response. "Awesome, because I can really use the help. I may be a go-with-the-flow chica, but this is pushing it, even for me."

Without stopping for a breath, she jumped into explaining the details, animatedly waving her hands. Tyler found himself leaning closer, unconsciously mimicking her gestures. His wife was a dynamo. Her excitement for these abandoned animals made him care, too. Now *he* wanted to adopt them all.

Simply being near her did something to him. Made him breathe easier, think differently, act better. Had him wanting to prove he could be the kind of man she deserved…if life were drastically different and a real relationship were feasible. A saying his dad taught him a long time ago came to mind.

Look for the game changer, son.

There was no doubt that Sherry Robicheaux would change the entire game if he let her.

The truth hit him like a stun gun.

"Tyler, are you listening?"

"Uh, yeah." He scrubbed a hand over his face, hoping the errant thought went with it. "It sounds fantastic. You're going to make a killing for this place. Put me where you need me."

"Hmm…" She chewed the corner of her lip in deliberation. "How about Master of Ceremonies?"

Anywhere but there…

Give him a guitar and he was good to go, but public speaking wasn't his thing. Accepting awards and hyping a crowd was part of the gig, but when Blue wasn't performing, Tyler avoided microphones like the plague. He was much better at singing than giving speeches. And improv? He straight-up sucked.

"Well…truth is, I hide behind a guitar for a reason. Trust me, sugar, you don't want me up there making jokes. I'll bore the poor people to tears." Tyler cleared his throat. "How about muscle?" he suggested instead. "Surely you can use some manpower, right?"

A look of surprise crossed her face at his admission, but she nodded, quickly accepting his counterproposal with a, "Oh, definitely."

Relieved, he smiled. "Good, then put me to work."

It wasn't until her gaze dipped to his fingers that he realized he'd been fiddling with his guitar. A habit of his whenever he was anxious. Or stressed. Or happy. Pretty much, it was what he did.

Sherry closed her laptop and leaned forward on the counter. "Tell me about *your girl*."

Her voice was so sweet, her wide eyes so sincere that Tyler couldn't *not* answer. Not without feeling like a dick, at least. Plus, strangely enough, he actually wanted to share part of his story. Let her see a small bit of the real him.

Fingers still strumming the strings, he said, "Mom had just gotten diagnosed, and things around the house were tight. We didn't have a lot of money. Just paying the bills was a struggle, and frivolous things like entertainment and hobbies didn't make the cut. But Dad, he knew my passion for music. He was a musician too, and he saw it in my eyes." He felt his mouth lift in a grin. "Anyway, he worked even harder than he already was, pulled more hours at the mill just to save up, and the day I turned thirteen they shocked the hell out of me. Handed her over with a big blue bow and said, 'Chase your dreams, son.'"

Sherry's gaze softened, and he played a quick riff from one of Blue's current hits to cover his discomfort. He wasn't ready to answer any questions just yet. When her lips parted, he hurriedly said, "You know, I've gotten tons of guitars through the years. Some I've bought, others given by companies wanting photos of Tyler Blue endorsing their brand. But this is mine. It's what I use when I write or just play for fun. This is me with strings."

Corny as hell, but the damn truth. He shrugged, slightly embarrassed, and she smiled.

"She's special," she said.

He nodded, ready to shift the focus away from him again. He'd shared a piece of himself, more than he'd shared with anyone in a while. That was enough for now. "What about you? Your brother and Emma both play. Are you a secret performer?"

Sherry laughed. "That would be a hard no. My musical career piddled out after third grade recorder and 'Hot Cross Buns.' Cane's the music guy."

But her eyes kept going back to his fingers.

"Maybe you just haven't had the right teacher." He waggled his eyebrows suggestively, and she rolled her eyes. "Come on," he urged. "One lesson. It'll be fun, I promise. Plus, isn't that Marriage 101? Thou shall learn each other's interests?"

"And here I never knew God wrote a marriage book." She smirked, but it soon transformed into a reluctant grin. Tyler slid her the puppy dog look that always worked on his mama, and she groaned, pushing to her feet. "Okay, okay. *One* lesson."

He pumped his fist in the air, and she laughed. "But not tonight. We, dear husband, already have plans for the evening." Sidling over to his side of the counter, an evil glint entered her eye as she asked, "Ready for the in-law inquisition?"

Chapter Ten

"Everyone's here." Sherry parked behind a Chevy in the long driveway of her childhood home, and thunder rolled as Tyler's eyes fell on the truck's bumper. Two stickers promoted the Magnolia Springs Fire Department and the local gym, Northshore Combatives. On the drive over from the house, she'd let it slip that one of his new brothers-in-law wasn't just the town's fire captain. He also owned the gym… and was trained in hand-to-hand combat.

So much for not being intimidated.

"My damn hands are sweating," he said with a laugh, wiping them on the rough denim of his jeans. He glanced across the console of her shoebox car. "And you're sure they bought your story?"

Lightning flashed, revealing her rolling hazel eyes. "In this case, it pays to be the addicted-to-love little sister." With a flick of her wrist, she killed the engine, and the blades swiping the rain from the windshield stilled. "Quick recap.

We met in the green room of the casino, completely hit it off, and spent the weekend together. Classic love-at-first-sight stuff. You swept me off my feet, and we just couldn't *stand* to have it end. Then, since I'm practically certifiable, I suggested we elope, which you thought was a fabulous idea, as most of my ideas are. So, we got hitched."

Glancing down, she straightened the diamond ring on her finger. "Anyway, the next morning, we parted ways. You headed back for a meeting in Nashville, and I came here to get our love nest ready. I feigned shock when the reporter showed up at my door because we hadn't wanted to tell anyone right away. You wanted to meet them first because you're traditional like that."

Tyler scoffed, but he had to hand it to her. The woman could spin a story. If she ever went into PR, she'd make a killing. "Wouldn't a traditionalist ask permission *prior* to the elopement?"

"Don't mess with the cover, rookie," she teased. "You're dealing with an expert."

Chuckling, he raised his palms in surrender. Already he felt lighter than when they first pulled up. "Wouldn't dream of it." The rain beat a steady rhythm on the hood, and he grasped the door handle, ready to run for it. "Prepare to see my eighth grade drama skills in action, Mrs. Blue."

She smirked. "Do try and keep up, rookie."

Laughing, he threw open the door and tore up the drive, expecting Sherry to be right behind him. But when he reached the front door and turned around, she wasn't on the porch. Confused, Tyler walked back a few steps and found her instead in the yard, face tilted to the sky, arms stretched to capture the liquid drops.

In his experience, women tended to get all Wicked Witch when it came to the wet stuff—they freaked if it touched them. While Sherry wasn't overly dramatic about fashion, he'd seen her tackle box filled with makeup and witnessed the application ceremony. If anyone would avoid the risk of messing it up, it'd be Sherry.

But then, as he always seemed to be when it came to this woman, he'd been wrong.

"What the hell are you doing?"

She stuck out her tongue like a kid catching snowflakes and closed her eyes as the rain pelted her once flawless face. Lowering her head with a grin, she said, "It's not like we're gonna melt. Haven't you ever danced in the rain for fun?"

"Danced?" Tyler edged closer to the end of the covered porch, shocked anew. Raising his voice over the torrent, he shook his head. "Can't say that I have."

His confession earned him a playful grin, and as she held out a hand toward him, she said, "There's a first time for everything."

Right now, he was dry. He was under a roof, warm and adequately dressed to impress the in-laws. But her smile was hypnotic. Placing his hand in hers, unsure why he was even doing it, he let her tug him into the storm.

As expected, it was cold. And wet. If anyone saw them out here—and with their photographic luck, people were definitely watching—they'd think he was nuts. But that didn't matter because his adorable, silly, crazy-as-hell wife dropped his hand and began dancing. Spinning in a circle, laughing at nothing, scrunching her nose and making a Mick Jagger face as she shimmied her shoulders and swirled those luscious hips.

It was mesmerizing.

"Dancing isn't a spectator sport," she called out, eyebrow lifted, twirling again. "Don't tell me you don't dance, music man. I ain't buying it."

Oh, he had some moves. Not *great* moves, mind you, but he could carry his own. So, with his sassy brunette watching and waiting, Tyler gave the quiet street a cursory glance, and then bopped his head.

"Niiice," Sherry teased, throwing her head back in a laugh. "Watch out, Timberlake."

Shaking his head, a smile twitching his lips, he added his feet. Pleasure filled her eyes as she followed his every step, so he also did a Michael Jackson moonwalk, complete with a crotch grab. That sent her into hysterics. And made him feel like a damn king.

There was no music, no beat other than the rain hitting the roof of the house and cars, but he danced anyway. They boogied together, in a storm, in public where anyone could watch (and the bodyguard parked out front definitely was). It was so completely *un*like him, and it felt ridiculous. Dumb and stupid…and completely free.

After another sidestep of her own, Sherry spun into his chest and slid her hands around his neck. "I've never seen you let go and be utterly silly before." She nodded slowly in approval. "It looks good on you."

"Yeah, well, don't get too used to it," he replied, slipping his thumbs along her cheeks to catch the runny lines of mascara. Even looking like a drowned rat, she was gorgeous. "From now on, I think I'll reserve wet and wild for only special occasions."

An emotion sparked in her eyes. Eyebrow lifted, she

dropped her voice to a seductive purr and said, "But you'll never forget your first."

Tyler swallowed as she drew her tongue along her lips to lick the moisture. Damn, what he wouldn't give to be truly alone. At his sprawling house in Nashville, acres of land to hide in, with zero chance of spying. Plenty of room to explore *other* rainy-day fantasies…

Her wicked grin said she'd read his thoughts, and Sherry stepped out of his hold. "Come on. The family awaits."

Family. Like the slightly intimidating brother he'd already met, and the one who ran into burning buildings for a living. Yeah, that killed his raging libido. Well played.

Desire in check, he followed Sherry back up the porch.

Sherry had said they'd all grown up in this house and inherited equal shares when their parents died, but this was now officially Cane's home. That didn't stop his little sister from walking straight in as if *she* owned it, though. Once she'd rung out her hair on the welcome mat, she pushed the door wide and called out across the open foyer, "Let the party start. The guests of honor are in the house!"

From somewhere inside, laughter drifted, sliding over the notes of smooth jazz. Tyler walked inside and stared at a giant fleur-de-lis, mounted above an old grandfather clock. It was as if he'd walked through his own childhood door. Chest strangely tight, he kicked off his shoes, noted the crucifix mounted over the door, and then followed Sherry across the hardwood foyer.

Just off the entryway was a cozy, informal living room. Cane, Angelle, and a man with dark hair were standing along one side, near a large window that overlooked the front yard. A fantastic spot to catch an impromptu dance recital in the rain.

That was one way to make an impression.

Angelle shook her head with a smile. "I'll go get y'all some towels." She looked them both up and down. "And wrangle up a change of clothes."

Following her gaze, he found a small puddle at his feet. Normally, jeans leaking water on hardwood would be strike two in the impression department—but then again, this was Sherry's family. Looking back up, he said, "Guess I can scratch rain dancing from the old bucket list."

Angelle laughed and scooted past with a wink. "Nice to see you again, Tyler."

He turned his attention to the two relatives remaining.

"Jason Landry," the unknown man said as way of introduction, grinning as he walked forward. He yanked a strand of Sherry's wet hair, and she playfully slapped his fingers away. "Welcome to the family," he said, taking Tyler's extended hand in a shake. "If you hurt my girl, I'll dismember you." Then he smacked his shoulder and smiled wide. "Want a beer?"

"Good Lord, the raging testosterone is giving me the vapors." Sherry fanned herself before elbowing Jason in the stomach and turning to Tyler. "Don't believe a word he says. These two cavemen are total teddy bears underneath."

"More like grisly," Cane said, joining the trio.

Tyler nodded, watching as the three went on teasing one another, unsure what to say or how to jump in. It was like the world was suddenly in fast forward. Or flip-flopped to a land where streaming water onto the hardwood and threats of bodily harm were normal occurrences. Maybe in Sherry's family, they were. It appeared the entire lot was as crazy as she was, and while he appreciated that, liked it even, that damn beer was sounding good about now.

"I'm sure he knows how it is," Cane said, grabbing a longneck from the coffee table and handing it over with a knowing look. "Have any sisters, Tyler?"

"Nope." He twisted off the cap and took a long pull. That was better. "Only child. Lots of cousins, though. In high school, I had to dunk a dude's head in the toilet for standing one up at her prom."

Cane nodded and exchanged a look with Jason. "Yeah, he'll fit right in."

Sherry peered up at him through thick lashes and gave the world's sweetest smile. He pulled her soaked body against his and squeezed tight, lifting his beer to his lips. So far so good.

In many ways, this felt familiar. The Robicheauxs reminded Tyler of his own family. Blue men loved to tease, to poke and push, never meaning harm, and they always looked out for their own.

Nostalgia slammed against his ribs. He grasped Sherry's hips, unprepared for the onslaught.

"Here you go," Angelle said, returning with a batch of towels straight from the dryer and a set of Cane's clothes. She held up a pair of workout pants and a tee. "I thought these could work. You're around the same height."

That was sweet and southern for saying Cane's jeans wouldn't fit, since the dude was twice his size, bulk-wise. But beggars can't be choosers. Kissing the crown of Sherry's head, letting the scent of her floral shampoo calm his racing heart, he thanked his host and ducked into the bathroom down the hall.

Closing the door behind him, he leaned against the wood and released a breath.

Performing and traveling the world kept Tyler busy. Kept him from thinking too much about home. But here, in this house, everything caught up with him at once. Memories of family parties filled with laughter and rowdy teasing. Dad playing music with his garage band, Mom on the covered swing, watching with adoration. On good days like that, they'd forget she was even sick. That her time with them was running short. Afterward, she'd head straight for bed, completely wiped, but his mom had lived for those stress-free gatherings. Tyler had, too.

Shaking away the wave of homesickness, Tyler emerged fully dressed and found a slightly older version of Sherry, minus the purple streaks and sassy smirk, leaned against the opposite wall.

"Hey there, I'm Colby. I'm tucked away in the kitchen but wanted to say hello." She shot a look in the direction of the living room. "And make sure the guys were behaving themselves."

"Nothing I can't handle," he assured her. Then, glancing down the hall, he asked, "Can I help you with dinner?" Anyone who knew him would laugh. His kitchen skills left a *lot* to be desired. But he wasn't ready to return to the group.

Colby smiled as she pushed away from the wall. "I never turn away extra hands."

Guilt, hurt, and fear roiled in Tyler's gut during the trek to the kitchen, stronger than they had in a long time. Those memories of home wouldn't shake. Fingers twitching for his guitar, he drained the rest of his beer and focused instead on the family photos lining the walls. It read like a visual timeline. Sherry as a baby. Her toothless school pictures. Costumed shots from dance recitals and drill team. Sticking her tongue out, flirting with the camera, and pretty much photo bombing the rest.

A grouping of each of the Robicheaux kids in their graduation gowns hung on the wall just outside the kitchen. The last one was of his wife. Her fingers were lifted in a rock-star salute, her other arm clasped around a woman clearly her mother. The familiar pang hit his chest again, and he rapped his knuckles against the frame.

Unsurprising for a family of chefs, the kitchen was huge. Dark oak cabinets, butcher-block island, and cast iron pots dangling from the ceiling. Over the sink, an aged sign read GET IT WHILE IT'S HOT, and an explosion of magnets covered the refrigerator. Garlic and basil teased his nose, making his mouth water. That ache in his chest deepened.

"This reminds me of my parents' kitchen." Rubbing a fist over his shirt, he willed the emotions away. He didn't know why they'd triggered, but he needed to pull himself together. Impressing Sherry's family, making sure they believed their story, was imperative for their plan to work. Looking at the spotless kitchen, a far cry from how it'd look if *he* were the one preparing supper, Tyler asked, "What's on the menu?"

"Lasagna." Colby slid up onto the island and grabbed a glass of red wine. "It's cooling on the stove, and the bread is in the oven. Emma helped me earlier, before the latest drama took her out back texting like a maniac. Only thing left is the salad." He scratched the side of his jaw, wondering why she'd accepted his help, and she shrugged. "Our family can be a handful. I figured you could use the breather."

At her understanding smile, the pressure in his chest

lifted a fraction, and Tyler walked to the sink. "Well, as much as I appreciate that, I'm a man of my word." He turned on the faucet and began washing his hands. "I'm making that salad." Then he hesitated and looked over his shoulder. "I can't screw that up too badly, right?"

"You'd be surprised," she replied, but smiled to show she was teasing. "The stories I could tell of what people do to harmless vegetables would make your toes curl. Lucky for you, a professional is standing by."

As Colby sipped her wine, she instructed Tyler on what to do. Soon he was too busy slicing, dicing, and spinning to think about home or anything else. While he built what was sure to be the best salad in the history of the world, Sherry's sister filled the silence with stories of her recent wedding.

"Who knew little things could add up so quickly?" She shook her head and grinned. "Guess that's one benefit of eloping. You miss the hoopla. Not to mention the huge dent in the bank account." She slid him a look. "But something tells me that wouldn't be such an issue for you. I do wish I could've seen my baby sister walk down the aisle, though."

She glanced away, a tight smile on her lips, and Tyler felt like an ass. Why, he wasn't quite sure, since the wedding wasn't *real*...at least not in the sense she meant. But already he could see how close this family was. If his marriage to Sherry had been legit, no doubt the church would've overflowed with relatives on both sides.

Not for the first time, he wondered about the ceremony. What it *had* been like. Clearly, not sentimental and romantic like Colby's, but definitely more entertaining. How could it not with a setup like theirs? And while he couldn't remember the particulars, there was the DVD he'd found in the hotel room.

Everything had been so hectic since he arrived. Getting on the same page, the studio worked out…he hadn't had a chance to tell Sherry it even existed. Now with things more settled, he was damn curious what it held. In light of their mutual hangovers, plenty of embarrassment. Sherry in that hideous veil, probably singing her vows off-key. Him stumbling and trying not to blow his cover. An Elvis impersonator officiating.

"Must've been some wedding." Tyler looked up from the salad bowl to see Colby's grin. "You're smiling like a lovesick dope. I should know. I do it all the time."

Unsure how to respond, he nodded slightly and returned to his work.

"Did Sherry tell you I was supposed to do the event that night?"

His head jerked up so fast he almost pinched a nerve.

She laughed. "Take that as a no." Studying him closely, she took another sip of wine. "I'm normally the one who handles those types of things, but I'd just returned from our honeymoon. Sherry stepped in, willing to go, and for once, I handed over control. Funny how things work out sometimes, huh?"

Tyler set down the chef's knife. "Yeah, funny."

Only, it wasn't. Imagining how different things would be had Sherry *not* been in that green room, laughter was the furthest thing from his mind.

• • •

"You killed it, ladies," Cane declared, slapping a napkin

on his scraped-clean plate. "You're gonna have to step up the workouts, Jase, with them both living with you." Emma beamed at her godfather's praise, and he tugged her ponytail. "You sure you're not ready for that job yet?"

Emma shook her head. "Still only twelve, Uncle Cane."

This was nice. Being with her family, acting silly, letting Tyler see this side of her…it was great. So far, they'd even done a decent job playing their designated parts. Their dance in the rain to start the night certainly helped. But ever since they'd dried off and changed, there was a sense of unease Sherry couldn't shake. Sure, part of it was guilt. She loathed hiding anything from her family, and lying to them felt even worse. But this was more than that. As she glanced around the table of bliss, she felt…wistful.

Colby and Jason were newlywed giddy. He anticipated her needs—more wine, or a second helping of salad. She rubbed the back of his neck as they spoke. They kept sharing little looks throughout dinner. And Cane and Angelle were just as bad. Whipped was a new look for her brother, and Sherry loved seeing it on him. In fact, she was so stinking happy for all of them. But that didn't mean it didn't hurt, sitting beside her *in-name-only* husband and pretending to be just as blissful as her siblings.

When would it be *her* turn to experience the real deal?

Would a man ever look at her with undisguised adoration, the way her brother and brother-in-law stared at the women they loved?

Sherry released a sigh, and Tyler placed his hand on her thigh under the table. Pressing a kiss against her hair, he quietly whispered, "Everything okay?"

No, not really.

What was worse was that her siblings were starting to notice. Normally, she ran the show. Cutting up, acting crazy to make them laugh, keeping the atmosphere light. But for some reason, she just wasn't feeling it anymore. She gave him a small smile and nodded. "Just tired."

That was the truth, if not all of it. She *was* exhausted… from keeping up their ruse. And they'd only just begun. Tyler stared into her eyes with a slight frown, clearly not buying her excuse, but when Angelle suggested a game of Taboo, he tore his gaze away.

"I think we have to pass."

Angie looked disappointed, and her suspicious stare grew sharper. Sherry was their group's perpetual night owl, teasing the others whenever they tried to duck out early. "Is everything all right?"

There was that question again, and suddenly, tears were building behind her eyes. Which, really, was just so ridiculous. Maybe she was premenstrual.

"Yeah, I'm fine," Sherry replied, making a production out of a yawn. "It's just been a long day. Finalizing the Humane event, recovering from the weekend in Vegas—"

"Enjoying married life at night," Colby teased with a sly grin. Jason cleared his throat, trying to hide his smile as he motioned toward Emma at the end of the table.

Her sister winced, and he chuckled. "Smooth, baby. Real smooth."

"Yep, you guessed it," Sherry replied brightly, perhaps *overly* brightly, as twin surges of heat shot up her face. Lord, she wished that were her excuse. It was a lot more fun than the truth.

Tyler chuckled low and deep in his throat, and she

squeezed her thighs together. His laugh was dark and seductive, and it tempted her to throw caution to the wind. To steal one night and take the edge off this craving. Watching her big, bad country boy get silly in the rain only heightened her desire…

But as amazing as a night would be, the fallout would hurt so much worse.

Raising her eyes, she found her so-called husband, her partner-in-crime, staring down with unmistakable mirrored want. She swallowed hard and pushed her chair back.

Definitely time to jet.

Everyone followed suit, standing and stopping at various points between the dining room and the front door. It was obvious they all planned to stick around and play the game, matched couples doing couple-y things. Well, other than Emma, but her niece was *twelve*. Sherry loved the girl to pieces, but she was ready to move away from the kid's table.

One day…the plan is still on. Just delayed, is all.

Hugging her sister tight, Sherry said, "Dinner was fabulous as always, *Coley*. Reminded me of Mom's."

Colby took a breath, the compliment obviously pleasing her. When it came to Cajun fare, there was no mistaking their father's culinary prowess, but their mom had kicked major pasta butt. "I clipped some of her rosemary for the sauce."

Next up was Emma and Jason, a two-in-one squeeze. "Bring that husband of yours down to the gym some time," he said, stepping back to shake Tyler's hand. "We'll even go easy on you your first visit."

Angelle cut in with a laugh. "*I* make no promises."

At Tyler's look of confusion, Sherry explained, "Cane

and Angelle both take Jason's ninjitsu classes."

"Great. So basically you're saying your entire family is trained to kick my ass if I step out of line."

Sherry tapped his chest with a smirk she didn't quite feel. "And don't you forget it."

"Well, except for me," Colby replied. "I leave the fighting to my man. I'd just slip something in your food."

Everyone laughed at that, and Jason pulled Tyler into a conversation about his class with Cane and Angelle. Emma stood as close as she could to her new "uncle," staring at him with the same wide-eyed adoration she once did Colby. Not that she'd ever stopped idolizing her stepmother, but the extreme fangirling had lessened over the last year. Evidently now finding an outlet in the caring, funny, hot-as-hell man wearing Sherry's ring.

The need to leave became an itch under her skin.

"Hey, Ty, I'm falling asleep where I stand."

The lighthearted smile he turned to her nearly buckled her knees. He was enjoying himself. Hanging out with her family, being cute with Emma. Cooking with Colby and joking with Jason. This day was seriously messing with her head. For heaven's sakes, the man left her a semi-love note on her mirror and freaking cuddled her puppy! Was the universe out to get her?

Tyler's eyebrows drew together and he reached for her hand. "Gentlemen, it's time I got my bride home."

Angelle and Colby visibly swooned as he tucked her under his arm and kissed her head, playing the part exactly as she'd asked him to. So then why were tears of frustration lumped in her throat? Clearly, she needed a nap.

Linking their fingers together, she tugged him gently

toward the door. Beyond the wood lay cool, clean air and quiet. Hopefully both would knock some sense into her. The knob was turned, salvation a few feet away, when Angelle said, "Oh, wait, one more thing."

Closing her eyes, Sherry exhaled and turned around.

Angie handed her a grocery bag filled with their wet clothes and a covered plate to take to their bodyguard, Tony. *Oh, right.* "So, Cane has a bunch of guys from the gym coming over Saturday to extend the back deck." She winced slightly, and dread pricked Sherry's neck. She already knew where this was going. "Normally, I'd be all for the company, and I'm definitely grateful for the help…but they're coming at *five* in the morning. With saws. And hammers. On my day off."

"Won't the neighbors be mad?" Tyler asked, clearly missing the bigger picture.

Sherry shook her head. "This house is in the middle of three acres." His eyes widened and she explained, "It was dark when we arrived, but the closest neighbors won't hear a thing. And the bayou runs out back."

"Bayou, huh?" He looked at Cane with an eager smile. "Good fishing?"

"The best," her brother confirmed. The dang dimple that made her friends gaga flashed in his cheek as he said, "If you want, we can take the boat out next week."

"Definitely," Tyler replied, at the same time Jason said, "I want in."

"Anyway." Sherry widened her eyes, really wishing the ability to read your spouse's mind came with the exchange of vows. "As you were saying, Angie."

"Right, well, I know y'all are in the middle of honeymoon

bliss, but do you mind if I stay in my room Friday night?" Rocking on her cowboy boots, she added with a hopeful grin, "I promise to keep ear buds in the whole time."

And that's when Tyler finally got it.

His dark head swiveled toward her, and Sherry would've laughed aloud, except no one else would've gotten the joke. She and Tyler would have to spend the entire night in her bedroom. At dinner, she came *this* close to attacking the man. Her hormones were running amok, tossing that stupid list of rules seriously sounded appealing, and in two days, they'd be sharing a bed. Lying side-by-side and breathing the same air.

Tyler's mouth curved in a slow grin, thoughts obviously aligned with hers, only not seeming that upset at all...

"Do you mind?" Angelle asked. Thanks to Sherry's reaction, her friend probably assumed she'd be interrupting wild monkey sex. Fabulous.

Swallowing hard, she broke away from Tyler's wicked gaze and said, "Not at all."

Lie number one thousand and ten.

Chapter Eleven

"You know what they say about a watched clock," Tyler said, leaning his back against the couch. Sherry transferred her anxious gaze to his and raised an eyebrow. "It never moves."

"Isn't that a watched pot never boils?"

"Close enough." He grinned and moved the guitar off his lap, holding out his hand. "Come over here and sit with me." After only a slight hesitation, she slipped her fingers in his, and he tugged her onto the floor beside him. The tension in her body kept her spine locked tight, and he reached over and kneaded the muscles of her shoulder, coaxing her to relax. "It'll be fine. I promise not to bite"—he glanced at her from the corner of his eye—"unless you ask me to."

She rolled her eyes in a *that's never gonna happen* way, but her shoulder began to loosen under his ministrations. Truth was, Tyler was anxious about sharing her bed tonight, too. Just not for the same reason.

Their plan was working. Every gossip site in the industry

was speculating over Tyler and Sherry's whirlwind romance, leaking pictures of that incredible kiss in her driveway. Arianne was like a cat that ate the cream, constantly sending him links with various messages, all renditions of, *I told you so.* The world was already in love with his sass-mouthed caterer, calling Sherry a "down-home sweetheart," and after the photos of their kiss, the latest polls speculated how long it would take until she'd be in the "family way."

Fat chance of that happening, rules or not. But the nonstop talk only fed his memories of Vegas. And three nights of sliding past each other in the hall, and three days of sitting shoulder-to-shoulder on the sofa, ratcheted their sexual tension to the point of insanity. He was on two-a-day cold showers as it was; an entire night of breathing her sweet-scented skin, hearing her soft sighs near his ear might very well kill him.

Lying in the dark stripped away pretense. Cut through the bullshit to what was real. But after only a week together, *real* was becoming a fluid concept. When Sherry took sex off the table, he'd hated it. He'd respected her decision but didn't think it was necessary. Now, he did. Keeping the line straight was crucial while they found balance.

It was another one of her rules, though, that he questioned—no romance in the house.

Was making out romantic?

Sherry moaned as Tyler pressed his thumb into a knot near the curve of her neck. If he didn't know better, he'd swear she was messing with him.

"Hey, Ty?" she asked a little later, her muscles practically putty in his hands. "I need you to promise me something."

Considering the last time she said that, he'd agreed to

enforced celibacy, he was hesitant. But unsure how it could possibly get any worse, he replied, “Anything, sweet thing.”

Sherry shifted her head to look at him. Fear and vulnerability pooled in her eyes. “If I throw myself at you tonight, or even suggest we push the boundaries of our relationship…” His fingers stopped moving. “I need you to turn me down.”

Aw, hell, was she serious? Did she think he was a candidate for sainthood?

But what could he say? No? As much as he wanted another taste—a kiss, a few more touches—what Tyler wanted more was for Sherry to want him, too. No regrets, no second-guesses. They had three more weeks together in this cozy house. He couldn’t afford to screw up now. “Rest assured, I’ll be a good boy.” He lifted two fingers in the air. “Scout’s honor.”

The last knot in her shoulders unkinked, and Sherry laughed. “You know, the heroes in my romance novels always say that. Scout’s honor. But they all later admit to never being a Boy Scout.”

“Not so with me,” he told her, purposefully steering the conversation toward a less *heated* topic. “Ages six through twelve. If you ever need a fire built, a knot tied, or a compass read, I’m your man.”

Rolling onto her hip, she gave him an impressed smile. “Never would’ve guessed it. I, on the other hand, while a Girl Scout, belonged to more of a Troop Beverly Hills deal. We camped in hotel rooms and learned about Mary Kay.” She laughed and wiggled her painted nails. “I may not know how to sew worth a damn, but I can give you one heck of a manicure.”

"Equally important life skills," he replied with a grin, glad to see her anxiety gone. At least for now. Hoping to keep it that way until Angelle arrived, he pulled his guitar onto his lap and removed a pick from between the strings at the neck. "Know what's another important skill? Learning to strum a guitar— "

"Kinda playing fast and loose with *important* there, aren't ya?"

Winking at her, he held out the pick. "If I recall correctly, you already agreed to a lesson." He plucked a few strings to illustrate his point, then nudged her with the headstock of the instrument. "What else are we gonna do to pass the time?"

Her eyes locked with his and she nodded. "Good point." Sighing dramatically, she said, "Fine, fine. Just remember when your ears start bleeding that this was *your* idea." She lifted to her knees and stared uncertainly at the guitar. "How should we do this?"

There were plenty of ways…but just now, only one sounded remotely appealing. "Sit in front of me."

She eyed him suspiciously as he kicked out his legs, then smirked as she crawled into position. "Sure, the way all good instructors set up."

"Exactly." He grinned, savoring the feel of her in his arms. Her back to his chest. Her hair brushing against his chin. Her floral perfume hit his nose, and he inhaled deep.

"Tyler…"

Her voice was a warning tease. Leaning forward, he whispered against her ear, "Rule number five, sugar. Enjoy the moment."

Her breath caught and his smile widened. Sitting back,

he swung the instrument over her lap, flush against her chest. "Now, let me show you how to hold it."

Mumbling something about hormonal whiplash, Sherry set her hands where he instructed, thumb of her left hand down low on the neck, fingertips curled over onto the strings, and her right hand gripping the pick.

"Good," he told her, covering her hand with his. "And you never have to push the string all the way to the wood. Just enough to press against the fret. These vertical lines are the frets, and you want to put your fingertips just behind it. Not on top of it, and not way back here, but right up against it, like this."

She pulled a face as she stretched her fingers along the neck, but did it perfectly. Tyler figured that deserved some sort of praise, and in lieu of gold stars, he slid his nose along her ear and kissed it. "Excellent."

She shot him a look. "Is that how you reward all your students?"

"Of course," he replied. "Are you questioning my methods?"

She shook her head with a laugh. "I wouldn't dare. Proceed, Teach."

After a quick anatomy lesson—*guitar* not human—and an explanation of pitch and tension—*strings* not sexual—he guided her right hand over the sound hole. "When you strum, do it parallel to the instrument, not pressing in, and keep the pick perpendicular to the strings with only a slight lean on the up and down strokes."

Hand wrapped around hers, he demonstrated the movement on the first string, then the second, followed by the third, fourth, fifth, and sixth. Sherry sat taller with each strum, her teeth trapping her bottom lip as excitement ignited in her eyes.

"You're a natural."

This time when she turned her head at the compliment, he pressed a kiss to her nose. Warm breath hit his throat as her lips parted, and he said with complete seriousness, "It's important to keep rewards consistent."

She laughed, and their lesson continued in much the same way. Innocent flirtations, creative rewards, and Sherry gaining confidence in strumming the strings and working the different frets.

"What string is this?" she asked during her fourth trip through the series.

"That's the D string," Tyler told her. "The low E is at the top, the second string is A, then it's D, G, B, and the last one is high E." A mnemonic device he once heard came to mind and, plucking the strings, he said, "Eddie Ate Dynamite… Good Bye Eddie."

Sherry scrunched her nose. "That's seriously morbid."

Tyler laughed and shifted his weight on his hip, coincidently closing the thin space between them even more. "Maybe so, but you won't forget it, will you?"

Her answering grin was quick and full of challenge. "I think we should test that theory. Quiz me."

Narrowing his eyes, he made it look as though he was trying to stump her. In actuality, he wanted nothing more than for her to succeed. To keep the smile on her face and the anxiety far, far away. "Okay, play the…B string."

He watched her silently mouth the phrase, her pick moving down the line until it landed on the second string from the bottom. She plucked it and looked back for approval. "Is that right?"

He nodded. "You got it."

"Ha!" Her ass wiggled against him in a victory dance, and Tyler bit back a groan.

It wasn't the friction or even the way her body molded to his. It was the pure joy in her eyes and the huge smile stretching her face...and it was knowing *he* put it there. This woman—this crazy, sassy, conflicting woman—got to him, pure and simple. Only there was nothing pure or simple about their situation.

She strummed through the series again, now completely solo, and settled against his chest. His hands hovered midair, hesitating and then sliding down either side of her trim waist. Roughened fingertips from years of playing skimmed across the smooth skin of her abdomen, exposed in her shrunken concert tee, and memories of kissing his way down her body taunted his mind. Sherry wiggled again, and his fingers inched closer to the waistband of her jeans...

"Dude, you're an awesome teacher," she declared, clearly *not* on the same page as his raging libido.

Clenching his jaw, Tyler leaned back against the sofa cushion. He took a deep breath of un-floral-scented air, trying to clear his head. "It's easy to teach what you love."

"I like that," she said, the smile evident in her voice as she continued her path down the scales. "I admit, watching you play every night is my new favorite thing. I don't know... it's like, this softness enters your eyes when you do it. The stress of the day melts away and you instantly find your happy place." Glancing at him she said, "It's sweet."

Sweet. Now there was a desire-inducing word.

Stifling a laugh at his severe lack of game with this

woman, he replied, "My happy place, huh? Well, yeah, I guess that's what music is for me." Her soft smile encouraged him to explain, so he did.

No game and a sudden habit of spilling his guts—watch out, ladies.

"Growing up, we didn't have money for vacations or travel. I worked whatever odd jobs I could find. Dad busted his ass. They did the best they could, and I had a great childhood, but we were always strapped to one place. Playing took me somewhere else. And now it gives me the chance to see the world."

Sherry's fingers fell silent. She turned to face him fully, setting the guitar down beside them, and confused, Tyler stared back, wondering what he'd said to add that strange look in her eyes. Slowly, she lifted her hand to cradle his cheek. "There's more to you than anyone knows, isn't there?"

Swallowing hard, Tyler watched her lids lower. Sat stock-still, afraid to move, as her body leaned forward. Her gaze flickered to his lips and then straight to his eyes.

Go for it?

Hold back?

The moment held as his mind warred with her list of rules.

Until the sound of a key sliding in the locked front door sprung them apart.

"Crap." Sherry leapt to her feet, and Tyler dragged his hands down over his face. So damn close. She stood there, her fingers on her unkissed lips, looking back and forth between him still on the floor and the door as it opened, ushering in a cold, stiff breeze.

That, at least, helped.

Tugging his guitar onto his lap, he smiled graciously as the redhead bustled in and slammed the door.

"Whew, it's cold cold tonight," she proclaimed, rubbing her arms to ward off a chill. The Cajun doubling of the word for emphasis reminded him of home, and he sighed. She and Sherry fell into an immediate conversation about Louisiana's unpredictable weather, Tyler all but forgotten… which, in view of his current state, was probably for the best.

It was ironic. This whole thing between them started with *easy*. Sherry's easy smiles. The way she made simply hanging out a breeze. It drew him to her in the green room, kept him coming back over the weekend, and it led him to believe this marriage idea could actually work.

But as his wife's conflicted gaze collided with his across the room, he had to admit that *whatever* this thing was building between them, it sure as hell wasn't easy.

• • •

Sweet Thing,

Did I mention you look HOT today?

Well, you do.

Kick some hostess ass. See you tonight.

Tyler

P.S. Charlie says you're our good luck charm ;)

Sherry spit the foaming toothpaste into the basin and rinsed her brush. Her eyes kept straying to the row of notes stuck on the mirror. For some reason, she hadn't removed that first one, and when she awoke the next morning to its twin, she'd decided to leave them both. Now there were three. None of his short messages overstepped any boundaries; they were simple but flirtatious. And adorable as hell.

After moisturizing, smoothing her eyebrows, and pinching her cheeks for a bit of color, there was nothing left to do but exit the bathroom. With each step down the hallway, her heartbeat increased. By the time she reached her bedroom, her pulse pounded in her ears. So much of their final night in Vegas remained shrouded in fuzziness… but the more time they spent together, the more their innocent touches became less innocent, the crisper a few key details became. In particular, the steamy ones just prior to her ungraceful exodus to puke.

Soft lamplight fell on Tyler when she opened the door, and she watched, mouth drier than the Sahara, as he reached back and tugged off his shirt. His jeans already discarded, he stood in the middle of her bedroom in nothing but a pair of plaid boxers. She must've squeaked, or perhaps moaned, because his head whipped up, and they shared a long, tense look.

"If you'd rather, I can sleep on the floor…"

He bunched the fabric of his tee in his hand, and she followed his gaze to a pallet of blankets and throw pillows near the foot of the bed. She smiled, touched, and shook her head. As soft as those blankets were, he'd be miserable come morning.

"That's silly." Glancing back, her gaze fell on his smooth, muscled chest. *But it sure as hell would be safer.* "We're adults, right?"

The corner of his mouth quirked. "Of course."

After another one of those dang delicious pauses, Tyler

tossed his shirt in the corner and turned down the comforter.

Sherry forced herself to look away. As she walked to the dresser for pajamas, sheets rustled behind her. Tyler sighed in what sounded like contentment at the eight-hundred-thread count Egyptian. Squeezing her eyes shut, she threw a mini-mental pity party. This was going to be the longest night of her life. With a sigh of her own, she opened them again and examined the contents of her drawer.

Skimpy or grandma?

Honestly, she didn't own much of the latter. Demure was Angelle's department—but she couldn't very well ask her friend for a loan. Settling instead for a thin tank and shorts combo, by far her least revealing option, Sherry spun around and found Tyler watching her.

"I'm just gonna"—she pointed toward the closet—"head in there to change."

Silently, his eyes tracked her movement until she closed the small door behind her. As her clothes fell to the floor, she gave herself a pep talk. She could do this. They *were* adults, and if she couldn't go eight hours sleeping next to a man—albeit an extremely hot one who also happened to be her husband—without having sex with him, then she had a serious problem. Tugging up her short shorts, she nodded firmly in resolve.

Tyler smiled as she exited, and she met it with one of her own. "Okay if I turn off the light?" she asked, padding across the hardwood.

"Go for it."

The moment she flicked off the lamp, she regretted it. What was it about losing one sense that made the rest so much sharper? The room felt smaller, more intimate, and the sound of his breathing filled the air. Or was that hers? She put a hand on the bed and climbed beneath the sheet, the soft cotton whispering across the bare skin of her legs.

As she fixed the bedding around her, their arms touched.

She shivered, and the movement brushed her calf against his. The dark curly hair of his leg tickled, and her belly dipped. Tyler didn't move a muscle, didn't make a sound, but she knew exactly where he was. His body heat pressed against her entire right side. Her eyes fluttered closed, and she imagined the sliver of mattress between them pulsating with energy.

Energy and memories.

The rasp of his hand sliding up her leg. A low chuckle bathing her ear when she squirmed. The graze of his fingertips finding the sensitive spot beneath her knee. His green eyes blazing as he moved over her. "You feel so good, sugar…"

"No romance in the house!"

Sherry slapped a hand over her mouth, mortified at her outburst. And although she couldn't see it, she could swear she heard Tyler grin.

The wall of heat shifted as he turned onto his hip, the bed dipping and sheets sliding. "There's an entire range of options to explore that have zero to do with romance."

His voice was gravelly and so close to her ear that wisps of hair moved with his breath. She shivered again. "That may be true," she replied, "but there's no way in hell we'd ever stop."

"We won't know until we try."

It was clear Tyler was teasing, but it was equally obvious he was waiting for a signal. All she had to do was hint that she was open to explore those options, take back that ridiculous request she'd made earlier, and he'd pounce like a lion. He never technically promised, she remembered with a bite of her lip. And while the prospect was tempting—so very, *very* tempting—her sense of self-preservation was stronger than she thought.

"Tell me about your parents," she whispered, almost laughing as he fell onto his back with a groan. She felt his frustration, and she wouldn't blame him one bit if he didn't answer her question. In fact, it seemed as though he wouldn't.

Then, "What do you want to know?"

Releasing a grateful sigh, she turned onto her side and put her arm beneath her head. "You said your father is into music?" She felt more than saw his nod, and she asked, "Is he any good?"

Tyler shifted again to face her, and the scattered light from her blinds lit his answering smile. "He's incredible. Taught me everything I know. His garage band was the first one I was in."

"Did he ever try and make it in Nashville, too?"

That smile fell from his mouth. Sherry hated to see it go, but she knew it meant they were finally getting somewhere. Her husband was a man of secrets. Something told her they weren't dangerous, like skeletons of drug abuse or jail time, but deep and personal. Painful. And for her to have a shot of getting to know the real Tyler Blue, the *man* not the star, this was where she needed to start.

"He never had the chance," he told her.

His voice was different. An edge was there that wasn't before, and she bit her tongue to keep from asking what had happened. Instead, she waited him out, the shadows on his jaw flexing, until he eventually continued.

"Dad's a writer, too. His band performed straight originals, and they played every local fair from Lafayette to Biloxi. They had a good-sized following; fans came to events just for them. Mom suggested he head out to Nashville, make a real go of it, and see what would happen. So, they started stockpiling cash. I even gave up my allowance to help the cause," he said with a laugh, but that hard edge was still there. "Six months later, everything was set. Dad had given notice at his job, Mom was making plans to take a vacation from hers, and soon school would be out for summer. But at the end of March, a couple weeks before my thirteenth birthday, we found out Mom had breast cancer."

Sherry's breath caught.

"It was nasty, too," Tyler said, shaking his head. "She battled it for five years. Of course, Dad gave up his plans. Nashville was forgotten while they went to doctor's appointments and he worked extra hours to pay the bills. I even started doing odd jobs for relatives to pitch in. I went to school, went to work, and then played music in my room. Dad would stay up late, after taking care of Mom, and we'd jam together. It was our release." He paused. "Our escape."

Sliding her hand across the mattress, Sherry searched for Tyler's hand. Finding his arm, she squeezed his bicep and scooted closer. "Your parents sound like they're incredibly strong."

He drew a breath and put his hand over hers. "They are. Mom…she, she's a fighter. Time and again, she kicked cancer's ass. Always with that smile on her face. It reminds me of yours, actually." The tenderness in his voice as he said that made Sherry's chest ache.

"She has more faith in her little pinkie than anyone I've

ever met," he continued with a slight shake of his head. "We thought it was finally over, that she'd finally won. Dad took her on a cruise and they celebrated their second chance at life. I'm glad they at least had that."

A muscle in his arm jumped beneath her fingers, and Sherry winced in anticipation. "Did you know there's a link between breast and ovarian cancer?" he continued. "A cruel joke life plays on a few women who've already given it all?" His voice was bitter and harsh, and tears welled in her eyes. "Turns out, Mom's stomach pain wasn't gas or IBS. But the amazing thing…she *still* hasn't given up. This time, there is no cure. There's no hope, other than keeping her comfortable until the end, but she fights every damn day anyway. And she refuses to let any of us stop living, either."

Tyler twisted onto his back and tugged Sherry with him. Laying her head against his chest, she skimmed her fingers down his arms, comforting him in the only way she could. Listening.

"One time, right after we got the last diagnosis, I passed on opening for Brad Paisley. It would've been our first big tour, a breakthrough chance, really. The guys didn't even blink. They understood. Mom was the one who didn't. She ripped me a new one when she found out. Told me if she ever heard of me staying on the sidelines again because of her, she'd fly out to Nashville and give me what for." He chuckled and brought his hand up to Sherry's hair, gliding his fingers through it as he said, "I don't doubt for a second that she would."

"What about your dad?" she asked after a moment, wanting to keep him talking. "What does he think about your success?"

"He's proud as hell. It was an old buddy of his, one of his former bandmates, who got my foot in the door. He'd ended up going on to Nashville as they'd planned and made it as a songwriter. As soon as I graduated high school, I took my father's dream and it became my own. With his help, I wrote songs for other artists while playing covers at local bars. Then I met Charlie, got a demo together, and got damn lucky."

"Not luck." She closed her eyes at the lulling feel of his fingers in her hair. "You're a hell of an artist."

Tyler tapped her under the chin and she looked up. "And how would you know?"

"I may've downloaded your albums," she confessed with a smile. She'd been listening to them non-stop, surprised at how much she enjoyed them. Maybe knowing the artist on an *intimate* level made a difference. "You're awesome, Tyler."

The smile he gave her was both humble and sad. "You should hear my dad." His fingers resumed their path through her hair, and Sherry resettled her cheek on his chest. "He's a hell of a musician, and he would've made it, too. Everyone says so. He just got dealt a crap deck." Tyler's chest expanded with a deep breath. "I know he loves my mom, and he has no regrets about staying behind. But when Mom got sick, he shoved his dreams to the background. *That's* why my career is so important to me. Why I asked you to do this insane scheme. I'm not just doing it for me, you know? I'm living *both* our dreams."

Sherry pressed a kiss over his thumping heart. She did know. In fact, she better understood everything after listening to his story. Who he was as a man. Why he was willing to go through all this craziness for his career. Why music seemed like such an integral part of his identity. It was his salvation.

They didn't talk again after that, but she didn't move, either. Tyler's fingers continued their trail through her hair and down her back, and she held him tight in her arms. Comforting him. Reassuring him.

Caring for him.

That was another revelation out of the darkness of the night. Lust wasn't the only thing fueling her desire. Their connection went much deeper than budding friendship. Sherry genuinely cared about the man she married…and, if she wasn't extremely careful during the next month, she could be in serious danger of falling for him, too.

Chapter Twelve

Robicheaux's was a lot like the family who owned it. Laidback, welcoming, and stuffed with energy. Tonight was the St. Tammany Humane Society event, and Magnolia Springs came out in droves. This was Sherry's element, and he loved watching her in it. She was totally in control; no problem shook her confidence. When a situation arose, she simply cocked an apron-clad hip, pointed a black-painted nail, and said how to fix it. People hopped to her bidding. Even him.

Her wide, gorgeous smile was the culprit. It was pure magic. Neighbors lined the parking lot, eager to empty their pockets, all so she'd shine that beam on them. And when she did, they walked away pleased as hell. Tyler had been to many charitable events in the past few years, but he'd never seen anything like this. Again, her enthusiasm was contagious, infecting everyone who walked through that front door. And as a result, the shelter was raking in serious cash.

Tyler had made his donation anonymously. Tonight, he'd enlist her opinion on other local organizations to support. For the next year or so, this was his community too, and he wanted to do his part. Earlier, he'd also made a call to step up his contributions to Ovarian Cancer National Alliance and Susan G. Komen. Seeing Sherry's giving nature in action convicted him. He already gave plenty and often, but he could always do more. Hopefully one day, women would no longer go through what his mother had.

A gray-haired woman snapped him out of his thoughts. As she shoved a roll of bills in the tip jar on the bar, she studied him over her spectacles. Tyler set down the keg from the back and smiled, wiping his hand on the towel tucked in the front of jeans.

"Can I get you anything, ma'am?"

"You that Nashville fella who married our Sherry?" she asked, pointing a gnarled finger.

"Yes, ma'am."

Funny how much pleasure it brought admitting that aloud.

"Thought so." Her smile was smug as she took a long sip of her dirty martini. After setting the glass on the mahogany bar top, she said, "That girl's heart is bigger than Texas." Her eyes narrowed. "And it's as tender as a baby's butt. You take care with it, you hear?"

The advice was nothing new. He'd lost count how many customers had shaken his hand, congratulated him and shared their favorite zany Sherry story, then issued a protective warning.

Weird thing was that after the other night in her

bedroom, Tyler wondered if he might be the one in danger.

He still couldn't believe what he'd shared. Other than his family, only his band and manager knew the details of his past. He couldn't risk his mom's struggle becoming a headline. But there was just something about Sherry. Yeah, he could trust her. More than that, she genuinely cared. She listened without pushing. Empathized rather than pitied. And went out of her way to look out for him.

As always happens when he's in the zone, he'd forgotten to eat dinner last night. Writing consumed him, and with three additional songs to produce for the new album, food rarely made the cut. Around nine o'clock he'd raised his stiff neck to pop it, the right word choice eluding him, and found a sandwich on the table. A sticky note attached to the plate ordered him to: *Eat!*

Tyler smiled at the memory. In another life, she'd be perfect for him. Sherry was exactly the kind of woman he'd want by his side. Downright crazy, absolutely no filter, just wild and fun with the biggest heart of anyone he'd ever met—and somehow a smile even bigger. Whenever she was around, the constant knot that lived between his shoulder blades vanished. Being with her reminded Tyler of how life used to be. How *he* used to be, before the fame. Before his mom got sick.

Catching her eye across the restaurant, he winked, and a pink stain crept up her cheeks. Another thing that made her perfect? She was adorable and sexy as hell. She lit him up in ways no woman ever had. Keeping his distance was killing him. Especially after a night of holding her in his arms. Connecting *emotionally*, not just physically.

Who knew simply talking, holding, sharing life, could

mean so much?

The *ding* of bells snapped her gaze to the door. An expression of complete shock transformed her features, and Tyler turned, wondering what was wrong. A dude walked in, arm slung around a cute blonde, and when he noticed Sherry a foot away, froze in place.

"Aw, crap."

At the sound of Colby's voice, Tyler tore his focus away from the door. His sister-in-law stood beside him, hip bumped up against the bar, and arms folded tight against her chest.

"Who's that?" he asked, turning back and watching as Sherry's surprise gave way to unbridled hurt. A rush of protectiveness clenched his fists. Whoever the guy was, he needed to go.

"That would be Ben-the-two-timing-ex," Colby replied with a sigh. "And that chick beside him? She'd be the other woman."

Tyler hopped the counter before she finished speaking.

Sherry had hinted at being burned in the past. Based on her Mr. Dull plan, and her need for their frustrating rules, he knew that betrayal cut deep. For the first time since their dinner at Cane's, Tyler could understand Colby's decision.

In the middle of making that salad, she'd asked if Tyler's lawyers did a background check on their family. When he admitted as much, she'd begged him never to reveal what he'd learned. Evidently, Sherry's siblings had spent years protecting her from their dad's infidelity. Hiding the details like she was fragile and unable to handle the truth. At the time, Tyler had been annoyed. It was as if he and Colby knew two different women. In his eyes, Sherry was a hell of a lot stronger than her family gave her credit for. From what he saw, she could handle *anything*.

But now, during her big moment, was not the time to test that theory.

Sidestepping customers, brushing past fans with a distracted smile, Tyler walked forward with a singular focus: comforting his wife. Shielding her from the man who once broke her heart. The line between her fairy tale and real life was blurring…but she was *his*. At least for the next couple years. And no one hurt his woman.

The route he took put her ex in his direct path. Almost to Sherry's side, Tyler glanced at the author of her pain and saw unmistakable longing on the man's face. Jealousy burned his core.

"What are you—?"

Sherry's question cut short as Tyler's mouth crashed down. The whimper in her throat said she didn't mind. It vibrated through him, and he clutched her close, her taste exploding on his tongue.

They could pretend when they were alone. Lie to themselves about what this was between them. Hell, he could invent a million reasons why he'd stalked over and staked his claim here. But the truth lay behind the sound of her moan and Tyler's answering groan.

Kissing Sherry wasn't about her damn rules.

It wasn't to save his career.

This woman was in his arms because he wanted her there. Because holding her chased his every thought since that day in her driveway. And because *nothing* felt as incredible as her nails scoring his back, her scent in his nose, and her curves molded in his hands.

Distantly, he realized people were cheering. The crowd around them was clapping. Sherry's giggle weaved itself into their kiss, and her smile against his mouth cooled his hunger. Transforming the moment into fun. Tyler slid a hand behind her head and set the other firmly at the small of her back, dipping her low.

Catcalls and wolfish whistles erupted, and their kiss broke into deep belly-laughter. Sherry, shy for the first time since he'd met her, buried her head against his chest. Giggles wracking her slender frame, and grinning like a mad man, Tyler raised an arm in acknowledgement of the accolades.

For her ears only, he whispered, "Rule one, baby," then nipped her tender lobe. She rolled her hazel eyes as he raised her to her feet, but the shadow of pain they once held was completely gone.

Tyler looked back and nodded with supreme satisfaction. So was her ex.

• • •

At this point in a romance novel, the heroine realizes she's falling for the hero.

Damn, Sherry hated being predictable. But honestly, she defied *any* woman to spend a night in Tyler Blue's arms, listen to the story of his past, and awake in the morning to his freaking Post-it notes, and *not* lose a piece of her heart. He'd just rocked her world, grinned like the devil, and then spun on his cowboy-booted heel back to the bar, the denim of his jeans doing delicious things to his backside. Now, like a lovesick stalker, she watched as he bent low to converse with little four-year-old Tansy. Her dang ovaries quivered.

Tyler being *here*, in her world, interacting with her people, brought everything to a whole other level.

The country star actually fit in. If it weren't for the constant whispers and the handful of autograph requests, you'd never know he was a celebrity. His Cajun accent was prominent, his laugh free, and his desire to help unmatched. For cripes sake, he'd even volunteered to do dishes!

Clearly, she'd had him pegged wrong in the beginning. Tyler was the furthest thing from the entitled, notorious player she'd once thought him to be. Unfortunately, something else was equally clear—the need to alter her original goal. Shift her focus from *eluding* damage to minimizing it, because escaping unscathed was no longer an option.

Eventual heartbreak was a foregone conclusion.

Sherry sighed. So her perfect plan wasn't so perfect. This wasn't the first time she'd gambled with her heart and lost. And experience taught her owning the problem was the first step to recovery. Second step? Keeping her dang wits about her. Remembering that her husband's soul-shattering kisses and wicked grins were for the sake of fulfilling their agreement. *Not* due to any reciprocated lovey-dovey feelings.

Tyler Blue's number-one objective remained his music. She should tattoo that on her butt.

After checking the kitchen, the bathroom, and behind the bar for any burning issues, Sherry quickly ducked onto the back deck. Though closed for the evening, this was her favorite spot in the restaurant. A secluded place she could think. The hidden gem of the north shore, and her daddy's pride and joy. So many nights she'd come out here through the years, the sun setting behind him on the bayou, and listened as he told stories and laughed with their customers.

Cane and Colby were doing an amazing job keeping his legacy alive…but nights like this, filled with electric energy and easy friendship, she missed her father something fierce.

A quarter-moon peeked through tall pines on the opposite bank, and fish jumped in the black water. The current lapped below the deck, the scent of honeysuckle and night jasmine filled her nose, and cool night air slid over her skin. Sherry breathed deep, hoping it would clear her head. It still felt fuzzy from Tyler's kiss. Truthfully, it'd been like that since she'd slept in his arms. If it hadn't been for her list of rules and a lock on her door, she'd have succumbed long ago.

But she *did* have those things, and she was also insatiably curious. What did the world think of Sherry Blue? Knowing full well that it was possibly her dumbest decision ever, but resigned not to follow her true desire to jump the man's bones, she'd pulled up Google and searched for the answer. The results were about as satisfying as expected.

On the plus side, country fans didn't hate her. Oh, there were snide comments about her dyed hair and size-eight curves, neither of those exactly shocking. Her dyed hair always got attention—hell, it's why she did it. And Nashville Barbie she wasn't. She was okay with that. For the most part, Sherry was confident in her curvy skin. But weight was her personal Achilles heel back from when she was young, and it never got easier to hear. Seeing the baby bump watches, thanks to her and Tyler's sudden marriage, didn't exactly help.

But honestly, *that* she could handle.

What surprised her…what hurt in that dumb way that makes zero sense…were the fan sites dedicated to who *should* be married to her husband. Other artists, actresses, and models they felt made a better match. Women such as Kristen Wilson.

It wasn't the first time she'd heard the blond goddess's name. It'd popped up in Sherry's first search, the night before Tyler arrived in Magnolia Springs and her world turned on its axis, and Tyler mentioned she was appearing on Blue's next album. In fact, she arrived here next week. When Sherry had heard that, her idiot self even volunteered to take the woman to dinner. But after reading those sites, her stomach felt hollow.

Kristen was everything Sherry wasn't. Tall, gorgeous, and successful. She understood his life, was country's sweetheart, and—according to Wikipedia—was a southern girl from Oklahoma. Who could compete with that? Certainly not Sherry. Her relationship with Tyler began with an expiration date.

When they made their agreement, Tyler vowed he wouldn't cheat. Quite frankly, even if he did, what could she say? He wasn't hers for *real*. But what gave Sherry pause, what put that empty hole in her gut, was wondering if the fans had gotten it right.

Muted bells dinged from behind, and Sherry turned to face the window. Brushing aside the hair lashing her face, she leaned against the railing and watched another group stream through the main door. This time, minus a cheating bastard ex.

Robicheaux's was rapidly approaching max capacity. People kept coming, pouring in all night, men and women she'd never seen before. And Sherry knew everyone in Magnolia Springs. She didn't know where they came from, but she was grateful. Judging by the latest numbers, they'd overshot their fund-raising goal. By *a lot.* She couldn't wait to tell Ms. Younis.

"All right, y'all, it's time for the next act."

Nicki Hargis's voice boomed through the mounted speaker, and Sherry pushed away from the rail. The pint-size dynamo was rocking the M.C. gig, keeping the crowd in stitches. And more importantly, entertained. Most of the planned lineup had performed, and if Sherry's memory served correct, Cane was up next. He was always a house favorite, and she loved watching him play. She walked back inside and slid onto a barstool just in time to see her big brother take the stage.

Only…Cane didn't get up there alone.

His new brother-in-law was right behind him, grinning as he swung the strap of *his girl* around his back. It was getting to the point where seeing Tyler without his guitar felt wrong. Sherry had even found him sleeping with the thing, back pressed against the headboard, evidently having fallen asleep mid-strum.

Good to know even superstars succumbed to exhaustion.

When Tyler grabbed the mic, the crowd went berserk. Tonight had been billed as a local-artists-only event. Laughing at the enthusiastic response, he glanced at Cane and shook his head. Her brother played a quick riff, mouthing what looked to be a teasing taunt, and Blue said something in reply. Turning back to the crowd, his green-eyed gaze slid across the floor. Then his deep voice boomed, "Howdy, y'all."

The roar of feminine screams was hysterical.

That sinful mouth twitched. "Not sure if y'all know this,

but recently, I got hitched." The applause swelled again, though perhaps with slightly less high-pitched squeals. Tyler's gaze sought hers and as the audience followed, he winked. "My new bride put this event together tonight, and I think she did a hell of a job. What do you think?"

The crowd hooted their approval. Patrons on either side of her thumped Sherry's back, and Colby wrapped a forearm around her neck from behind the bar. Pleased yet embarrassed at the attention, Sherry waved meekly, then covered her mouth to suppress a cheesy smile. Tyler beamed with pride from the stage, and that look, more than his words, made her heart full.

Good Lord, he was adorable.

"Now, I thought it'd be nice to play one of my wife's favorite songs, since it's her big night, and it just so happens, one of my own made the cut."

Sherry burst out laughing at his mock-shocked face. His fingers strummed the beginning chords of "Next Time"—indeed, her favorite from the ones she'd downloaded—and she blew him an air-kiss.

The crowd, hanging on their entire exchange, went nuts again.

Tyler and Cane launched into the full song with the help of the house band, and the excitement about tore the roof off the place. Singing along, Sherry grabbed her cell phone from her pocket, a sneaking suspicion tapping her foot. She opened Twitter, where, sure enough, she found a tweet he'd sent about an hour ago.

Tonight: Impromptu concert at my beautiful wife's restaurant, Robicheaux's. VERY worthy cause. Do Not Miss!

Attached was one of her fliers. It listed the address and

gave the St. Tammany Humane Society even more exposure. Warmth spread throughout her limbs. Sherry bit her lip, trying to contain the emotion, knowing even as she did that it was no good. She was glowing like a flipping lightning bug.

Minimize the damage, her heart screamed out, giving one last battle cry...even as her eyes lifted to steal another glance at her man on the stage, and her shoulders shimmied to the music.

Chapter Thirteen

"AHHHHH!"

A shrill, feminine scream shot through Sherry's sexy-time dream, waking her with a jolt. Widening her eyes, she focused on the blurry clock, dazed and in disbelief. Five-fifteen a.m. That time actually existed. She could've sworn it was an old wives tale, right up there with crickets in your house equaling good luck. Not happening. Unless its name was Jiminy, critters better stay the heck back. Insects were insects, and if they couldn't sing and dance, they got squished.

Closing her eyes, she listened again through the thick, inviting fog of sleep, and past the thump of her heart, positive she'd imagined the strange shriek.

But then she heard it.

Elvis's yap…Tyler's deep, gravelly baritone…and Angelle's perky country accent. Only, it didn't sound so perky just now. More like freaked and confused.

Crap on a flaming stick.

Fully awake now, Sherry tossed back the comforter. Explanations exploded in her mind. Rational excuses for why Tyler was catching z's in her friend's bed and not her own. She took off for the door—only the sheets twisted around her body hampered her momentum.

Her torso went forward, one foot stayed behind, and suddenly, the ground rose to meet her. And she was eating floor.

Pain burst through her left hip, and her right knee smacked a metal bracket on her bed. Her teeth clashed together—thankfully, without slicing off her tongue—and her little toe throbbed with a pulse.

"Are you kidding me?" she asked the room at large, groaning as she curled in the fetal position. She knew no good could come before nine a.m. "Can't a chica catch a break?"

The increasing *clack* of puppy claws in the hall said evidently not, as company was clearly on its way. A few seconds later, Tyler's voice preceded a gentle rap on the door.

"Hey, babe..."

Sherry lolled her head back as the door opened, and an upside down Tyler appeared. Hair mussed from sleep, chest bare, and a pair of unbuttoned jeans slung low around his hips, he looked way too hot for sunrise. He took one look at her on the ground and lifted an eyebrow. "Uh, are you all right?"

Lifting a hand in the universal sign for *OK*, she replied, "Peachy. Just got my cardio in." Then, glancing beyond him, she offered Angelle a feeble smile. "Morning, sunshine."

Her former roommate stared back, her sweet face

marred with a frown. "Sorry for the hassle. Came to get some gear I left behind for a defense seminar Jason is holding this morning at the gym, and accidentally fell on Goldilocks here in my bed."

Sherry winced. If memory served correct, Angelle's gear was stored in the closet. Right beside every item of clothing Tyler had brought to Magnolia Springs. The evidence was building.

Sure, she was the queen of misdirection. She could say she and Tyler got into a lover's spat, or invent some other non-embarrassing explanation. *I needed the closet space for my shoes?* The ship hadn't sailed on this marriage gig just yet. But it was hella early, her body was twisted, and she simply didn't have the energy for another lie.

Was there any possible way out of this—other than the truth?

Tyler squatted beside her and brushed her hair behind her shoulder. Quietly, for her ears only, he asked, "What do you want to do?"

"Not sure we have much of a choice, music man."

Angelle was a smart girl. Tyler's gear aside, based on their sleeping arrangements and over-the-top reactions, it was clear *something* was going on.

"Don't worry. If it comes down to it, my girl's like Fort Knox."

Well, that wasn't exactly accurate. The woman couldn't lie worth a damn. Her big green eyes gave away her every thought. But she never intentionally broke confidences. If no one directly asked her about Sherry's marriage—and no one would, since up until now she'd sold this thing—everything should be fine.

Besides, she could use some advice about now, and *that* her bestie rocked.

"Well, all right then." Pushing to his feet, Tyler raked a hand through his messy hair. It flopped back in place, bangs falling across his forehead, and Sherry itched to touch the silky strands. Even in the midst of the sky falling, the man turned her on. She was hopeless.

"I guess I'll let you two talk. If you need me, I'll be at the studio." He bent down and kissed her softly, a chaste peck that seemed equal parts instinct and ruse, then snapped his fingers together. "Be good, ladies."

Angelle smirked in reply and silently watched his awkward exit. She waited, lips pursed, until his footsteps faded down the hall. Then, turning back to Sherry, she said, "Normally, I'd say this is none of my business. A couple's marriage is their own affair. But, honey, you two look guiltier than a pair of streetwalkers in service on Sunday."

Even grumpy and sore, Sherry couldn't help but smile. "That's my usual look."

"Uh huh. And your handsome husband was sleeping in *my* bed because…?"

"Because we had a fight last night?" Her voice lifted at the end, question-like, and Angelle raised an eyebrow.

Bah. This conversation was going to require caffeine.

"Fine." Sherry lifted her hands in the air, symbolizing a white flag. "Nosy minx, I will reveal all. But please, a little patience? Mama needs her coffee." Glancing at her smarting knee, she added, "And a Band-Aid. Just give me a few minutes and I'll scrounge us up some breakfast. Then I promise, I'll explain."

Angelle snorted. "How about *I* make breakfast, and

you tame that wild nest on your head? If you cook, we'll be eating charcoal biscuits and burned grits."

Sherry rolled her eyes and grinned. "Fair enough."

Lifting a hand to the mattress, she pulled herself up and withheld a groan at her friend's intelligent stare. "I'll see you in the kitchen in five."

Angelle nodded and left the room.

The entire time Sherry got ready—brushing her teeth and fixing the chaotic mess she called hair, tugging on clothes and, well, *stalling*—she considered what she'd say. What reason she could give for newlyweds who exhibited zero signs of illness or sleep apnea to sleep apart. Any way she sliced it, the choice was embarrassing. Either she and Tyler were fighting two weeks into their quickie marriage, which she'd done a horrific job of selling a few moments ago, or they were lying to everyone. Neither option cast her in the adored, fairy-tale light she'd wanted for herself.

After sitting on the closed lid of the toilet for what felt like an eternity, Sherry stood up, knowing it was time she faced her too-smart friend. So much for her relaxing day off. She straightened her shoulders, determined to do her best whichever path it took—fact or fiction—and marched into the kitchen.

On the counter sat two plates filled with fluffy eggs, buttered toast, and sliced strawberries. Her stomach groaned. *Loudly.* Two steaming mugs of chicory coffee scented the air with a heavenly aroma, and her synapses fired in response. Behind all that was Angelle, forearms bent against the granite top, a suspicious grin curving her mouth.

"So, I've been thinking."

That's not good. Whenever women uttered that phrase,

all signs pointed to hell. Sherry would know; she used it often. Wrapping her palms around the mug closest to her, she let the heat infuse her skin, inhaled the earthy scent, and took a tentative sip.

"Oh, yeah?" She lowered the cup just enough to blow along the surface before taking another hit. "And your conclusion?"

"You're hiding something," Angelle replied. She let that declaration hang in the air as she leisurely cut her fork into the pile of eggs and savored a heaping bite. After chewing and swallowing, she dug in for a second one. As she lifted the fork to her mouth, her eyes flicked to Sherry. "My instincts say you're as happily married as I was engaged two months ago."

Female intuition was a bitch. Sherry frowned, ready for a rebuttal, when Angie set a giant box of Nerds on the counter. Tyler's Nerds. Which meant Angie had gone exploring.

See, that was another flaw in their plan. It wasn't *just* Tyler's clothes in Angelle's room. It was everything he owned. His prized guitar, his collection of lyric-filled notebooks, and his perpetual stash of Nerds. They'd moved every bit of it back after Angelle stayed over, never once thinking she'd return so soon.

Excuses were now irrelevant. The jig was officially up.

"Please don't tell anyone."

It was as good as a confession, and the slight widening of Angelle's eyes suggested she was surprised. Maybe because she figured Sherry would stubbornly hold tight to her story. Maybe she hadn't been certain of her theory. It didn't matter why. Sherry had just broken her own rule, but maybe this is exactly what needed to happen.

Setting down her mug, she sank onto a barstool, ready for some sound advice.

"Tyler really *is* a great guy. Awesome, in fact. And we *did* get married in Vegas. That much, at least, is true. But everything else? It's…" A disaster? A mess? Heartbreak waiting to happen? "A runaway train is what it is."

Angelle put down her fork, giving the admission her full attention, and Sherry dropped her head onto her folded arms. The weight of a boulder seemed to have lifted from her shoulders…only now, a raging battle churned in her stomach. Her chest pinched painfully.

"We…have an agreement," she explained, staring at the counter's speckled pattern. Black and white dots morphed before her eyes. "The marriage thing was a whim. One that, honestly, neither of us even remember. But Tyler needs this relationship to save his career. And I…well, I need to keep from being a joke. At least, that's how it started."

Lately, however, saving face and fairy-tale dreams took a backseat to her wacked-out feelings for her husband.

"And a lot of what we told you *did* happen," she continued. "We met in the green room, we hit it off, and we spent the weekend together. An amazing weekend." Sherry lifted her head. "Angie, I didn't know things like that existed. I think, maybe, I started falling for him even then. I don't know. But that last night, things got wild. We drank too much, somehow wound up hitched, and here we are." She licked her lips and dragged her teeth along the bottom. "If the press discovered what *really* happened, I'd be nothing but a pathetic headline. And Tyler's career would be in the toilet."

The pale skin between Angelle's eyes furrowed. "Honey,

I have no room to judge here. You know what happened between your brother and me at Thanksgiving. I get self-preservation, I do." She paused and seemed to choose her next words very carefully. "But sweetie, I know you. I know your heart. And I have to wonder, in *this* case, if it's not worse living the lie."

A humorless laugh escaped Sherry's lips. "I'm not sure I even know what's real and what's not anymore."

Picking up her mug and taking a fortifying sip, she then caught her friend up on the events of the last two weeks. Tyler's proposition and her list of rules. The kiss out in the driveway. His guitar lesson and parts of the night they slept in her room. Not his mother's illness—that wasn't her secret to share—but enough for Angelle to get a clear picture of the man she married. And the mess she'd landed herself in this time.

Luckily, Angelle Prejean was a good egg. A sweetheart, loyal to the core. Once she and Colby straightened out their mess last summer, and stopped sorta going after the same man, Angie had been like a sister to them both. Soon, she'd be one for real. There was no judgment in her eyes. Not even censure or amusement at her latest failing. Only compassion.

"Well," Angelle said once the story was over. "It's not the most conventional of beginnings…but it could make a heck of a story." Grinning softly, she took Sherry's hand. "What is your heart telling you?"

"That organ hasn't exactly been the most helpful in the past." Sighing, she squeezed her friend's hand with a forced smile and released her grip. She pushed back from the counter and meandered to the coffee pot. "For as long as I can remember, I've looked for the best in people. Colby got cynical in college and Cane started chasing skirt"—her future sister-in-law grunted, knowing full well what a womanizer he'd been—"but I was a fan of love. I'm *still* a fan." Her mug refilled, she leaned her back against the cabinet. "I just don't know if I buy it for myself anymore."

Angelle offered a gentle smile, silently encouraging her to continue.

"I'm the town's heart-wide-open wild child," she declared, rolling her eyes at the stupid title. "That's what people see when they look at me. For a while, I even embraced it." She looked down at the hot brew. "But my heart's been burned beyond recognition. Late last year I realized I *must* be crazy, because I kept doing the same thing again and again, expecting a different result. Fishing in the wrong hole, luring the same kind of guys. Cheaters, jerks, playboys..." She made a face and raised her head. "The type of guy I'd pegged Tyler to be. But that's *Blue*. The Tyler I know is so much more than I ever expected."

Angelle gave her a smug look, and Sherry threw her head back, knowing what was coming. It was easier to admit the truth to the ceiling.

"What is your heart telling you?" Angie repeated, emphasizing the last two words like Sherry was being intentionally thick. She huffed a laugh because she kind of was.

"If I were to follow my heart, I'd like to see where this could go," she confessed to the cobweb floating in the corner of the ten-foot room. She'd have to come back in with a broom later to knock it down. "But honestly, where *can* it go? Nashville? Traveling the U.S. via tour bus?"

She looked down to see Angelle shrug. "Yeah, if that's

what you want."

Sherry opened her mouth and then closed it.

Was that what she wanted?

Starting a new business—the long-held dream she'd finally begun taking more seriously—would be a challenge out on the road, and she'd miss her family like *whoa.* But tours didn't last forever. Maybe this was exactly what she needed. A chance to stretch herself, live out loud. See what lay beyond Magnolia Springs.

A strange bubble of hope rose in her core, a tingling warmth that sparked in her chest and spread throughout her limbs. She fought to contain the answering smile, and the result ended up being a squinty-eyed smirk. "I do love a good adventure."

Chapter Fourteen

A slightly overcast sky was overhead, and a stiff wind blew the canopy, but Tyler Blue Day in the city of Opelousas was nothing short of perfect. The people's adoration and appreciation for Tyler rivaled the attention you'd expect of royalty, showing up en masse with sparkly signs and tall banners, proclaiming their love for their hometown stud. They overfilled the folding chairs and set up blankets on the lawn, stretching out on either side. Sherry couldn't have been any prouder.

The last week had been insane. Finalizing the details along with his publicist, Arianne, and her contact with the Louisiana Music Hall of Fame, and trying desperately not to step on any toes. They'd had a great event planned—small and intimate, a few songs, and the announcement. But it just hadn't been enough. Not for Sherry. It wouldn't only be former neighbors and stalker fans showing up today. Tyler's parents were coming, too. And for them, this had to be a party to kick all other party asses. No one said the words, but those in the know understood the truth. This could be the last time his mother saw him before the end. Anything short of spectacular wasn't an option.

Sherry's gaze sought the woman out now, looking frail, peaceful, and so very proud of her son, seated right in front. The pure elation shining from the woman's eyes brought tears to her own. Every second of stress had been worth it.

"You did good."

Dabbing her eyes, Sherry turned to smile at the man beside her off to the side. Charlie Tucker was Tyler's bassist and his best friend. Getting to know him had been her second goal of the day.

"Thanks," she replied, watching as an adorable little boy with a mega voice left the stage. "I wanted to do something different. A fun way to get the town in the mix honoring Blue." She grinned as the boy's mother swooped him up in her arms. "What I didn't count on was them stealing the show. That kid freaking rocked!"

Charlie huffed a laugh and propped his foot against the DJ wall behind them. "First thing you learn in this business: there's always someone younger and cuter ready to steal the spotlight."

The boy and his family walked past on the way back to their seats, and Charlie held his palm out for a high-five. The young kid smacked it. "You killed it out there, buddy."

As he posed with the family for pictures and signed the boy's flier, Sherry couldn't help but feel proud. Call it sheer brilliance, community outreach, or *Opelousas Idol*—a somewhat cheesy title the local press coined—the opening to Blue's show today was genius. Last Sunday local acts auditioned and a select handful won coveted spots to perform. Grandmas in gingham, cute kids in bowties, and all walks in between sang covers of the band's many hits over the last hour. With Tyler finishing his round of interviews in the back, the final performer took the stage.

Charlie let a whistle rip as a young woman with long, platinum blond hair, her white dress swishing just above her cowboy boots, grabbed the mic.

"Friend of yours?" Sherry asked, amused. "Or past conquest?"

Tyler may not be the playboy she'd once pegged him for, but his best friend more than earned the title. In between acts, as Tyler made the rounds, Charlie had entertained her with stories of the road. In particular, the tales of his many hookups. Normally, that sort of thing would've disgusted her. He represented every bad boy she'd ever chased after. But Charlie's secret power was his charm. A wicked wit, a slow smile, and a unique way of giving you his undivided attention, making you feel important. It was a lethal combination.

Thank God she hadn't met *him* in the green room at New Year's. He was trouble with a capital T. But as an ally, he might just make a good friend.

"I wish," he replied, flashing her a playful grin. "That's Sadie Hart. Our agent represents her too, and we met at a few industry parties. Nolan got her out here for some extra exposure."

Sherry watched as the woman closed her eyes and took a short centering moment. She was gorgeous in that fresh, natural way, the kind that made you just a little jealous, but put you at ease right away. Impossible not to like. "Is she any good?"

Charlie grinned as the familiar intro to "Next Time" rolled over the crowd. "You tell me."

Sadie launched into the upbeat ballad, her powerhouse, *female* vocals bringing a fun twist to Tyler's lyrics. The song was about heartbreak and learning from past mistakes, being better in the *next* relationship, and the female spin brought a new edge to the once male lines.

Sherry nodded her head with the beat. "Yeah, she's really good."

Charlie smiled, and the two of them moved to the music, thriving on the crowd's energy. It wasn't until a group on the far edge began twisting their heads, gesturing and whispering to each other, that Sherry looked over and saw another blonde make her way toward the stage. This one, however, she knew. They may not have met yet, but Sherry could recite the woman's stats verbatim.

Kristen Wilson stopped beside Tyler in the roped-off media section. She told the reporter something that made him smile, and the photographer took a picture of the country duo. When the last of the journalists made their exit, Kristen's lips twisted in a grin. The woman leaned close, whispering something near Tyler's ear, and he threw his head back in a laugh.

Sherry's breath caught. Seeing him laugh like that gutted her.

She wanted to be the one to make him laugh. It was foolish and silly, yes, but that was *her* thing. Or she'd thought it was her thing. The fact that Kristen could make him laugh was just one more point in the girl's favor.

Last week, she'd admitted that she'd like a future with Tyler. Three weeks ago, she'd agreed to live in the moment and not discuss what happens next. But he left in seven days. A large part of her wanted to be making plans to go with him. But as she stared at the striking pair that Kristen and Tyler made together, Sherry's tummy tightened, and she couldn't help but wonder…

Was *this* his future?

Charlie nudged her side. "You're pretty cool, you know that?"

Sherry tore her gaze away from the stage. "How so?"

He shrugged. "Just a lot of women in your place would be insecure."

That stung, since she *was* insecure, and was totally being a head case at this very moment. But she also had no right to be. Charlie was one of the few who knew the truth. Before she could say that, however, he gave her a pointed look.

"Yeah, I know the story," he told her. "But I've also seen the difference in him this month."

Lord, she'd love to believe that. If her husband felt even an iota of what she did, it would give her hope. But hope could be a very dangerous thing.

Charlie narrowed his eyes, considering her, then turned and lifted his chin toward the huge crowd. "This gig comes with a lot of benefits. Fame and money. The chance to do what you love and get paid for it. We're damn lucky. But it's not easy. Finding a woman who's willing to put up with the rumors, to stay by your side despite the distance and the constant stress…" He shook his head. "It's practically impossible."

If the man's goal was comfort, he sucked at it. This was not helpful, nor was it calming her nerves one bit. Her gaze strayed again to the stage.

What made this that much more comical was knowing this had been Sherry's brainchild—or brain-fart, depending on your take. Originally, Kristen hadn't been scheduled to perform. It'd been her idea to give the crowd a sneak peek of the new album. But hey, what was that old saying? *Keep your friends close and your enemies closer?*

"Don't tell me you believe the hype."

Sherry winced at the disappointment in his voice. So much for her being *cool.*

"The look on your face says you've been doing some fishing. Trust me, darlin'. All that's gonna catch is trouble." She looked at him, and his narrowed gaze bore into hers. "You should know better than anyone how these things go. How little truth matters. The media lives to drag people in the dirt and cause trouble where there is none. Don't let those vipers in your head."

The audience went crazy with applause as Sadie's song ended. Charlie pushed away from the wall. "Look, I don't know what's going on with you two. Ain't none of my business. But you should know that man hasn't stopped staring this way all morning."

Sherry looked at the stage and found Tyler's gaze locked on her. Had he really been watching her? She'd been so busy since they arrived: setting up, meeting contacts, trying extra hard not to hover. But the thought that *he'd* been watching *her* sent a warmth trickling down her spine.

"He's a good man," Charlie told her, "and a better friend than I deserve. He's worth your faith." A mischievous tone crept in his voice as he added, "Besides, you're our good luck charm."

Whatever else she'd been about to say flew right out of

her head. She looked away from the stage and asked, "Huh?"

Whistling, Charlie began the trek to the front. Blue was up next.

"What do you mean I'm a good luck charm?" she asked, dogging his steps unabashedly. She recalled one of Tyler's sticky notes had said that very thing. "Has something happened?"

He sent her a sly grin. "You'll see soon enough."

With that, he left her on the sidelines and took the steps two at a time to the stage. Tyler said something to his agent, Nolan, then grabbed her wrist. "Don't go anywhere."

"Are you kidding?" she asked, squeezing his hand. "And miss my first Blue concert? Never."

That smile slid across his face. Not the one she saw online or earlier when he mugged for the cameras. The one she was starting to calls *hers*. Lighthearted, flirtatious, almost boyish. It reached his eyes and made the corners crinkle. Earning that smile made her feel invincible.

He glanced over at Tony, the bodyguard who'd all but become Sherry's shadow in the last month. The man never said much, and he rarely smiled, but she had to admit, he did make her feel safe. "Keep an eye on my girl here," Tyler said, lacing their fingers together.

Tony lifted his chin. "Of course, sir."

Charlie began strumming a beat and the drummer kicked in, and still Tyler held her hand. He brought it to his lips, pressing a kiss across her knuckles, and her belly fluttered. A keyboard came in, the music swelled, and finally, he winked. "Enjoy the show."

Hand to heart, Sherry watched her man take the stage and swallowed hard. Oh, she was such a goner. Feeling the weight of a stare, she turned to meet his mother's eyes. The woman smiled softly and mouthed, *Thank you.*

Sherry's chest squeezed as she shook her head. "Thank *you,*" she said in return.

The crowd cheered as Tyler took the stage. Sherry knew the set-list, and the exact moment everything would happen, but still, she was nervous. Twitching with energy. After Blue performed their current top-rated single, they'd have the awards and announcement, and then the band would play a shortened set of fan favorites...plus a couple top-secret ones from the new album, including the duet with Kristen Wilson.

Tyler's smooth voice crept over her skin as he began to sing, and Sherry closed her eyes, letting the lyrics wash over her. Her shoulders found the beat, her hips swayed, joining the party, and she'd almost lost herself completely when—

"Exciting, isn't it?"

Sherry's eyes popped open at the sweet drawl at her ear, shocked to find Kristen Wilson standing beside her, beaming at her as if they were old buds. And, she reluctantly noted, looking even more beautiful up close than in her pictures.

Jeez. Couldn't the woman at least have a zit or something?

"We haven't had a chance to say hello," the Oklahoma beauty said, turning to give Sherry her full attention, "but I'm Kristen. Tyler told me it was your idea for me to perform today, and I just wanted to say I appreciate it. That duet is a huge step for my career, and I'm thrilled to help celebrate his special day."

Sherry forced a smile, unsure how to respond. What does one say to a possible rival, anyway? *Hey, girl, stay away from my man?*

What about when the man in question wasn't yours...at

least not yet?

"We're happy to have you," she said instead.

Kristen leaned forward, close to her ear. "Don't say anything, but really, I was most excited to finally meet you."

Positive she heard that wrong, Sherry asked, "You wanted to meet *me*?" When the woman nodded, she tilted her head in confusion. "But…why?"

"Are you kidding?" Kristen widened her eyes dramatically. "The woman who snagged the un-snaggable Tyler Blue?" She winked to show she was teasing and laughed. "No, seriously, the way that man talks about you, I honestly felt like I already knew you. Which, if you think about it, is epically unfair, since we haven't officially met. So, here I am."

She thrust out a hand and Sherry looked down, a dopey, hopeful smile curving her mouth. Biting the corner of her lip to try and contain it, she took Kristen's hand in her own and said, "Nice to meet you, Kristen. *Officially*."

The final note of Blue's song faded away, and both women turned to the stage. Tyler handed off his guitar to a technician and shook hands with two men as they joined him, one wearing a belt buckle to rival his own—country boys and their bling—and the other a dark pair of shades. Sherry bounced slightly on her toes, radiating confidence now thanks to Kristen, and smiled over at her new friend. "Here it comes."

The music lowered, and Belt Buckle Man stepped up to the mic.

"It's my supreme pleasure," he proclaimed, looking indeed very pleased at the turn out, "to declare today, January twenty-second, as Tyler Blue Day." The crowd went nuts, and the mayor grinned. Clearly, he was a showman. "And to officially recognize our proud city of Opelousas, Louisiana, as Tyler Blue's hometown!"

As expected, the roar was deafening. Tyler looked almost embarrassed, and extremely humble, as he accepted a key to the city where he was raised. Looking back, Sherry saw his mom swipe a tear, and felt her own begin to build.

"Now," the mayor continued, "I'd like to introduce to you all the president and CEO of the Louisiana Music Hall of Fame, who has his own special present."

Tyler laughed as the audience went crazy again, knowing how special today was. He put a hand over his chest, bowed his head slightly, and mouthed a heartfelt *thank you* to them before placing a quieting finger over his smiling lips. His fans did as requested, falling silent almost immediately, which made his smile widen. He sought Sherry's gaze, and she blew him a kiss, her eyes teary.

Gah. She had nothing to do with his accomplishments, but she was so stinking proud regardless.

The man with the shades stepped forward and said, "We won't keep you waiting for long. We know you're all eager to hear this young man perform. But before he does, on behalf of our proud state and our rich history of music, it's my honor to officially announce Tyler Blue as a member of the Louisiana Music Hall of Fame."

A plaque materialized out of nowhere, and Charlie played a quick lick on the bass. Family, friends, fans, and neighbors clamored to their feet and applauded, screaming and cheering with pride. Even from where Sherry stood, she could see the tips of Tyler's ears burn red. It was adorable. And his quiet confidence as he shook both men's hands and thanked them for the attention was freaking *hot.*

"Thank you," Tyler said, this time addressing the audience. He held the microphone so close, his lips likely brushed it as he spoke. "If it weren't for all of you, for your support of our albums, we wouldn't be here today. I've received a handful of awards in my short career so far, but this one is truly the greatest honor. I'm proud to be from Opelousas and proud to represent Louisiana music."

He paused as the praise rose again, and his green-eyed gaze caught hers. Sherry felt the warmth in his eyes to her toes. It wasn't sexual, which in some ways would've been easier to handle. No, his gaze was filled with affection. And her dopey, lovesick heart swelled right with the applause.

Chest tight, belly fluttering so much it felt like a flock of birds was throwing down, Sherry held tight to the railing as his gaze penetrated hers.

"Certain events are markers. Stones set in the timeline of your life that you just know will stay with you. Change you and become a part of your DNA. This month has been one giant marker and, without a doubt, I know that I've been irrevocably altered."

Sherry blew out a slow, controlled breath. She had to play this right. Media lined the grounds and a dozen cameras were pointed at her face at that moment, capturing her reaction. A small voice whispered *that* was why Tyler had said that. He was fulfilling his end of the bargain even now. But another voice—one that dared to hope—screamed out, *what if he means it?*

What if?

She didn't know how, but she must've reacted visibly because suddenly, Tyler's intense gaze widened. He scanned her face as the thick knot in his throat bobbed. Then, tearing his gaze away, he focused again on the crowd.

"Now, what do y'all say we get on with the music?"

• • •

Tyler held tight to Sherry's hand. Navigating through his parents' backyard was a sensory overload, even more chaotic than the concert. By the time they arrived here, having gotten stuck finishing interviews and signing autographs for fans, the party was already underway. The place was packed. Kids yelling, people laughing, and Uncle Bill manning the barbecue. Country music played on the radio, and snippets of a dozen conversations blended into one.

After nodding and mumbling his thanks to another distant cousin stopping to congratulate him, Tyler led her past the back deck. The familiar green-and-white patio set had been shoved in the corner, making room for instruments. A drum set, a keyboard, and the old mic stand from the garage were out just waiting to be played, and front and center, propped next to his own prized Takamine, was his old man's Gibson.

A lump rose in Tyler's throat.

"Man, you people don't play around with reunions."

He tore his gaze away from the makeshift stage, and Sherry smiled up at him. She jutted a thumb at the abandoned sneakers and multi-colored socks lying haphazard outside a giant jump house. "I never got this when I was a kid. My parents were only children, so our parties were total snooze fests. But I always wanted a huge family." As her wistful words seemed to catch up with her brain, her steps faltered and she turned to him with wide eyes. "Not that *this* is my family. You know, like for *real* or anything. Just making conversation."

If it weren't so awkward, it'd be adorable.

God, Tyler could kick himself. It'd been like this ever since the concert. Stilted conversations. Sherry off, stuck in her head. Thinking about his dumb speech on stage, he bet. Where that verbal diarrhea had come from, he had no clue. Normally, he had the opposite problem.

Writing lyrics that made women weep was easy. Looking someone in the eye—looking *this girl* in the eye—and speaking the words in his head was impossible. Or so he'd thought until today. But affection was proving to be a dangerous thing. It prompted him to speak when he should keep his damn mouth shut. After he'd spewed his guts, he saw the flare in her eyes, even with the shadows falling on her face. *Panic.* It's why he'd ignored Charlie's advice and cut their other new song from the set list.

If his pathetic fumbling made her this uncomfortable, *that* would've been a disaster.

"Oh my word, something smells divine." Sherry tugged on his hand, and Tyler smiled at her enthusiastic attempt at misdirection.

As he led her around the corner of the shed, the tang of garlic hung heavy in the air. His stomach rumbled loudly. Gluttony was a given whenever the Blues got together; if you weren't singing or dancing, you were stuffing your face. But even he was impressed by the tables packed with food. Fried chicken, coleslaw, jambalaya, macaroni and cheese… you name it, his aunts had brought it. And Tyler had a hunch as to why.

"Is your mom still lying down?" Sherry asked, as if she could read his mind.

After glancing at the empty covered swing just off the deck, he nodded. She squeezed his hand tighter.

"You know, she found me before they had to leave." She rested her head on his arm. "The excitement may've worn her out…but Tyler, she is so dang proud of you."

He closed his eyes, not sure if that helped or made it worse. He'd talked to his mom briefly too, before the performance. And during it, he'd sought out her serene, joy-filled smile. Wondering when her chair would be *empty* was what killed him.

Releasing a ragged breath, Tyler opened his eyes. He refused to do this now. This was a party, a celebration, and his family was here en masse. Kissing the crown of Sherry's head, he asked, "Want a beer?"

Before she could respond, he was striding to the icy cooler. He plunged a hand inside, the freezing temperature a welcome shock to his system, and withdrew two Bud Lights. Uncapping one, he handed it over. "Bottoms up."

Sherry studied him for a moment before clinking their bottles together. "Cheers." Then, tilting her head back, she lifted the beer to her lips and chugged. Tyler watched her delicate throat work to pull the liquid down and then took a long sip of his own, sliding his gaze lower.

Sophisticated rocker chic. That's what she'd called today's look when she walked out of her bedroom. Tyler just called it hot. A dark purple blouse, almost the same shade as her hair, hugged the curve of her chest, and a deep V hinted at cleavage. And a plum, lacy bra. A flirty black skirt skimmed her hips, and sexy heels encased her feet. With her hair in a messy bun, eyes smoky and dark, she was like a siren. An illusion tempting him with what he couldn't keep.

Making him wish he could push for more.

But Tyler had no room in his life for a relationship. Too much was on the line to risk splitting his focus now. This had always only been a temporary arrangement. A *fairy tale*, Sherry had called it. Real life was touring and craziness and everything she'd never want. And everything *he* needed.

"You know, I met a few of your relatives at the concert," she said, snapping his gaze back up. She grinned, clearly enjoying the fact he'd been checking her out.

"Oh yeah?"

"Yep." Her pouty lips popped on the *p*, and it was a Herculean effort to keep his eyes from falling again. "They seem really cool. Sweet, welcoming…*fun*." Her eyebrow quirked, a smile full of mischief tilting her lips as she asked, "You sure you aren't adopted?"

He choked on his beer with a laugh. Swiping his mouth with the back of his hand, he said, "Are you implying I'm *not* fun? Woman, you seem to have forgotten my Jackson moves in the rain." He did an impromptu moonwalk just in case, not the easiest feat in grass. "And my acrobatic skills in Vegas. Baby, I've got fun cornered." He looked her up and down and grinned. "In fact, why don't I— "

"Told ya he'd be back here!"

"—show you now…" he finished, trailing off with a shake of his head. So much for that. "Well, all I can say is, if you thought my family was fun before, consider this your warning." At her questioning look, he waggled the beer in his hand. "Now they're liquored up."

She laughed, free and full, and the stress in his back

melted away. Oh, his life was beyond screwed. His family was eager to meet a wife who wasn't really his, and everyone was smiling a bit too much. Pretending his mom wasn't napping inside, weak and feeble. The one thing he really wanted to do—grab Sherry and lose himself with her for the next week—was off the table. But she *was* by his side. Gifting him with a never-ending supply of her smiles. Filling him with that calm, *easy* feeling he craved.

A moment later, his godmother popped around the corner, signature pink, rhinestone-covered cowboy hat obviously still going strong. "Boy, you should know better. If you're trying to hide, don't do it by the food." She tossed Sherry a wink. "It's the first place any of us will look."

"See, what'd I tell you," Tyler stage-whispered. "Drunk as a skunk."

He grinned to show he was teasing. The woman didn't shy away from booze, but he'd never seen her lit a day in his life. She could drink any of them under the table.

"Besides, would I ever hide from you, Aunt Lettie?"

"You could try, but I'd always find you," she declared with a wide smile, walking right up and cupping the side of his face. Her smile softened as she looked in his eyes and asked, "How you doing, honey?"

"Good." Up close, it was hard to look right at her. The resemblance to his mom was so pronounced. Ignoring the pinch in his chest, he asked, "How's she doing?"

Of course, Dad had given him the health report earlier, but he liked to add a positive spin. Aunt Lettie always shot him straight.

"It's getting close," she admitted, eyes growing misty. "She's ready, though." After letting the pain of that settle in his bones, Tyler nodded and she stepped back, taking his hand in hers. "She's so happy you're finally settled, though, and I couldn't be more grateful that she got to see it."

Unaware of the way her words tore at him, Aunt Lettie smiled and glanced back and forth between them. "You be good to each other."

When Sherry's conflicted eyes found his, Tyler cleared his throat. "We will."

More relatives descended, well wishes and gifts piling on the ground around them, the after party transforming into a pseudo-wedding reception. He had no proof, but this had his mom written all over it. Sherry took it all in with her famous wit, making his entire family fall head over boots in love with her. Tyler wasn't surprised.

Uncle Bill clapped him on the shoulder. "Congratulations, kid. Couldn't be happier about all the good coming your way. You deserve it."

Tyler's smile felt fake and plastic, but he said, "Thank you, I appreciate it. Don't know if I deserve it, but I'm certainly trying." When the crowd shifted, he locked eyes with his dad and added, "I inherited some rather large shoes to fill."

At that, his old man howled. That full-body laugh had gotten Tyler through years of doctor's appointments, sleepless nights, and waiting for test results; it held a bit of magic, too.

"Now you're just talking nonsense," Dad said, stepping forward. He grinned at his new daughter-in-law and took her hand—the man was an unrepentant flirt. "Don't let him fool you, darlin'. He's got more talent in his left pinkie than I ever had. But I tell you what. All those fancy awards and that big bank account of his can't keep a man warm at night. That's why his mother and I are sure glad he found you."

The flash of insecurity in her eyes was so quick Tyler doubted anyone else noticed.

But *he* had.

"Oh, my man *knows* he's lucky," Sherry said, rallying with a confident grin. Maybe a shade too confident. She slid an affectionate hand over Tyler's chest and added, "I got a pretty good deal, too."

His family laughed appreciatively, and Tyler drained the rest of his beer. That tension from before? It was back. Big time. And he had not a clue why. It didn't make any sense. His dad was just trying to make Sherry feel special, and she was playing the part as agreed. But none of that stopped a muscle from popping in his jaw.

Sherry stepped in front of him, wrapping her arms around his neck in a hug. His hands slid to her lower back as she whispered in his ear, "Maybe you two should go for a walk."

That was the last thing he wanted to do right now. Even as he knew she was right, he fought it. He twirled his empty bottle behind her back, circling it between his thumb and forefinger, looking to put off the inevitable. But in the end, he agreed, because she *was* right.

Inhaling a breath, Tyler nodded, and the queen of misdirection smiled.

She spun in his hold and, back pressed to his chest, said, "All right, y'all, my husband seems to think his family can cook. But see, *mine* owns a restaurant," she said, sass in full effect. "To satiate this palate, you gotta bring your A game." Although he couldn't see it, he could tell she'd winked playfully, and his family ate it up. "Any suggestions what dish I should try first?"

As expected, his aunts surged forward, racing to ply her with a plate and promising theirs was the best. She nodded and teased and, over their heads, gave him an encouraging smile. He glanced over at his dad. Dad's forehead was lined; his eyes narrowed a bit in concern. Tyler had no plans of admitting the truth. He'd promised Sherry he wouldn't, and after what the old man and his aunt had to say, it was best he kept it that way. But he did need answers.

"Want to take a walk?"

Dad tilted his head and shoved his hands in his pockets. "Sure." He waved toward the back of the property and said, "Lead on, son."

Nodding once, Tyler turned and aimed for the rear fence. His father fell in step beside him. "Mom still gardening?" he asked, needing to fill the silence.

"Every day she can," Dad answered with a tight smile, shifting to look over the landscape. "It centers her, she says. Helps her remember what's important and stop thinking about what's to come."

They stopped near the fence line, and he grabbed hold of a plank. Tyler had replaced the thing last year, so the wood was new. Freshly painted white to offset his mother's flowers. *White is the perfect backsplash*, she always said. Tyler tore his gaze away from her row of camellias.

"Something tells me you're not wanting to discuss flowers, though," his old man said, shooting him a wry look. "What's on your mind?"

Tyler scrubbed a hand across his face and squeezed the back of his neck. Where to begin? "I guess I never realized you and Mom worried so much," he said, giving the board in front of him a gentle kick. "You talked about my career like it's empty. But you didn't seem to feel that way a few years back."

"Now, I didn't say it was empty. It's just that I know it can be lonely. Non-stop touring on the road can be isolating. That's not the life your mother and I wanted for you."

Tyler's hand clenched around his neck. He'd never known his old man to lie, but...

"How can you say that?" he asked. "Dad, it was the lessons you paid for and the contacts you had that got me here. And hey, I'm grateful. Thanks to you, I'm living both our dreams, and I'm doing better than I ever imagined. That's for damn sure. But I don't get how you can stand here and say this isn't what you wanted. This is *exactly* the life you pushed me toward."

Awkward silence fell, and Tyler winced. He'd tried to contain it, but the words had just come out. Here he was busting his ass every day fulfilling a dream his father instilled in him, and the man acted as if he'd missed a memo. His dad made a rough sound in his throat, and releasing a breath, Tyler cracked his knuckles and faced his old man.

Blue eyes stared at him under bushy brows. "Son, you need to know I'm proud as hell of you. I saw that spark in you, the same spark I once had, and I encouraged it. I admit I never expected it to amount to all this"—he held out his hand—"but we're thrilled you achieved your goals. That's all I wanted, for you to succeed in a career that you obviously had a God-given gift for." Tyler's shoulders sagged a bit in relief, until his dad added, "But success can be fleeting. More than that, it can be lonely. That's why I hoped you'd find the same happiness in life, in *marriage*, that I have."

Grasping his ball cap, Tyler tugged it off and shoved his hand through his hair. He scratched the side of his jaw, twisted the cap around, and returned it to his head. But he couldn't look his old man in the eyes.

"How..."

He squeezed his eyes shut and coughed. Could he actually ask him this? They'd always told each other anything. Total open-door policy. But even while everything inside Tyler screamed for an answer, would asking it gut his dad?

Opening his eyes, he saw his father's mouth curved in a small, understanding smile. He nodded once, subtly, and Tyler said, "You still feel that way, even with Mom...?"

He didn't need to finish the thought for his dad to understand.

"Absolutely," he replied, voice filled with conviction. He put a hand on Tyler's shoulder. "I never once felt like I missed out. Yeah, things got hard earlier than expected. We lived the sickness a lot more than the health. But she's my sunshine. My angel. The undisputed love of my life. Earlier, you said you were living both of our dreams. And I still wonder now and then about Nashville, what would've happened had I gone like I planned. At one time, I wanted that almost more than anything in the world."

Tyler caught the *almost* and swallowed hard.

Dad looked him straight in the eye. "That would've been a heck of a journey. You know I love me some music...but son, I love your mother more. A life with *her* was always my dream."

Chapter Fifteen

Tyler laughed humorlessly and tossed his phone onto the bed. Ridiculous. One article turned his entire life upside down and, almost one month later, another one set it to rights. At least musically. Along with the Exclusive First Listen of Blue's new album, Tammy Paxton sang Tyler's praises today on the magazine website, not so subtly tooting her own horn. Being in love *did* make him a better writer, she claimed.

Singling out "Rain Dance" for its "vivid imagery of the early stages of love, when everything is new and beautiful and exciting as hell," she'd gone on to say that their third album was the best to date, and credited Tyler's recent marriage for the change. "Blue's early work was full of fun and flirtation, but it lacked that vital core of truth. Now it has it in spades. We at *Country Music Weekly* congratulate Mr. and Mrs. Blue and wish them many years of happiness."

Many years...or two days. That's all they really had left.

Where in the hell did an entire month go? Just over three weeks ago, he'd woken up in his hotel room hungover and in the middle of what he thought was the worst mistake of his life. Now he couldn't imagine anything worse than leaving. But he had to. He had a job waiting, an album to promote, and an agreement to keep. Despite what his dad had said, marriage wasn't the goal for everyone.

At first, the old man's words had rocked his belief system. How could Tyler have misread his father so badly? He hadn't lost himself or given anything up. He'd married his dream. But that didn't really change anything for Tyler. Music might not have been his dad's dream, but it sure as hell was *his*. It's all he'd ever known.

More than that, music was Tyler's life, and it was no life for Sherry. She deserved more than months on the road, trapped on a tour bus and a different hotel every night. She had a new budding career of her own. The Humane Society and Hall of Fame events had generated tons of buzz, and a huge, soon-to-open bridal shop had already contacted her, wanting help planning their launch. Now wasn't the time for her to leave.

Just as he couldn't let marriage split his focus now, Tyler refused to get in the way of Sherry's dream. Her goals.

And a relationship, much less a marriage, couldn't survive if they were always apart.

Tyler slumped to Angelle's bed, a hand scrubbing across his face. God, he was exhausted. He'd put it all out there musically, writing three songs that were in fact his best yet. He'd lived as a husband…though not biblically…and formed a real friendship. Whatever else she wasn't, Sherry was his friend. He cared about her. Wanted the best for her.

Hell, maybe even loved her.

Elvis darted through the crack in the door and hopped onto his legs. "Hey, boy."

Picking up the puppy's soft weight, he fell back on the mattress, Elvis planted on his chest. "I'm gonna miss you, too. Our daily walks helped me think, yes they did." Laughing, he rubbed behind a fluffy ear. "Your mama's even got me speaking baby talk." Warm puppy breath hit his chin and the dog's upper lip twitched. "You gotta take care of her for me, okay? You're gonna be the man of the house again. Don't let any strangers inside; attack any burglars." He thought for a moment. "Attack any dates she brings home, too."

The very real possibility—no, *guarantee*, that Sherry would be dating again hit him like a brick. She was too beautiful, too lovely, too perfect to stay single. She'd go on eventually and find someone else to give her the fairy tale, and he'd be left alone. Like he wanted.

He looked into Elvis's eyes and scratched under the dog's chin.

"Knock, knock."

Glancing over, Tyler watched Sherry slide the door fully open and smile. The sight never stopped slaying him. She shifted her weight and shoved her hands in her back pockets. "So, I was thinking..." Her gaze fell on his open suitcase and the light vanished from her eyes. "You're packing already?"

He almost laughed. In many ways, they were totally compatible. A similar sense of humor, shared interests, and off the charts chemistry. But Tyler's need for order, and Sherry's need to wing it, was definitely not one of those compatible areas.

"Just getting a head start," he said. "You know me. I

never wait to the last minute." He winked to show he was teasing, but she didn't respond. She nipped at her bottom lip, and he pushed to his elbows. "You were saying you'd thought of something?"

"Oh. Right." Sherry leaned her back against the wall and raked her fingers through her hair, seeming to debate for a minute before squaring her shoulders. "I've been thinking Arianne might need some help while you're on the road. Setting up venues, promoting, things like that. Maybe I could come with you for a while." Her gaze flittered to the far wall. "It'd probably be good experience for me."

A selfish warmth hit Tyler's chest, even as pressure built behind his eyes. She wanted to come with him. Leave her family and friends, put a pause on her budding career, all to travel the world by his side. And *God*, did he want her there. Just the thought of waking up to her easy smiles, hearing her infectious laugh, made him excited for the tour. He'd been dreading it every calendar day that passed, knowing it meant saying good-bye. That wasn't fair to his guys, to Charlie.

But if she came with them…

No. Tyler squeezed his eyes shut. What kind of man would he be if he said yes? A selfish one, that's what. Sherry deserved better than him and the life he could give. From what he could tell, she'd always put the needs of her family and friends above her own. This was *her* time now. Saying yes, letting her come with him, would mean letting her choose his dream over hers.

Staying in Magnolia Springs was for the best.

"I'm pretty sure Arianne's got it covered," he replied.

When her shoulders slumped, Tyler reached a new level of self-loathing. But he convinced himself he was doing the right thing. Relationships couldn't last without roots. If Sherry joined him on the road, they'd only be prolonging the inevitable. He was far gone in this girl already, and he saw how she watched him. The only shot he had of not completely decimating her was ending it now. A clean break, just like they'd agreed.

"Besides, you don't need experience," he added, hiding away his pain. Camouflaging emotions was a necessary survival skill in the entertainment industry. "You've got clients coming to you."

He willed her to look at him, so she could see his forced smile and they could pretend everything was fine. But when her hazel eyes turned his way and locked on him with pooled hurt, breath *whoosh*ed from his lungs.

Sherry's gaze tracked his face, eyes narrowed in search. Maybe she was looking for assurance. Maybe she hoped to discover how he felt about her. Tyler stared back, expressionless even though it killed him, and watched his beautiful wife's face shut down.

Unable to stand it any longer, especially when everything in him wanted to retract his words and beg her to come with him, Tyler pulled a true dickhead move. Stretching his arms above his head, he yawned big and fake. "Man, I'm beat." He rolled his shoulders and sighed heavily. "I think I'll turn in early. Get some rest for the parade tomorrow."

She nodded once and wrapped her arms around herself. But still she didn't budge.

In the same breath he wanted her to leave, he also needed her close. Was desperate to soak up as much time with her as he could. So even though he should've been pushing her away, discouraging a greater attachment, he asked, "Are you still going to watch from the stands?" She nodded again, this time with a forced smile, and the tightness in his chest eased a fraction. "Good. I'll be looking for you."

She pushed away from the wall. "I even got a new dress for the ball," she told him. "Need to wow the press for our last hurrah, right?"

Tyler winced at the slight edge to her voice. "Right."

Fingers drummed against her thigh as she hesitated by the opened door. "All right then, I guess I'll let you get some rest." When he didn't argue, she looked away. Raising her voice an octave, she called, "Coming, boy?"

Elvis sagged against his chest. He'd been glued to Tyler's side ever since he'd arrived, sleeping in his bed, cuddling on his lap on the sofa. Sherry shook her head softly and mumbled, "Traitor."

A fluffy white tail ticked in response, and Sherry raised her eyes to his. "Night, music man."

He hated that it sounded so final. But he guessed, in a way, it was. "Good night, sugar."

• • •

Well, you wanted a clear sign. I think you got it.

Sherry closed the bathroom door and leaned against it. Lord, she was an idiot. She'd gone into his room, completely believing she was prepared for any outcome. Of course, she'd hoped for the best. Hell, she'd even expected it. But she was a big girl.

If Tyler had said yes, then that would've been awesome. She'd have gladly stood at her next book club meeting and proclaimed she'd been wrong. Happily ever after really *did* exist outside fiction. And, if he'd said no, well, that would've been okay, too. It would've hurt, sure. But it wasn't like she was in *love* with the guy.

Swallowing hard, Sherry rubbed the left side of her chest, soothing the throb that screamed, *Liar*.

Tyler was wonderful, and she cared a lot about him. She enjoyed his company, liked the way he made her feel. Loved the sound of his laugh and the strum of his guitar. Without his stealth cleaning operations, the clutter on her counters would return, and she'd have to hide all her shoes from Elvis—he liked to chew on or pee in them when he was angry, and he'd be pissed when Tyler left. Her baby had totally chosen sides, and it was *not* hers.

But those things didn't equal love.

Love was pure passion and complete insanity. It was terrifying, intense, and fickle as hell. It made her second-guess her every thought, every move, and held her brain hostage. It didn't feel comfortable, peaceful, or *tender.* Not in her experience, anyway.

Tyler made her tummy flip and her skin prick, but he also made her laugh. He danced in the rain and taught her how to play guitar. They had fun. Just sitting on the sofa with him made her feel safe and warm and happy, and watching him with Elvis filled her with joy. Sure, they had passion in spades, and the way he made her feel was incredible.

But again, that wasn't *love.* At least not the sort that existed outside of fiction. It wasn't sustainable in real life.

Was it?

Beneath Sherry's palm, her heart lurched, and she shoved away from the door. Ugh, why couldn't she have just kept her dang trap shut?

Sliding over to the sink, she turned the spigot, needing a shot of cold reality. As tepid water flowed over her hands, she lifted her eyes to the beveled mirror. A neat, ordered row of Post-it notes floated before her vision.

Sugar,

Do you know, I've laughed more since I met you than ever before?

You always make me smile.

How do you do it?

Tyler

That nugget was from last week. Pressure mounted behind her eyes as Sherry shifted her gaze, this time landing on a note from a few days prior.

Sweet lips,

You look way too good today.

For the sake of our rules, please go change…

Just kidding. See you tonight.

Tyler

On and on they went. Twenty-eight days' worth of notes, each filled with flirtation and friendship, and a strong dose of desire. But that's all it ever was. Staring at them now, a stupid tear leaking past her lashes, Sherry felt ridiculous.

These notes didn't mean anything. Not to *him*. They were just Tyler being Tyler. The soft look he'd sometimes get when he thought she wasn't looking? It was probably just dust in his eyes. It wasn't affection. Or, if it was, it wasn't enough. She'd read too much into everything. Let herself believe and get her hopes up. Whatever was causing the erratic pulse in her chest—affection, love, or simply a huge, honking crush—it was all on her end. For Tyler, this had only ever been a job. Another role to play, a masquerade.

And she'd fallen for the game.

What a lovesick dope.

She'd waltzed into his room tonight, sure as shit, willing to put her heart on the line and give her marriage a real shot. And he wasn't even interested. That speech he'd given on stage about being changed really *had* been for the press. And she'd lapped it up right along with them.

At least with Ben, and every other cheater she'd ever dated, she'd had her anger to strengthen her. Heartache was bearable when you knew you were better off without them. But Tyler hadn't cheated. He'd been faithful to her and home every night, without ever getting anything in return. He was kind, smart, talented, and genuinely *good*. An amazing man who simply didn't want her.

She almost rather he *had* cheated.

Sherry hung her head as heartache washed over her anew. She hugged it, wallowed in it, let it saturate her pores. This was what she always did. Fell for men who didn't love her back. It was her thing. *Lord*, it was her thing. Shaking her head in self-loathing, she gripped the basin in front of her and opened her eyes.

There were two ways she could play this one going forward. She could end it now. Go and stay at Cane's for the next two days, say to hell with the parade and the fancy ball, and hide out until Tyler left Magnolia Springs. *Or* she could savor the short time she had left with him. Go to the parade, play the role of doting wife, and wear a dress designed to make him swallow his tongue. Then, after the last photo snapped and the champagne was gone, she could take Tyler back to the suite the parade organization had gotten him… and seduce her husband.

Yeah, she'd be breaking a rule, but dammit, they were *her* rules. She wouldn't beg Tyler to stay or push for more when he clearly wanted out. But she could take one night for herself, a memory to cling to when he eventually left her.

A night, this time, she fully intended to remember.

Chapter Sixteen

"You seriously haven't heard it yet?"

Sherry met her sister's gaze in the mirror and shook her head. "Not the biggest country fan, remember?"

Colby pulled a face. "Uh, yeah, but this is your *husband* we're talking about, and the freaking song is about you." She sighed and sat on the bed, a mock scowl on her face. "Both of you hussies have songs written about you. Where's *my* damn song?"

Angelle laughed as she held another set of earrings against the red dress on the hanger. She'd yet to find the perfect pair for Sherry to wow the crowd. What her bestie didn't know was that she was *also* trying to wow Tyler. At least enough to bed him.

"My song will never be on international airwaves, though," Angie tossed back. "Or inspiring a bazillion hits on YouTube."

Sherry purposefully kept her eyes averted. She wasn't

in the mood to force another smile. Nope, she *hadn't* heard Blue's latest single, and she had no wish to change that. Not until after he was long gone at least. If the song really was about her like everyone was claiming, listening would only make today harder. She was barely holding it together as it was.

Besides, she might have a song…but she didn't have the *guy*.

Colby, of course, was still in the dark about Sherry's marriage. Angelle believed everything was now hunky-dory. Well, things were neither hunky, nor dory, and quite honestly, she was *this close* to an ugly cry—but losing it wasn't a luxury she could afford. Sherry Robicheaux-Blue was a fighter, and when she made up her mind, she gave it everything she had. Right now, that meant keeping her cool, donning her best bra, and looking hotter than hell.

Tonight, she was claiming her man.

The decision made even more sense in the light of day. By the time Colby and Angelle had arrived to help her prep, she'd had the eye of the tiger…and Katy Perry playing on repeat. For twenty-nine *long* days, she and Tyler had been good. They'd courted, held hands, and shared a scant handful of steamalicious kisses for show. He'd never once tried to push her no-sex-rule—and she'd been too chicken to act. But that ended now.

"Lord, I wish I had your skin tone."

Sherry blinked her newly applied fake eyelashes and released her death grip on the lipstick.

Angelle smiled warmly as she leaned in to inspect Sherry's makeup. "Gorgeous. When the world sees pictures of you in the morning, they're gonna forget all about that famous husband of yours. They'll be asking, *Hey, who's the dude with that hottie?*"

Sherry snorted. "Right." Out of her many concerns—and boy, did she have a ton—fan reaction wasn't a blip on the radar anymore. Strangely enough, the media and all that other nonsense had become white noise.

"I'm serious," Angie pushed on. "Tyler's gonna take one look at you in the stands and abandon his kingly duties." She waggled her auburn eyebrows mischievously. "I hear the suites at the Roosevelt are romantic."

From the closet, Colby added, "And have thick walls."

Shocked, Sherry glanced back where her sister was selecting the perfect pair of heels. Colby shrugged, but a playful smile twitched her lips. "What? You look like a screamer."

Other than the night in Vegas, which didn't count since Sherry couldn't remember much, she didn't know the last time she'd *screamed.* But she was positive Tyler could inspire her. Heck, if he accepted her offer, who knew what noises would be coming out of her mouth? Animalistic mating calls, high-pitched squeals, or curses that'd make a sailor blush… at this point, anything was possible.

With a final check of her makeup and hair, Sherry tugged the knot of her robe. Time to get her night of seduction underway. Releasing a slow exhale, she walked to the garment bag hung outside the closet door. Each step closer made her plan more real, more concrete, and sweat pricked her skin. Before she left for the parade, she'd need another swipe of her deodorant.

Why am I so nervous?

Now was the time for bravery, not stupid cowardice!

There was nothing left to fear. She was already butt-crazy in love with Tyler (that ship had sailed), and he was most definitely leaving tomorrow. His bags were packed, ticket bought, late-night show appearances booked. Whether she slept with her husband tonight was irrelevant. Saying good-bye would tear her apart regardless.

Steeling her spine, her last bit of resolve solidified. Sherry unbelted her robe and let it fall to the floor with a gentle *whoosh*. Shaky fingers lifted the plastic covering the gown, and she slid the straps from the hanger.

• • •

People in suits and fancy ball gowns hobnobbed on either side of her in the viewing stands, a weird and striking contrast with the casually dressed crowd packed like sardines below. Sherry hadn't been to a downtown parade in years (she preferred the smaller, family-friendly ones on the north shore), but this was definitely the way to do it. Access to a private bathroom, plenty of refreshments on hand, and enough legroom that her new shoes wouldn't get trampled. Now, if only she could turn off her brain, she'd be set.

Horses trotted down the blocked-off street and costumed riders tossed trinkets to the crowd. Sherry blew on her hands to warm them. She hadn't factored in the weather when planning her wardrobe, but oh well. At least the bluish tint to her skin went with the dress. And she looked *hot*. No less than five men had hit on her since she arrived in the Quarter, enough to give her a boost of confidence for the night. But then, reeling men in had never been her issue. Keeping them was another story.

The drumbeat from a local high school's marching band thrummed heavy in her stomach. As the dancers shimmied, stomped, and did their thing, her body kept time with the music, her gaze seeking Tyler's distant outline. The king's float was next.

A Krewe of Erato program was wedged underneath her arm, but Sherry didn't need it. She'd had the parade order memorized for hours, having zipped to the website upon finding today's sticky note on the bathroom mirror.

Sherry,

You deserve the life you've always dreamed of.

Never settle for less.

But for at least one more night, you're mine.

Tyler

No pet names this time. Direct, simple, and if she had to guess, a shade apologetic. That first part was Tyler's way of letting her down gently, easing the sting of his embarrassing rejection the night before. But she didn't need apologies. Didn't want pity, either. She wanted what she'd set out to experience, a fairy tale, and in lieu of stepping into the pages of her very own story, she'd settle for chasing a manufactured one.

Besides, everyone knew a good romance needed a hot sex scene. And fortunately for her, the second part of his note was much more promising.

The king's float turned off Canal, and as Sherry's anticipation escalated, so did the bob of her head. Butterflies flew loop-de-loops in her belly and the ache in her chest bloomed...but there was no fighting her smile at Tyler standing tall and proud atop a gaudy green, purple, and gold papier-mâché display.

The float was comprised of every recognizable Mardi Gras emblem she'd ever seen, and the centerpiece structure was a huge carnival mask. Tyler's throne sat just below that, but she doubted his butt had touched the seat once. He was clearly having a ball—wiggling his hips, waving to the crowd, tossing goodies their way. And looking damn fine doing it all.

Strands of multi-colored beads were his only nod to the holiday. Otherwise, he was dressed in all black. A button-down with sleeves rolled up and a snug pair of jeans. Sherry knew he'd change into a tux for the ball, but she liked him like this. Rugged, real, and sinful. The crowd on Tchoupitoulas screamed his name, and Tyler laughed as he chucked beads and doubloons at their heads.

Mardi Gras was kind of sadistic.

Since she never once looked away from his face, she knew the exact moment that he saw her. She *was* hard to miss in the front row, clutching the guardrail and staring unabashedly, but she'd prefer to think he was simply as attuned to her as she was to him. His gaze held hers for a long moment, then he stooped and said something to one of his assistants. The float crept forward until it slowed to a stop in front of the stands, and Tyler walked toward the edge.

The camera from WWL-Channel 4 swung her way as her husband leaned forward. A sizable gap remained between them. Close enough to touch, but not quite close enough for him to kiss her…though the way his smoldering eyes lingered on Sherry's skin, it felt as if he had.

A young man popped up beside him, the same assistant he'd spoken with before. He handed over a bundle and said,

"Here's the special throw."

Tyler accepted it, and then turned to Sherry with a grin. "You know, this is called a *throw* because I'm supposed to toss it at you." After testing the weight in his hand, he leaned back on his heel and took in her dress again. "But seeing as how I've got plans for you tonight, I'd hate to hurt you."

Sherry's eyes widened. It appeared as though Tyler had been sampling the punch. A shocked laugh escaped her lips as she scanned the crowd. The television crew was on the other end of the stand, and the street noise was deafening. No one, other than the few people on either side of her, could hear their banter. Even if they did, they were married anyway. The flirtation worked in their favor.

And it sounded as though Tyler's *plans* remarkably aligned with hers.

Pressing her hips against the metal railing, Sherry bent her torso toward him, grinning at his small intake of air. The neckline *was* a bit scandalous. "You gonna tease me with your *package* all night?" she asked with a wicked grin. "Or are you gonna give it to me?"

This time Tyler widened his eyes, followed by a deep, throaty chuckle. It carried over the noise of the street, settled in her core, and sent her heart racing. Something must've flashed in her eyes because suddenly his amusement died. And awareness took over.

Tyler's gaze sharpened on her face. The thick knot in his throat bobbed as he swallowed, and his dark eyebrow lifted. Knowing what he was asking, Sherry stared straight ahead. She nodded subtly, and his mouth parted.

"You're sure?"

She smiled. A lot of things between them remained in

the air, but of *this*, she was certain.

Tyler snagged her wrist, encircling it with his calloused fingertips. The hold was gentle, but the effect staggering. Her knees went weak and she was grateful for the support of the rail. Flashes went off at their clutch, and the media drew in, trying to capture the moment happening between them.

They'd officially delayed the parade, but presently, clearly neither of them gave a damn.

"Tonight we're breaking the rules," she told him, hoping he didn't catch the slight waver of emotion in her voice.

He glanced down, his chest expanding with a breath, and she briefly wondered if she was about to be rejected again. But then his green eyes found hers, heat where doubt had once been, and he held out his other hand. "I've never wanted anything more."

Excitement ignited under her skin. Sherry accepted the throw, acknowledging its weight without looking down, and then watched as the float crept forward, the parade begun once again. Several long beats later, Tyler broke their stare and resumed his kingly duties, and only then did she study the gift—the special *throw*—he'd given her.

A purple lace garter, a string of coveted Erato-signature beads, and a single perfect rose, wrapped around a thick bundle of yellow Post-it notes. Sherry smiled. It was so uniquely and wonderfully him. Her dopey, lovesick, gone-pecan heart convulsed inside her chest.

• • •

The Superdome was a madhouse. Bodies were everywhere, marching bands were dueling, and huge floats were coasting down the floor. Somewhere in this chaos was Sherry, and if Tyler didn't know Tony had personally escorted her here, he'd be flipping the hell out. As it was, he was about ready to crawl out of his skin.

He raised his cell phone and gritted his teeth. Of course, he had no reception. Luckily, he'd thought ahead and instructed the bodyguard to meet him on the Plaza level at Gate D, so that's where he headed. Nodding distractedly at the fans calling his name, apologizing for not stopping to take a photo. If he did, he'd never make it anywhere.

And after what happened on the parade route, he needed to see Sherry *now*.

Tyler hadn't slept in more than twenty-four hours. He'd been haunted by the look in her eyes when she'd left his room. Leaving her was the right thing—she needed to pursue her own dream, and life on the road was insane. But that didn't make saying good-bye any easier.

Selfishly, he wanted to hold on while he still could. Time wasn't on his side. His plane to L.A. left in fourteen hours…and drunken idiots were tripping over their own feet all around him. Sidestepping a group of cackling women leaving the bathroom, Tyler pushed on, gaze fixed to the sign for the gate. He was so intent on ignoring the mayhem and finding Sherry that he almost walked right past her.

"In a hurry, music man?"

His feet registered the voice a second before his ears. As a result, he nearly knocked out a young woman walking dazedly behind him. He helped her catch her balance, grateful she was either not a country fan or too liquored up to care, and turned to search for his wife.

There she was, back leaned against the wall, her mouth

curved in a smirk. "Miss me?"

An unintelligible sound rumbled up his throat.

Sherry had looked incredible on the parade route, but a metal wall, the edge of the float, and a dozen security guards had blocked his path. Now, only a few short feet separated them. And their one, lone guard was smart enough to keep his distance.

Beginning at her feet, Tyler slowly traced the length of her crimson gown. His gaze lingered on the high slit up her thigh. Paused at the plunging neckline of the bodice. And rested on her parted lips before finally reaching the mesmerizing pools of her eyes.

Her words from the viewing stand hung in the air. *"Tonight we're breaking the rules."*

God Almighty, he needed her.

"Yes," he answered without a trace of flirtation in his voice. "I did miss you."

Her mouth tumbled open, as if in surprise. "Well…uh." She shifted on her feet. "That's good."

That slight hesitation, her small flare of uncertainty, prompted him into action. Two steps closed the distance between them, and he never once broke eye contact. Sherry needed to see the desire in his eyes, *feel* what she did to him. Their future was iffy at best, improbable more likely, but he'd always wanted her. *Would* always want her. Probably long after she'd forgotten about him.

He pressed his body into hers, and they shared a gasp. Sliding his arms up against the wall, he caged her head on either side. Then he ducked down, tilted her chin, and kissed her.

The response was immediate.

Sherry's hands latched on to his forearms as he devoured

her lips. Sweet, soft, and wet, her lips had filled the majority of his dreams. The memory of their taste would drive him insane on the road. Impatient, Sherry opened her mouth beneath him, clutching his arms as she invited him to delve inside...but he waited. Something he'd wanted so badly for so long was finally within his grasp. Tyler intended to feast.

Sherry moaned, frustrated, and the softened bite of her nails through his jacket made him grin. "Ty..."

"You burning, baby?"

She nodded as he slid his nose along her jaw, inhaling her scent until he reached the gentle lobe of her ear. He tongued the delicate skin, sucked it into his mouth, and then whispered, "Me too."

She moaned again as he leaned his head back, inadvertently crushing his hips against hers. He hissed a breath. "Ready to go?"

Her thick lashes were slow to lift. Rimming her bottom lip with her tongue, her gaze skated over his tux. "But... you're the king."

The breathlessness of her voice made him ache with desire. "I did a ton of interviews this morning," he told her, "and made a speech for the execs a few minutes ago. The news got plenty with our halftime show in the stands." At that, she grinned wickedly, and he chuckled. "My duties here are over."

Sherry's dazed eyes met his as his words sank in. Then, with a curt nod, she replied, "Let's get the hell out of here."

Chapter Seventeen

The moment the driver closed the door, Sherry hiked up her dress and straddled Tyler's lap. High slits rocked.

"I think..." His voice trailed off as she simultaneously slipped her hand beneath his shirt and sucked the skin of his neck into her mouth. Beneath her lips, she felt him swallow hard. "I think maybe we should talk first."

Isn't that supposed to be my line?

"No," she replied, a bit forcefully. Talking was the *last* thing they should do. "Kiss first."

The stubborn man went to protest, and she pushed up on her knees. She licked a trail down his neck, returning the favor he'd given *her* ear in the Dome, and he hissed a breath as he clutched her hips.

Talking was overrated. It led to problems, questions, and revelations about feelings. Since she had the messy love kind for Tyler, and he didn't reciprocate, *that* would lead to her doing the ugly cry. So not attractive. No, if talking had to happen, it'd be after sexy time. After they ended their month-long fairy tale with a lovely memory she could cling to.

Tyler's fingers pressed into the satin of her dress, massaging and grasping her curves. Sherry loved her body. Getting to that point had been hard earned, and she owned her confidence with pride. But her husband was the first man who made her feel as though *he* loved her body, too. Not just liked her curves, but *reveled* in them. That feeling was like a drug.

The limo came to a stop, and Sherry glanced out the window. They were still a block from the hotel. "Just a red light," she whispered, bringing her mouth down again.

The imagined *tick* of the clock counting the seconds until their relationship's eventual demise made Sherry's motions frantic. She assaulted Tyler's mouth, ground her hips against his, and tugged the silky strands at his nape. But he wasn't a meek participant. Tuxedo pants whispered against the leather seat as he fought to wrest control, and the rest of the limo ride blended into a blur of grunts, moans, hisses, and touches. Such wonderful, tingle-inducing touches.

When the car came to a stop, Sherry waited until the last possible moment to lean back and put her dress to rights. The driver rapped on the window.

"We're ready." Tyler's searing hot gaze ripped through her, as his words hinted at so much more.

"Hell, yeah, we are," she replied, twisting off his lap with a wicked smirk.

The Roosevelt Hotel on Baronne Street was un-freaking-believable, like something out of a fairy tale. Though the setting was fitting, Sherry didn't give a flip. As her heels clacked on the marble, her gaze swept the high ceilings and fancy digs with one thought in mind. "Where's our room?"

Tyler's response was a firm tug on her hand toward the elevator bank.

As they stood waiting for the lift to arrive, he pulled her back flush against him. The rigid feel of how much he wanted her shot through her core like lightning, making her weak in the knees and clutching the tight arm around her waist. His lips nipped at her ear. *Soon*, they seemed to warn.

Bring it.

Finally, the sleek doors popped open. They rushed inside, and Sherry turned in Tyler's arms, ready to pick up where they left off. Only, just before the doors closed, a very elegantly dressed elderly couple snuck on board. At her groan of frustration, Tyler winked.

At their floor, the halls were silent. Empty. And thank God for that, because she practically mauled the man. His palms held her head as his mouth descended, walking her backward as his lips drank from hers. She gripped his biceps, clinging for balance. Her heels caught in the lush carpet and she kicked the suckers off. That was better.

A few feet down the annoyingly long hallway, Tyler backed her against a wall. As his hand snaked into his coat for the key, he rained kisses along her jaw, making a path to her ear. "Tonight, you're mine."

A picture on the wall shook as her head fell back. "That's the plan," she replied breathlessly. Fire licked her veins, her body one giant inferno. Had she *ever* felt like this before?

Would she ever again?

She squeezed her eyes shut and dove for his mouth, but

Tyler evaded her. Opening her eyes, she found him watching her, pupils dilated so wide only a thin circle of green remained. Breaths sawed in and out of his chest as his hands flexed on her waist. *Uh oh.*

"Look, about tomorrow..."

Sherry threw out her hand. A familiar pressure sprang in her sinuses and blood pounded in her ears. Her desperation not to hear what followed those words was almost manic. She couldn't even *think* about tomorrow, and she refused to do so now.

"One rule break at a time, okay?" She widened her eyes, begging him to drop it. He was about to ruin everything. "Tonight, let's just live in the moment, like we said. Take what we can. Enjoy each other."

To accentuate her point, she arched her back, bringing her hips flush against his.

"Can we do that?"

His penetrating gaze studied her as a muscle ticked in his jaw. Desire transformed the sliver of green into jade, dark and hypnotic, and she hoped to God he'd say yes. She wasn't sure she could survive if he didn't.

The muscles in his throat moved as he swallowed hard, and he shifted a hand to her hip. Threading the fingers of the other through the strands of her hair, he pressed his forehead against hers. Mint and bourbon scented breath hit her lips. "We'll talk in the morning."

Relief washed over her and Sherry nodded. Then her husband took over the seduction.

• • •

Sunlight from the opened curtain they'd forgotten to close spilled across the room, and with it, the knowledge that the fairy tale was over. Pain sliced fresh in Sherry's chest and she buried her face in a pillow to muffle her sob.

Last night had been amazing. Every bit as hot and sexy as her Vegas flashbacks had promised…and surprisingly tender and romantic like her heart longed for. It had been the perfect ending to their story. Only now, she had no clue how she was supposed to leave him.

Long after Tyler had fallen asleep, arms wrapped around her as she lay on his chest, Sherry stayed awake watching him. Mapping the shadows as they shifted along his face. Memorizing the dark slashes of his eyebrows, the gentle slope of his nose, the almond shape of his eyes. The perfection that was his lips. She wanted to remember everything about him. Not Tyler Blue, international celebrity whose face she could study on Google, but the one lying beside her. The man who even in his sleep held her close. Her music man.

Her heart was irreversibly gone. Claimed by her husband. That's what sex with Tyler had felt like—a claiming—and she was his. Permanently, forever, and whether he ever knew it—or even *wanted* it—or not. Love was a strange beast. It came in many forms, and that's why at first she hadn't recognized it. What she felt for Tyler, even before last night, was so drastically different from anything she'd experienced before. This love was empowering, and it gave Sherry the strength to do something so completely unlike her. Be selfless.

Oh, with friends and family, local charities, she gave rather than took. She strove to meet their needs without being asked, and worked for whatever was best for the cause. That made her feel good, and she took pride in that fact. But in relationships, she tended to look out for herself. Whenever she felt the guy slipping away, she'd cling tighter. She was so terrified of being alone, unloved, that she chose to stay with men who treated her poorly, and often guilted others so they wouldn't leave her.

Tyler deserved better. He deserved to live his dream, conflict-free, without her bringing him down. Last night, she'd glimpsed the turmoil in his eyes. Whether it was a trick of the shadows, silly hope, or even the truth, she'd also seen affection. Obviously not enough, and clearly not to the extent she felt, but enough that he didn't want to hurt her. She refused to let guilt trap another man, and especially not *this* one. The selfless thing to do, the *loving* thing to do, was walk away.

Feeling another sob rising, Sherry squeezed her eyes shut. The pain was intense, and she knew it'd only get worse. She needed to leave, and she needed to do it before Tyler woke up. Shifting slowly out of his arms, she slid across the mattress. The *swish* of cotton was magnified in the quiet, and she paused, eyes trained on the steady rise and fall of his chest. Convinced she hadn't woken him, Sherry got up and dressed quickly.

Dress on, she grabbed her new pack of Post-its. Shoving a thick section of hair behind her ear, she uncapped a pen.

Where to begin?

Sherry wasn't a writer. She filled her house with books and married a lyrical poet, but making sense of her jumble of thoughts was impossible. Especially when it came to the man who'd stolen her heart. With the sun rising behind her, and Tyler's internal clock ticking against her, she decided to borrow from the expert.

Music Man,

YOU deserve the life you've always dreamed of.

I wish you nothing but the best.

Thank you for the fairy tale.

Sherry

P.S. The house will be empty. Keep the key. You're welcome any time.

Biting her lip so hard she could taste blood, trapping the sounds of her crying, she stuck the note to the television in plain sight, and then hurriedly slipped out the hotel room door.

• • •

Tyler's head felt hollow. Pillow over his eyes, he sensed the sunlight hitting the bed and knew it was time to get up. But he wasn't ready. Unlike the last time he'd awoken in a hotel, his daze was a result of lack of sleep—not too much alcohol—and he knew exactly what to expect when he opened his eyes.

He was married to a beautiful woman. She made him laugh and smile, more often than he could ever remember. Challenged him to dig deeper, be better. His accountant was now used to Tyler's frequent calls with yet another charitable donation. She'd inspired him to create the best songs of his career.

And yet, he was leaving her in a mere matter of hours.

"Time to wake up, sugar." He wasn't surprised when

Sherry didn't reply. The woman slept hard, and if he was dragging ass this morning, *she* was going to be an interesting sight. Why the thought of that made him grin into his pillow, he didn't know.

"Sweet lips…" Tyler spread his hand out on the mattress, prepared to feel soft, sexy female. All he got was luxurious cotton. Prying a corner of the pillow away from his eyes, he squinted into the lit room and found the other half of the bed empty.

The woman and her constant bathroom trips. Her pea-sized bladder was why he'd started with the notes on the mirror. Early on, he'd discovered it was the one room she visited the most. And the only one guaranteed where she'd find anything. The kitchen was hit or miss. The living room too big a disaster to see a note, much less anything else. And slipping into her bedroom every morning would've been too tempting.

Chuckling, Tyler slammed the pillow back over his head, and a floral scent hit his nose.

Making love to Sherry had been incredible. It hadn't just lived up to his fuzzy-edged memories of Vegas—it obliterated them. Holding her, hearing his name on her lips, he'd almost said too much. Let emotions run away with him and asked for more. That would've been dangerous. Tyler was a plan man. He didn't live on impulse. Nothing about their circumstances changed overnight. She still had a career to start here…his was elsewhere. But damn, he'd miss her like crazy.

He grabbed his cell phone from the nightstand and checked the time. He had to be at the airport in a couple hours. Another few minutes passed with no sound from the bathroom.

"Sherry?"

When she didn't answer this time, a spasm rocked his chest…and he knew. A confused, hurt glance about the room confirmed the truth when he saw a Post-it stuck to the television.

Sherry was gone.

Chapter Eighteen

Green rooms were forever ruined. Even swank ones like the room backstage at *Late Night with Jennifer Marr*. It'd been a month and two weeks since Tyler had set foot inside a place like this, prepared for another bland meal of pasta, and discovered a Cajun feast laid out in the middle of the desert. Served by a sass-mouthed waitress who'd rocked his entire world.

"Thirty minutes."

His fingers stilled on his laptop. He'd been responding to emails, trying to keep his mind occupied. Arianne waved her cell phone, signaling she was stepping out to answer a call.

"You're on in thirty. Be sure to lose the gloom and doom by then."

Gotta love empathy.

Of course, to the rest of the world, Tyler Blue was a happily married man doing his job. Traveling, promoting his band's recent release, gearing up for their gigantic tour.

But his publicist knew better. *She* knew that Sherry wasn't simply waiting at home for him to return. In fact, Tyler didn't know when he'd see his wife again. If ever.

The truth of that fell over him and settled like a rock in his gut. He missed her. So damn much. Missed hearing her laugh, seeing her smile, the sweet scent of flowers in her hair. He hadn't even gotten a chance to say good-bye—although that had probably been her intent. Good-byes sucked, and he couldn't blame her for wanting to avoid it.

But not being able to say it?

Not holding her in his arms *knowing* it'd be the last time?

That was proving to be torture.

This was what he'd claimed to want the entire time. Blue was back on top of the country charts. In its first week, their new album had sold more copies than any of their others ever had, and the single, "Rain Dance," had shot to number one. Critics loved the record, concert stadiums were selling out, and Tyler's musical future was secure.

So why did it feel empty?

Why did performing that song hurt so badly? Why did his so-called dream suddenly feel less than? He was doing his job the same as he'd done every other day prior to meeting Sherry Robicheaux, only now, it felt hollow. Like an essential piece of himself had been left behind in Magnolia Springs.

With a curse, Tyler snapped his laptop closed. That distraction hadn't helped. What else did he have?

Desperate to get thoughts of his wife, her dog, and her sleepy hometown out of his head, he set his boots on the coffee table and opened his messenger bag. He kept it filled for whenever boredom struck in situations like this. Or, you know, when he couldn't escape memories of Sherry.

He vetoed the notebooks and legal pads (those just reminded him of the last songs he'd written), and he'd already read the latest *Men's Health* cover to cover. Twice. Settling for his beat-up copy of *Catcher in the Rye*, Tyler grabbed the book, only to find something shoved within its pages.

A DVD entitled "Our Wedding."

Damn. He'd forgotten he'd put it in here.

Yeah, he'd just been complaining that he needed his thoughts *off* Sherry, but curiosity was too powerful. With a quick glance to make sure he was alone, Tyler slid the DVD from its case. He popped it into his laptop and, grabbing his ear buds, settled back on the sofa, eager to see Sherry's face.

Unlike the hollow ache he felt any other time he'd seen her picture or answered a question about her from the press over the last fourteen days, Tyler expected to laugh at their drunkenness. Remember the crazy weekend they'd shared. Perhaps fill in a few missing gaps.

The classic, romantic anthem of "Love Me Tender" swelled through his ear buds, and the black screen transformed into an interior shot of a standard, run-of-the-mill chapel. What wasn't so run-of-the-mill? The circa-1950s Elvis in black leather at the end of the aisle, standing beside a top-hat-wearing Tyler.

Where in the hell had he gotten *that*?

On-screen, Tyler suddenly smiled a toothy grin, and the camera panned to show Sherry waltzing toward him. Her white lacy veil and a bouquet of white roses screamed bridal. The jeans and sweater combo? Not so much. Coming to a stop beside him, she stage-whispered on screen, "I'm so glad we got young, hot Elvis. The white jumpsuit version is depressing."

The officiant's top lip twitched in a smile.

Tyler felt his lip twitch, too.

Fascinated, he kept watching, waiting for the moment it became obvious they were out of their skulls. Unaware of what they were doing. Making a giant mistake. Only…it never really happened.

Oh, they were clearly intoxicated. The Tyler on video never once stopped smiling; Sherry kept cracking jokes. When Elvis asked if she'd take "Tyler Blue to be her husband," she wrinkled her nose before bursting with laughter. "Your name is *Blue*? Like the lead singer's? What a coincidence!"

Yeah, sober Sherry would've been quicker on the uptake.

But for all their smiles and laughter and over-the-top flirtation, neither of them looked confused. They weren't falling down or stumbling. They didn't slur their words. They appeared completely lucid and excited. In fact, when the ceremony ended, and it came time for his on-screen self to plant one on his bride, Tyler lifted Sherry in his arms and said, "Now it's too *late* to say no. You're stuck with me."

Real-life Tyler's feet hit the ground.

Suddenly it all came back to him. The casino floor and the hot streak at the craps table. Dancing in the middle of the crowded sidewalk, staring up at the neon lights, and looking down into her wide, joy-filled eyes.

It'd been *his* idea to get married.

This whole time, both he and Sherry had naturally assumed it'd been hers. Between the facts and, well, their personalities, that much had seemed like a given. Shock rippled over him…along with the strangest feeling. Almost as if he'd somehow known all along.

"Oh, good, the mope is gone."

Dazedly, Tyler looked up, and Arianne winked from the doorway. "It's show time."

When he nodded in acknowledgment, she slipped into the hall. He glanced around the room, scrubbed a hand over his face, and huffed a humorless laugh.

What in the hell am I doing?

Drunk Tyler was so much smarter than the sober version. He'd known how special Sherry was and scooped her up before it was too late. God, was it too late *now*?

Powering down his laptop, he shoved it into his bag, mind whirling.

His career had always been his dream. It had been all he'd ever known. But that was before Vegas. Before he'd spent a month with an intoxicating woman who surpassed any high performing could've brought. His job may very well be on the road for the next few months, but his heart and his life remained wherever his wife was. He finally understood what his old man meant.

Sherry wasn't a distraction. She didn't split his focus. She *was* his focus. And without her, music didn't matter.

The walls of the green room faded as scenarios filled his head. Ways to persuade her to come on the road, options for her to build her career while doing so. Setting down roots, splitting time between Nashville and Magnolia Springs. Doing everything he could to make *both* their dreams come true…and in the end, whenever that wasn't possible, knowing that for him, Sherry was the ultimate dream.

Memories collided with exciting new possibilities for

the future as Tyler joined Charlie behind the sound stage. His best friend glanced over and nudged him in the ribs. "You okay, dude?"

Tyler nodded distractedly. "I will be."

The P.A. standing behind the curtain held a palm to her ear. "And…we're out for commercial. Blue, take the stage."

The crew sprang forward, ready for the first televised performance of their new single, but Charlie stilled him with a handle to the elbow. "You awake yet?"

Tyler blinked away thoughts of Sherry swollen with child—*his* child—and stuffed animals on the tour bus. He quirked an eyebrow in question, and Charlie chuckled.

"Man, you've been asleep since we left Louisiana." He released his grip on Tyler's elbow and shrugged. "We all see it. You're not here. You're back *there,* with your wife." He shot him another look. "Where you *should* be."

"Guys! This is live to tape. Move your asses!"

Arianne's stressed voice floated from the other end of the stage, and Charlie slapped him on the back. "Go get your woman, kid."

Tyler smiled, the first one that felt real since the day he left his heart behind. "I intend to."

"Good." Charlie glanced at the stage and cocked his head. "Just, maybe wait till after the show." He slapped him on the back, and Tyler laughed.

"Kinda figured that'd be best," he replied with a shake of his head.

But as soon as the segment was over, Tyler was out of there.

Decision made, a weight lifted from his chest. Tension in his shoulder blades, the knot that lodged itself when he'd left her side, loosened. The fog that had filled his vision evaporated and he exhaled as he nodded toward the stage. "Let's do this."

• • •

"Will you shut your trap? Sherry's hubby is about to be on the television."

Poor Earl frowned into his mug of beer. "Old coot. Maybe you need new hearing aides."

Despite the plastic smile on Sherry's face, the anxiety knotting her chest, and the strong desire to bolt from the premises, she had to stifle a laugh. Between Mrs. Thibodeaux's yelling and old Earl's muttering, it was hard to wallow in heartache. It was like watching a sitcom from the 60s: *The Extremely Incompatible Couple.*

Angelle sidled up behind the hostess stand and glanced around the packed restaurant. "How you holding up?"

Sherry shrugged. "As good as expected, I guess."

When she'd come in for her shift that afternoon and heard the buzz in the air, she knew something was happening. About an hour ago, patrons began pouring in, eager to watch Blue's late-night appearance together as a community. Supporting their newest member.

"It's not like I can turn it off without explaining why," she said with a sigh. "And honestly, I *want* to see it. I do. It's just..." Sherry threw her head back and released a heavy breath. "This will be the first time I've seen him since that night. I mean, it's through a screen. And it's not even live... they taped the show hours ago. But pre-recorded, live-to-tape is as close to the real thing as I've got." Swallowing past a lump of fear, she nibbled her lip and then gave voice to her true fear. "What if I can't handle it?"

"Aw, sweetie." Angelle promptly wrapped her in a hug and squeezed her close. "You are the strongest person I know. You can handle *anything*, you hear me? You're amazing, and tough, and kickass." She leaned back and looked her in the eye. "Don't you forget it."

Sherry laughed humorlessly. "Gotta say, not feeling that kickass tonight." She dragged her fingertips beneath her eyes, wiping the black residue on her apron as she scanned the gathered crowd. When her gaze landed on Will Trahan, Mr. Boring himself, seated at the bar, she froze.

His soft gaze was on hers, and he tipped his beer in her direction. His smile was nice, kind, sweet—and dull as dishwater.

Had she really convinced herself a life with no sparks, no *excitement,* could ever make her happy?

She hung her head and admitted softly to the ground, "I miss him, Ang."

"Of course you do." Sherry lifted her gaze to her friend's understanding smile. "You're in love with him." At her shocked open mouth, Angie lifted a shoulder. "People say *I* have no poker face. Sweets, the moment you hear that man's name, your eyes are a dead giveaway."

Well, that was reassuring. If Tyler had found her as easy to read, that explained why he hadn't chased after her. Or even contacted her in the last two weeks.

Yeah, she'd left *him* that morning. It was part of her new selfless M.O. The more time that passed, however, Sherry decided she wasn't a fan. Part of her honestly thought he'd fight for her. Realize he was in love with her too, and fly back to snag her. The big Hollywood ending.

She sighed. First thing in the morning, she was bringing her entire library to Goodwill. This was what reading did to you—gave you silly, ridiculous schoolgirl hopes.

"Oh, turn it up!" Tootsie, the big old flirt who owned the dog spa, turned around and flapped her hand in the air. "Turn it up! Blue's up next!"

Cane reached behind the bar and dialed the volume higher. A commercial for toilet paper so soft it felt like a million angels kissing your *arse*. Why anyone would want celestial beings snogging their bottom, Sherry didn't know, but she was thankful for the strange and random distraction. Unfortunately, it was short-lived.

The late show returned, and the spunky, adorable host, Jennifer Marr, smiled on screen. "My next guests are a country singing phenomenon. Their latest album just released, and the first single, 'Rain Dance,' debuted at number one."

The camera panned, and Sherry's breath locked in her lungs. There was Tyler. Her music man. Wearing the flipping belt buckle; snug, low-slung jeans; and a denim shirt. His guitar was strapped around his chest, his eyes were steady, and he'd never looked better. Her chest ached for him.

"Now, before the guys play it for us, I thought we'd get the inside scoop." Jennifer turned to Tyler and grinned. "I'm a big fan of yours, have been since the debut album, but I've got to say, this song blew me away. It's much more emotional than your previous songs. Care to divulge why?"

Tyler chuckled at the ground, almost looking embarrassed. The shy, adorable thing only made him hotter. Lord, she was whipped on this boy.

"Well, as you know, Jennifer, I recently got married."

Angelle clutched Sherry's hand as the crowd at Robicheaux's cheered.

Tyler grinned at the studio audience's enthusiasm. "Thank you," he said with a small nod to the crowd before turning back to the host. "This was the first love song I've written since truly learning what love is. My wife, Sherry, opened my eyes." He paused and swallowed hard, a look Sherry had never seen before on his face…vulnerability mixed with determination.

She leaned forward, heart galloping in her chest, pulse thrumming in her ears, and the weight of her family's stares on her cheek. Pants of breath escaped her lips as he scratched the back of his neck and glanced at Charlie. Then, staring straight into the screen, he said, "She's home now, back in Magnolia Springs, but I hope she's watching tonight. Sugar, if you are, this one's for you."

His fingers caressed the strings of his beloved guitar as he nodded to the band. Jennifer Marr turned to the camera and as she stepped back with a wide smile, held her arms out and said, "Blue, everybody!"

The crowd cheered appreciatively as the song that he'd supposedly written about *her*, that he said she'd inspired, began. And as she listened to it, the lyrics about a beautiful woman who danced in the rain and captivated the heart of the man who secretly adored her, Sherry's broken heart knitted together.

All it took was one verse, one cycle of the chorus, for her to make up her mind. Yeah, the hero often made the grand gesture in the end and fought for the woman he loved, but it wasn't solely a man's job. She was the heroine in this story—

and it was time to get her man.

Whipping off her apron, she turned to her friend, who was smiling with her arm already extended to take it. "Go," Angelle said, nodding toward the door. "Be happy. You deserve it."

Hope tingling beneath her skin, electrifying her veins, Sherry bounced on her toes and grinned. "You know, I think I do."

Cane held his hand up to his ear from behind the bar, signaling for her to call when she arrived in L.A., and Colby blew her a kiss. Her heart swelled with the love and support of her family, and it gave her that last boost of confidence she needed to bolt for the door.

Only, before she could reach the knob, it opened for her…

And Tyler barreled in.

• • •

His beautiful wife stared at him, mouth dropped in shock, as she glanced back and forth between him and the television. She swung her head back a final time, purple strands lashing across her lips, and said, "You're here."

Nodding, he took a step toward her. "I took the first flight I could out of L.A."

The door closed behind him, jingling the bells again, and this time, the patrons who'd previously been glued to the show noticed him. Gasps and whispers of *"He's here,"* broke among them.

"I needed to see you," he admitted, stopping in front of her. He reached out and skimmed his fingers over her cheek.

She leaned into his touch, and he said, "Seems I figured something out today."

Sherry smiled, the soft skin of her throat sliding against the heel of his palm. "Oh yeah? What's that, music man?"

Tyler raised his gaze to see practically the entire town of Magnolia Springs, including her whole family, unabashedly listening in. He chuckled and said, "You know I hate big speeches, darlin'. I tend to get tongue-tied and awkward, and I've always preferred to let my lyrics speak for me. But it seems, once again, you inspire me."

He swallowed down the small lump in his throat, the knot of insecurity telling him he'd waited too long, and said, "I'm miserable without you, Sherry. I never should've left you here"—he glanced at the listening crowd—"waiting for me to return while I went on the road. My career, the awards and recognition, hell, even the music, it's meaningless without you. It's empty. And today, I realized why I push myself so hard."

He placed his other hand on her sweet face, now cradling it between his palms, and her gaze implored him to continue. "I'm always chasing the next goal. The next achievement. Trying to fill that void and find the happiness I've only ever felt once in my life." Tears welled in her hazel eyes. "With you."

A sob escaped her parted lips. "Really?"

"Apparently, happiness has been hiding behind exuberant smiles and rain-soaked dances," he answered with a grin. She laughed at that, and a tear slid down her cheek. He brushed it away with his thumb.

"I'm not saying a life with me will be easy. The road is chaotic and the media is fickle." Tyler glanced again at the eavesdropping customers and locked eyes with Cane. Swallowing hard, he nodded at his brother-in-law and turned back to his wife. "But if you'll have me, I promise to spend the rest of our lives putting you first. Spending equal time here, in Magnolia Springs, with your—*our* family. Making sure that incredible smile never leaves your face."

Another fat tear fell down her cheek, followed by another and another. Sherry laughed as her hands clamped around his wrists, tugging him even closer. He gladly closed the distance between them and pressed his lips to hers…a brush, a slide, a sweet caress…then pulled back, chuckling at her frown.

When he let go of her face and got down on one knee, right there in the middle of her family's crowded restaurant, that frown was replaced with a gasp.

"Our marriage began a bit unconventionally," he said with a smile, raising his voice to include the *aww*ing crowd, and they laughed in appreciation. "And though I wouldn't change a single moment of the last month, I believe I owe my beautiful bride here a real hometown wedding."

That, as expected, got an enthusiastic response. Neighbors cheered, and Sherry slapped a hand over her mouth as Tyler took her left one. The one *already* wearing his ring.

"Marry me again?" he asked, staring up into her eyes. Lowering his voice for her ears, he added, "This time fully sane and rational?"

Sherry laughed, full and free, and that breathtaking smile curved her mouth. "Baby, you should know by now I'm *never* fully sane and rational." Sinking down to her knees, she brought his hand to her mouth and kissed his knuckles.

"But Tyler, I'd marry you again in a heartbeat. You *are* my fairy tale."

Releasing a breath he hadn't realized he was holding—*she said yes!*—he crushed her body to his chest and brought his mouth down on hers. Her lips were salty with tears and tasted of forever, and he threaded his fingers in her hair. He'd been an idiot for so long. *Too* long. Music may be his passion—but this, right here, was his dream.

When his lungs burned for air and he *had* to draw back, he broke away.

"God, I love you," he whispered roughly, pressing a kiss against her forehead before leaning his forehead against hers.

Sherry bit her lip, a half-laugh, half-sob sound escaping. She closed her eyes, head hung limp as her hands clutched tighter on his back. Exhaling against his neck, she looked up again, those mesmerizing eyes flaring with emotion.

"And I love *you*, music man. You are my happily ever after."

Then her mouth claimed his again, and the entire restaurant erupted in applause.

Epilogue

18 MONTHS LATER...

"I'm *pregnant*," Sherry explained as she took a seat at the table on the tour bus. "Not incapacitated."

So she'd stumbled walking from the master in the back. Big whoop. Their current house was on freaking *wheels*. Her balance would've been off even if she weren't carrying the equivalent of a giant basketball in her stomach. But she was indeed with child—a future soccer player or Rockette if kicks were any indication—and her baby-daddy was a worrywart.

"You should be lying down," Tyler grumbled, sliding on the bench beside her. His expert fingers immediately found the throbbing knot at the base of her spine. It had been spasming all day. "Please humor me. You're due in a week, we're at the tail end of a tour, and for all my luck, you're gonna pop in the middle of a concert." The pressure from his hand eased as he kissed her temple. "I just want you to be safe."

Gold in Fort Knox isn't guarded as safely, she thought with a chuckle. Honestly, though? The über-protective, clueless-future-father vibe was hot. Seeing her music man worry over her, fuss, make sure doctors were on call in every city they toured...she'd be lying if she said it wasn't a turn on. Tyler loved her. Truly, completely, totally loved her, and he showed it every minute of every day.

Who knew happiness like this existed outside of books?

Deciding to cut the man some slack, she smiled and grasped his slightly stubbled chin. She tugged him down for a kiss on the lips—that temple business so wasn't cutting it—and said, "I *am* safe. A bodyguard trails my every step. Arianne is back in control of Meet and Greet duties, and Angelle is handling everything with *Fairy Tale Endings* in Magnolia Springs."

As a second wedding present, Tyler had purchased her rent-to-own cottage, making the site where their love story began officially theirs. They went back as often as they could, considered it their home, and spent the entire fall and Christmas season with her family. That was when Blue created their latest album, and when they created the baby she affectionately called *Whopper.* That's all this thing craved—meat, meat, and more meat. In between runs to the nearest Burger King, she'd also set up a thriving event planning business and recently hired Angelle as her partner.

"I'm fat, happy, and practically living in bubble wrap," she continued with a grin. "And Elizabeth Angelina Blue would be blessed to enter this world while her daddy's kicking butt on stage. Some of his best lyrics are inspired by a fabulous woman." Her husband scrunched one eye and sized her up, then flashed his crooked grin. Expert fingers moving again, only this time decidedly *south* of the base of her spine, he murmured his agreement. "Can't argue with that. A hot woman, too."

"Good God, I'm eating here!" Charlie made a production out of gagging, but she saw through his act. He was going to make an amazing honorary uncle. And, hopefully, occasional babysitter. "I thought you two would've gotten all the gushy, mushy, love crap out of your system after the last tour."

"Sorry to disappoint you," Tyler replied. "But hey, look on the bright side. All this gushy, mushy, love crap is the reason our last two albums kick such ass." He slid his arm around Sherry's shoulders and cuddled her close. "Embrace it, my friend."

"Better yet, get your own woman," she suggested, smiling despite the increased pain in her back. It was an ongoing joke between them. Charlie was the eternal playboy with a heart of gold. One day he'd settle down and make a fabulous boyfriend. For now, she'd just tease him into submission.

"Yeah, yeah." Charlie rolled his eyes and shoved a spoonful of Cap'n Crunch into his mouth. Loud crunching soon filled the bus.

Sherry shifted her enormous weight on the bench. Man, today was a doozy. Pregnancy had been relatively easy on her thus far. A few bouts of morning sickness in the beginning, fatigue around the second trimester, and her obsession with meat (and unattractive waddle) in the third. Mostly, though, she was enjoying the hell out of this thing.

Today, however, she'd awoken with a dull pain in her lower back that wouldn't go away. In fact, hours later, it seemed to be getting worse.

Lord, what would actual labor feel like?

Just then, another spasm rocked her core. Teeth clenched, she gripped Tyler's thigh as she breathed through the cramp.

"Still in pain?" When she nodded jerkily, Tyler swung his gaze about the bus. "Want me to grab the heating pad?"

"No." Thankfully, the spasm was easing. After a few more moments of deep breathing, all that remained was a dull ache. A low laugh bubbled in her throat as she slumped against the seat. "I'm fine. I think Whopper's just punishing me for the Chinese last night. Sticky note to self: only burgers until I give birth."

"Uh, Sher?"

Sherry glanced at Charlie to see his head tilted, gaze darting between them.

"You think maybe you're in labor?"

"No." She shook her head forcefully. "Oh, no. I'm not due for another week. Besides, it's almost all in my back."

Cereal bowl forgotten, he grabbed for his phone. "Are the pains lasting longer and longer?" he asked, eyebrows raised. She nodded reluctantly. "And coming frequently?"

Well damn. When he put it like that…

"But it's only in my back," she repeated.

Charlie shrugged. "Five older sisters, twelve nieces and nephews, and only a few had traditional contractions. The rest all had back labor." His gaze flicked to Tyler. "What? I'm a good brother. You find the nearest doctor, and I'll go tell the driver."

Without another word, her husband leapt from the bench. He went to the back of the bus, Charlie stalked to the front, and Sherry sat there, staring at the tabletop.

"But it's only in my back!"

This was not happening. She'd done her research, read her books, and every stinking one of them said she needed a birthing plan. So, by God, she'd actually made one. And it was already an epic fail.

For starters, she looked a mess. Far too many photos existed of stringy-haired, sweaty women holding their babies, and that business was supposed to end here. *Her* baby's first photo was going to show a darling angel, a proud papa, and a glistening mama with full-on makeup.

Currently though, thanks to the dull ache she'd had all morning, the only thing Sherry was rocking was cherry-flavored Chapstick.

Also, Merle Haggard? *So* not in her birthing plan. No, she had a playlist prepped, ready, and filled with girl power. Katy Perry, Beyoncé, even old-school Madonna. Music to empower her, give her confidence, and keep her sane until the good doc arrived with drugs. No trains, tractors, or whiskey involved.

Sherry's gaze swung to the dead phone holding her beloved playlist hostage.

Why could she never remember to charge the bloody thing?

As if in agreement, a new spasm shot up her spine, rocketing her off the seat. Instinctively, she curled forward to shield baby Whopper from the pain, and breathlessly called out, *"Babe?"*

Her voice was so low she doubted he'd even heard her, but a moment later, Tyler marched back down the hall, duffel bag in one hand, functioning cell phone in the other. "I just called Colby and they're on their way." Eyes wide and alert, he tossed the bag on the counter, scooped her into his arms, and said, "The nearest hospital is two miles away. Hang on, sugar, we're almost there."

If she weren't in so much pain, it'd be adorable. Gripping his shoulders tight, she lifted her chin in acknowledgment and exhaled.

Strong fingers pressed into her back. The silly lessons her Lamaze coach taught them came flooding back, the ones she'd sworn she'd never do because they looked so dumb. But when the pain continued, Sherry decided dumb or not, *anything* was worth a shot.

"He he hooo." Yep, complete and total idiot. "He he hooo." But dang it if she cared.

The breathing exercises continued until, a few moments later, the contraction passed. "Holy crap." Sherry sagged against her husband and huffed a laugh. "Yo, labor ain't no joke."

She shook her head and then raised it to find Tyler's mouth curved in an awed smile. A mix of anxiety and wonder filled his green eyes, and he gently slid a palm around to cradle her stomach. "You're about to be a mama."

Happy tears sprang to her eyes as her heart melted all over the floor. She touched a hand to his cheek and said, "You're about to be a daddy."

His gaze lowered to his hand on her swollen abdomen. The muscles of his jaw flexed and her hair fanned with his exhale. Locking his gaze with hers, he said, "Thank you."

She knew he meant more than for just this moment. This was emotional for both of them, wishing their mothers could be there. But in their own way, they were. And their daughter would forever honor both her namesakes: Elizabeth Blue and Angelina Robicheaux.

Sherry smiled, feeling the slow glide of tears on her cheeks. "Thank *you.*"

Charlie cleared his throat behind them. The bus came to a stop, and Sherry glanced out the window. The doors for Meadow Crest Hospital were just beyond, and already a few people were gawking in their direction. Apparently, tour buses didn't roll up here that often.

"Sorry to interrupt," Charlie said, "but we're here."

Sherry rolled her shoulders as the chorus of "Roar" started in her head. She looked up at Tyler and asked, "Ready to do this, Daddy?"

His answering smile, while still a bit anxious, was also full of excitement. "Ready for the next adventure with you? Definitely."

Both men grabbed a hand and helped her down the stairs. For once, she didn't mind the fussing. Face-planting out of a tour bus in front of a crowd was most certainly not a part of her birth plan. When she reached the ground, she grabbed hold of her husband's steadying arm and said, "Just think of the songs you'll write after this."

"Already on it."

Unsurprising, Tyler withdrew a pad of sticky notes from his pocket. What was surprising was that the first sheet was already filled with words. A boyish grin replaced his usual confident one as he handed her the note.

My Gorgeous Wife,

Marrying you was the best decision I ever made.

Our future child is the best gift I've ever received.

Thank you.

Tyler

P.S. I hope this girl's as crazy as you are.

Tears fell freely now, and Sherry didn't even bother to swipe them. Sniffling, she looked over and said, "I'm crazy, huh?"

"Certifiable." His response was immediate and seemed sincere. But before she could get all riled up, he added, "And I wouldn't have you any other way."

She laughed aloud and reached down to link her fingers with his. Then, hand in hand, they walked through the emergency room doors, ready for their next adventure.

Rain Dance

With just one smile
You make me wanna stay awhile
Your eyes, they tease
But it's your heart I want to please

Held me captive in her stare
I knew then I didn't have a prayer
Pouring rain she starts to dance
Yeah I never really stood a chance
Dancing in the rain put me under her spell
So damn beautiful it's no wonder I fell
A wild child with a heart of gold
Please be mine to have and to hold

With just one glance
You make me wanna give this a chance
Lord knows I've tried
But I don't wanna get off this ride

Held me captive in her stare
I knew then I didn't have a prayer
Pouring rain she starts to dance
Yeah I never really stood a chance
Dancing in the rain put me under her spell
So damn beautiful it's no wonder I fell
A wild child with a heart of gold

Please be mine to have and to hold

With just one touch
You make me feel so much
My hopes are high
Lets just give this a try

Held me captive in her stare
I knew then I didn't have a prayer
Pouring rain she starts to dance
Yeah I never really stood a chance
Dancing in the rain put me under her spell
So damn beautiful it's no wonder I fell
A wild child with a heart of gold
Please be mine to have and to hold

With just one kiss
You make me feel your bliss
I wanna make you mine
Tell me baby, where do I sign?

Held me captive in her stare
I knew then I didn't have a prayer
Pouring rain she starts to dance
Yeah I never really stood a chance
Dancing in the rain put me under her spell
So damn beautiful it's no wonder I fell
A wild child with a heart of gold
Please be mine to have and to hold

Before I Met You/Maybe Baby/Maybe

"Before I met you, love was a dream somewhere down the line.

Before I met you, yeah, my life was just fine.
I didn't know there was somethin' missin'.
Marriage was another thought I kept dismissin'

But maybe, baby, this was meant to be.
Maybe, you're my perfect melody.
Yeah maybe, baby, you were made for me.
Maybe you're my perfect melody.

Before I met you, I thought love would be harder to find.
Now that I've met you, am I out of my mind?
Yeah, you've got me breaking all of the rules.
I was always one of those wild, crazy, love sick fools.

But maybe, baby, this was meant to be.
Maybe, you're my perfect melody.
Yeah maybe, baby, you were made for me.
Maybe you're my perfect melody.

Now that I've met you, I know some fairytales do come true.

Now that I've met you, my old dreams will never do.
I found out what I was really missin'
I don't wanna go another day without your kissin'

So, maybe, baby, this was meant to be.
Maybe you're my perfect melody.
Yeah, maybe, baby, you were made for me.
Maybe, you're my perfect melody.

Acknowledgments

When I sat down to plot this book, I had such a smile on my face. It's no secret that Sherry has been a fan favorite since day one…truthfully, she's my favorite, too. I couldn't wait to dive into her world and give her the happy ending she so rightfully deserved. I hope you enjoyed the outcome!

Writing the Love and Games series has been such a thrill. This was my first foray into adult romance, even though I've been reading the genre since I was a young girl swiping books from my mama's shelf. Words don't exist to thank you for the incredible welcome I've received, so for every reader, reviewer, and blogger who's taken a chance, for every sweet message and letter I've received, and for every friend I've made on this journey, just know that I adore you. You are my daily dose of inspiration and gratitude.

Rose Garcia, thank you for sharing your sweet mother-in-law's story with me. Char Ryken was a courageous woman who battled peritoneal cancer but never lost her spunk.

Peritoneal cancer acts and is treated in much the same way as ovarian cancer, and it is Char's story that inspired Tyler's mother. For every woman who has faced a similar battle, and for every loving family member who has held their hands, my prayers and thoughts are with you.

Ashley Bodette, assistant extraordinaire, you are the cure for my insanity. Thank you for speed-reading these pages as I write them, and then reading the second, third, and fourth drafts if I can't seem to get a certain scene right. Thank you for not laughing too hard at my crazy plot outlines, for your keen insight into the editing process, and for all the laughter.

Trish Wolfe and Shannon Duffy blessed these pages with their notes and love—best critique partners ever! Also a shoutout to Trish for the character name inspiration J Jessica Mangicaro blew my mind with her beta notes (and love for Tyler, *mwah*). And I can't thank Caisey Quinn, Megan Rigdon, and Staci Murden enough for their enthusiasm and fabulous feedback. Love you, girls!

Cindi Madsen, my completely adorable sister in love, I don't think it's possible for me to write a book anymore without a dozen text, Facebook, and phone conversations with you. Thank you for getting me, for all the advice and brainstorming sessions, and for letting me borrow your character for this story—I can't wait to see Sadie shine in her own book!

Lisa Burstein, our jaunt down the Vegas Strip not only inspired the beginning of this book, but it remains one of my favorite nights ever. Any excuse to hang with you is a blast, and I'm so grateful to call you friend.

Melissa West, Christina Lee, Heidi McLaughlin, and Stina Lindenblatt…your belief in this book and in me are a gift. I love sharing this bookish life with you talented ladies! Thank you for loving Blue and for all the giggles.

To the Cool Kids Mafia…secret handshake, chin lift, sly wink.

Mega shoutout of gratitude to Rhonda Helms, Megan Erickson, Tara Fuller, Wendy Higgins, Cole Gibsen, Lea Nolan, Veronica Bartles, Cindy Hale, Ophelia London, Mindy Ruiz, AJ Pine, Lex Martin, and Mary Lindsey for all the support and friendship. It means the world to me.

Arianne Cruz and Fizza Younis, two of my fabulous street teamers, thanks for letting me use your names!

Debbie Suzuki and Kelly P. Simmon of InkSlinger PR are my lifesavers. They are crazy talented and their ideas never stop amazing me. Thank you for believing in me, ladies. Your tireless efforts are so very much appreciated.

Stacy Cantor Abrams, you rock my socks. I count my lucky stars every day that you snapped me up from the slush pile. The past few years have been a wild and exciting journey, and it is all because of you. I can't wait to see what the future holds in store!

Jessica Cantor, your covers are flipping phenomenal!! Thank you for giving my stories the best possible chance. I couldn't ask for a more talented artist. Mary Kate Castellani, thank you for your incredible wordsmith skills, and Alethea Spiridon-Hopson, thank you for your fabulous notes. And finally, Alycia Tornetta, thank you for being a constant cheerleader and champion of my stories. So, so blessed…

Speaking of being blessed, my family rocks! My husband always helps plot my books, and he has inspired every single one of my heroes…but Tyler is the most like him. Gregg, you inspired Tyler's sweet Post-it notes with the thirty notes you've stuck to our bathroom mirror, filled with words of love and encouragement. You show me what a true hero looks like, and I'm a very lucky woman. My daughters, Jordan and Cali, are so forgiving of when Mama needs to write, and they are the best publicists an author can ask for—they tell everyone about my books. And I do mean everyone. Angel Girl and Sweet Potato Bug, I love YOU more! My mom, dad, and brother live right next door, so they hear about these characters almost as much as my husband does...which is saying a lot. They also provide free babysitting! And my mother-in-law is a member of my street team and my number-one book pimp. I love all of you to pieces.

Giant tackle hugs to every blogger, reviewer, and reader of Taste the Heat and Seven Day Fiance. Your #JasonIsADemiGod and #CaneIsMine tweets made me smile and laugh, and I hope you fell just as in love with Tyler Blue. Double tackle hugs go out to The Autumn Review, Good Choice Reading, Night Owl Reviews, Ramblings From This Chick, Stuck in Books, Lovin' Los Libros, Imperfect Women, Jenna Does Books, A Bookish Escape, Meredith and Jennifer's Musings, Library of a Book Witch, Pandora's Books, Crystal in Bookland, Tsk Tsk What to Read, and Just a Booklover for going above and beyond as always.

No list of acknowledgments would be complete without a mushy, sentimental thank-you to my street team, the Flirt Squad. Your enthusiasm for my books, your love of these characters, and your unending support mean the world to me. Thank you for laughing and sharing life with me—I adore each and every one of your faces! Extra gooey love goes out to the rock stars who went above and beyond supporting my last release: Meagan Rigdon, Valerie Fink, Mi-Mi Nguyen, Saleana Rae Carneiro, Heather Love King, Maliha Khan, Fatima Tariq, Jenna DeTrapani, Angelique Gouvas, Katrina Tinnon, Maura Trice, Denice Cordero, Gaby Navarro, Jennifer Stasi, Patricia Lopez, Vi Nguyen, Mary Hinson, Holly Underhill, Bette Hansen, Francine Soleil, Ciara Byars, Cynthia Bolasina, Cindy Ray Hale, Kathy Arguelles, Chrissy Wolfe, Veronica Bartles, Myra White, and Linda Townsend.

And to everyone reading these words right now, a heartfelt thank-you. It's never too late to chase your dreams!

About the Author

Rachel Harris writes humorous love stories about sassy girls-next-door and the hot guys that make them swoon. Emotion, vibrant settings, and strong families are a staple in each of her books...and kissing. Lots of kissing.

A Cajun cowgirl now living in Houston, she firmly believes life's problems can be solved with a hot, sugar-coated beignet or a thick slice of king cake, and that screaming at strangers for cheap, plastic beads is acceptable behavior in certain situations. She homeschools her two beautiful girls and watches way too much Food Network with her amazing husband.

An admitted Diet Mountain Dew addict, she gets through each day by laughing at herself, hugging her kids, and losing herself in story. She writes young adult, new adult, and adult romances, and LOVES talking with readers!

Other Books by Rachel Harris

<u>Seven Day Fiance</u>

a Love and Games novel

Angelle Prejean is in a pickle. Her family is expecting her to come home with a fiancé—a fiancé who doesn't exist. Well, he exists, but he definitely has no idea Angelle told her mama they were engaged. Tattooed, muscled, and hotter than sin, Cane can reduce Angelle to a hot mess with one look—and leave her heart a mess if she falls for him. But when she ends up winning Cane at a charity bachelor auction, she knows just how to solve her fiancé problem.

<u>Taste the Heat</u>

a Love and Games novel

For Teen Readers

<u>My Super Sweet Sixteenth Century</u>

<u>A Tale of Two Centuries</u>

<u>My Not So Super Sweet Life</u>